TH[illegible]
[illegible]
W[illegible]O
COULDN'T
SEE
FACES

C. J. BOWDEN

MARSHALL BROWN

THE GIRL WHO COULDN'T SEE FACES

ISBN: 978-1-7392810-1-4

Contact: marshallbrownenquiries@gmail.com

PART ONE

Chapter 1

SOME PEOPLE HAVE a happy face. Some people have a kind face or a friendly face. But I think I must have a particularly serious and sullen-looking one, because random strangers are always calling out things like: *Smile, it can't be that bad!* Or *Cheer up love, it might never happen!*

And although I'll always smile back politely, like I'm grateful for their kind advice, I know that what they're really trying to tell me is: *Stop moping around and being such a Debbie Downer.*

Almost as bad as *Cheer up love* is its close cousin, *A penny for your thoughts.* But trust me, after an exhausting twelve-hour shift in A&E, having vicious abuse hurled at me by frustrated patients, and then getting away late because I had to clean up after a drunk who climbed onto the bed and urinated all around the cubicle, you really don't want to know what I'm thinking.

So I tend to keep my eyes lowered when I'm walking to avoid all these helpful remarks. And more importantly, it also helps prevent the embarrassing awkwardness of blanking someone I might know.

Which is why, when a woman carrying a bottle of spirits steps out of the 24-hour corner shop ahead of me, I've got my head down. Surreptitiously studying her in the periphery of my vision I notice that she's not wearing a coat, even though it's a really chilly October evening. Instead, she has on one of those long, buttonless edge-to-edge cardigans which are always flapping open, paired with baggy tracksuit bottoms and worn-out Ugg boots which are clearly a couple of sizes too big for her.

I watch her shuffle through the jaundiced puddle of light spilling from the shop window, clutching her bottle of vodka tightly under her arm, and feel a sharp pang of pity: yet another sad alcoholic living rough on the streets of south London. We get them all the time at work. They come into A&E with head injuries, pancreatitis, or some other alcohol-related illness, and I always find it heart-wrenching to see a life ruined by alcohol.

The woman waits right in the middle of my path, trying to catch my eye as I approach, but I keep my gaze stubbornly fixed on the cracks in the pavement. Just when I think I've managed to safely navigate past, she calls out an irritated, sardonic '*Hello?*'

I look up at her for the first time and let out a little *oh!* in surprise. I couldn't have been more wrong: she's the least alcoholic-looking person imaginable. Instead of the grubby, ruddy, prematurely-aged face of the alcoholic that I was expecting, I'm looking into the immaculately made-up face of a girl about my age, with long, dark brown, freshly-straightened hair.

'Trying to avoid me?' she asks, half-joking, half-offended.

'Sorry, I was miles away.'

She obviously knows me, but I've no idea who she is. A neighbour? One of the nurses or therapists from hospital perhaps? Maybe she's an ex-patient?

'Hard day at work?' she asks reproachfully.

I'm not sure how to respond. I could tell her *yes,* ambulances were queueing up in the loading bay all day, the waiting room was so packed that people had to sit on the floor, then we had casualties from a four-car pile-up on the M25, and then a stab victim was admitted and is still in a critical state. Quite busy for a Friday, but nothing out of the ordinary, and if she works at St George's she'll know all this already. So, I just say 'Mmm, yes,' and wince at my basic reply.

I must seem like such a dull person, but better that than admit I don't recognise her. People get really offended when I tell them I don't know who they are. Like I've deliberately chosen not to bother making the effort to remember them. And even if they're not offended, it's often just too complicated to explain.

'Come on then, it's freezing out here!' she exclaims, pulling her cardigan tighter and slopping off up Tooting High Street in her over-sized boots. I hurry after her, wondering where she's heading. She must live locally if she's come out without a coat.

'Doing anything tonight?' she asks.

'I'm going for a drink in Balham. With my boyfriend, Alfie. It's our one-year anniversary,' I explain, slowing my pace because we're approaching the corner of my road.

'Got time for pre-drinks?' she asks, jangling her bottle of vodka like it's a handbell, like she's trying to hypnotise me into saying yes.

'Thanks, but I've got to get home,' I reply in a regretful tone, jerking my head in the direction of the flat.

There's an awkward moment as she stares at me, wrinkling her brows in puzzlement. Then she gives a feeble, pitying laugh, like I've just made the worst joke she's ever heard, and sets off up Brudenell Road — *my* road — calling over her shoulder: 'Are you coming?'

It's then that I realise who it is: my flatmate Claire.

The instant I know it's Claire, her face seems to undergo a transformation. It's hard explaining it exactly. Nothing's changed physically of course, but as we pass under the yellow haze of the streetlamp, this unrecognisable, meaningless face suddenly becomes imbued with a significance it didn't possess before. In an instant she transforms from a stranger waving a bottle of vodka at me, to a thirty-one-year-old home-counties girl, who works in PR, who I've been living with for the last seven months after answering an advert on *SpareRoom*. Who also owns a pair of old Ugg boots which she often slips on to go to the corner shop.

My problem is face blindness. It's a neurological disorder which affects around two percent of the population. People with a milder form of the condition are usually able to recognise someone after meeting them a few times. But my facial cognition skills are so poor that no matter how many times I see a face, it just won't stick in my memory. I'm unable to recognise my friends, my family, or even my own face.

Which is why, when everyone else seems obsessed with taking selfies and pictures of their friends, I never take photos of people. After all, who'd want to fill their phone with pictures of faces they will never recognise? And apparently watching TV with me is an intensely irritating experience because I have no idea who anyone is and have to keep asking.

Alfie teases me about my condition all the time. He calls me *The Girl Who Can't See Faces*, like I'm a character in some sort of moral fable, who you just know is heading for a sticky end. I keep having to explain to him that *yes*, I can *see* faces, and *no*, it's not like there's a pixelated blur where the face should be, it's just that I can't recognise them. But he doesn't get it. Or maybe he just pretends he doesn't.

The best way I can explain it is like this: imagine you're looking at a bowl of fruit. It's easy enough telling an orange from an apple or a banana, but unless they've got some particularly distinguishing blemishes, most oranges look pretty much the same. Well, for me, faces are as unmemorable as fruit.

In fact, I didn't even realise that it was possible to use faces as a means of recognition when I first started school. My new classmates would call out each other's names in the playground, and I couldn't figure out how they were doing it. I was utterly mystified. I thought they must possess some sort of hidden super-hero power which allowed them to identify each other.

It's hard forming connections with people when they all look the same, and I struggled to make friends. I'd spend my break-times hiding out behind the toilet block, wishing someone would let me in on the big secret. I guess that's where my shyness stems from.

You might think I'd be able to recognise people by their voice, but unless there's something particularly unusual about the way a person speaks, their voice conveys surprisingly little information to me. So over time I've learnt to identify people by picking up on other, more visual, clues. Like how a person walks, how they stand, how they do their hair, what they're wearing.

It's all a process of elimination, a bit like the game *Guess Who?* we had when I was a child. It had these little plastic cards with pictures of faces on them, and you had to guess who was on your opponent's card by asking questions. Like: *Is it a man? Does he wear glasses? Is he bald?*

I go through the same thing whenever I encounter someone new, mentally flipping down little plastic cards in my head until I've narrowed down all the possibilities. Only, as I'm getting older, the game's becoming harder to play. The flawless make-up some girls wear gives them a smooth uniformity which is very difficult to read, while boys like to hide their faces behind thick woolly beards that make it impossible for me to tell them apart.

It's not so bad at work because we have to wear name tags and colour-coded uniforms and there are procedures in place to ensure we're dealing with the correct patients. And because the hospital employs so many people — in A&E alone there are about 150 nurses on the rotas — no-one could be expected to recognise them all. But out in the real world, encountering people without any sort of context, it's a minefield of misunderstanding.

I guess that's why I've always been most comfortable around people with really distinctive features. At school I was drawn towards the weird looking kids — the fattest, skinniest, misfitiest ones with buck teeth, big noses, untameable hair and bad acne. I didn't exactly run with the cool crowd.

I get the sense that Claire doesn't think I'm cool enough for her crowd either. In the seven months since I moved in, she's not once invited me out with her friends. But who can blame her when I come out with such cringe stuff all the time?

When we get back to the flat, I take a shower to wash off all the grime and grossness of a twelve-hour hospital shift. Then, in my bra and pants, I lay three outfits out on my bed, and stare at them, paralysed by indecision, unable to choose what to wear this evening.

Should I go with the dark green dress with the flowery pattern which I've had for years? The black one with the silver trim, which is classier, but perhaps a bit too officey? Or the new electric blue dress I bought after Alfie chided me for dressing like a frumpy nun, but which I wasn't going to wear until I'd lost a few pounds?

I really hate my body sometimes. Nothing ever seems to fit properly. My breasts are too large, my bum's too big, and the bits in between could probably do with some toning. I wriggle snake-like into the new blue dress and study my reflection in the mirror. It's maybe a bit tight, and I'm not sure about the amount of cleavage on display. I hunch my shoulders and pull in my elbows to make my breasts look smaller, but now it just looks like I've got stomach cramps and desperately need the loo. I'm torn. I really do like this dress; I'm just not sure I like it on *me*. Then again, what do I know? I've never been any good at judging what suits me.

Claire and Beth are lounging on the sofas in the sitting-room.

'D'you think this looks okay?' I ask, turning a little pirouette.

'Mmn, you look great!' Beth replies in a cheerily upbeat tone.

'Really?' I ask doubtfully, smoothing the tight material over my hips, suspecting that she's only being polite.

'Honestly,' she nods, making the tips of her new French bob do a feathery little flutter across her cheeks.

Claire combs her fingers through her long tresses as she considers my outfit. She screws up her nose and sucks her teeth before finally delivering her verdict: 'It's too tight on the bum.'

She's right, it is too tight. But does she really have to sound so smug about it? 'It's a 12,' I tell her defensively, which is a big fat lie because it's actually a 14. 'Does it look that bad?'

Claire stares at my size 16 bottom squashed into my size 14 dress, and although she doesn't actually say anything, she doesn't need to. The non-committal *mmeh* noise she makes under her breath says more than any words could. Looks like it'll have to be the green dress again.

On my way out of the room Beth asks — perhaps to make up for Claire's brutal honesty — 'Phoebe, are you free next Saturday? It's Caroline's birthday, and a bunch of us are going clubbing.'

My first invite! Yay! I feel honoured. Except — to be honest, clubbing isn't really my thing. Especially with a bunch of people I've never met before. I'm not much into bars or pubs either, truth be told. I'm more of an evening-in-front-of-the-TV-glomming-a-wildlife-documentary-box-set-on-NetFlix kind of girl. But a pity-invitation is still an invitation, and it'd seem rude if I turned it down. Plus, they might never ask me again.

'Would it be okay if Alfie comes?' I enquire, figuring that I wouldn't feel so overwhelmed if I wasn't on my own.

Beth exchanges a quick little glance with Claire.

'Oh. If it's a problem —'

'No, of course he's welcome,' Beth replies quickly, turning to Claire to ask: 'That's okay, isn't it?'

Claire twists her hair between her fingers, then flicks it behind her shoulders before answering: 'Why not? The more the merrier.'

'Great! I'll ask him tonight and let you know.'

But half-way back to my room I remember that Alfie's busy on Saturday. I do a one-eighty in the hallway, but stop in my tracks at the door when I overhear Claire complaining in a peevish voice: 'Did you *have* to ask her?'

'Why not? I don't know why you have such a problem with Phoebe.'

'I don't. I mean, she's not exactly the most fun person to live with. She walks around with this miserable expression all the time —'

There's a burst of laughter, then Beth's voice: 'Ooh, harsh!'

'It's true! Even the neighbours have noticed. But it's not her I have the problem with. It's her boyfriend.'

'Same!'

'There's something about him that *really* creeps me out. He's such a fake. When you first meet him he's all smiley and sincere and everything. But then you catch him looking at you in a really unnerving way. Like this —'

'Eeurgh!'

'Plus, he dresses like a cross between a gangsta rapper and an eight-year-old boy.'

Another shriek of laughter, and then Beth says: 'What I hate is when he stays over, and Phoebe goes off to work at the crack of dawn, and you're never sure if you've got the flat to yourself or whether he's suddenly going to appear —'

'In his pants.'

'Yes! Just wearing a pair of boxers, scratching at his armpit, and asking *is there anything to eat?* Like it's your job to make him something. He's a complete mooch.'

'D'you think we should have a word with her?'

I can't bear to hear any more, and scurry back to my room, my cheeks burning with embarrassment, indignation and shock. Mostly shock because I had no idea how they felt. Yes, it hurts to hear them bitching about me, but I accepted a long time ago that I'm not the world's wittiest person. And it's true that I do avert my gaze when I walk down the street to avoid the embarrassment of not recognising our neighbours. But to slag off Alfie like that is *so* unfair when they don't really know him.

When he chatted me up in the Sainsbury's checkout queue twelve months ago, with some goofy quip about the tin of marrow fat peas in my basket, I was instantly hooked. We get on so well. I'm not saying he's perfect of course. He can be a bit moody, his timekeeping is terrible, and occasionally he gets funny about money. But when you find out what a hard childhood he had, you have to be prepared to make a few allowances. He never knew his father, his mother was never home, and it fell to a kindly neighbour to look out for him.

Claire and Beth have no idea what it's like growing up poor. It's so easy for them to sit there and mock because they were raised in nice middle-class homes with nice middle-class parents and have never had to worry about money.

That's the trouble when you move in with strangers. You hope you're going to become best friends, but nine times out of ten it doesn't work out that way. It's not like I haven't tried really hard to fit in either. I do the washing up whenever I find dirty dishes by the sink; I empty the kitchen bin whenever it's full; and I always change the toilet roll when it runs out. I've even baked them my world-famous gooey salted caramel brownies, which everyone who's ever tried says are the best things they've ever tasted. But Claire and Beth have known each other since school and can be quite cliquey at times.

Which is why, this evening, I'm going to ask Alfie if he wants to move in together. I think he'll say yes. I really hope he does, because it's so tiring having to tiptoe around Claire and Beth, like I'm just a guest in their house.

Chapter 2

I DECIDE TO ignore Claire and wear the blue dress anyway, reasoning that I'll be sitting down most of the time, so who's going to notice if it's a teeny bit too tight, right? But as I totter along Balham High Street, I feel the seams straining across my buttocks, and I pray that I find the bar before I suffer an embarrassing wardrobe malfunction.

Here it is at last: *The Butcher's Block*. I nearly walked right past because it has the façade of a traditional butcher's shop, with wooden trestle tables in the window piled high with sausages, and glistening carcasses of meat twisting slowly on hooks. Not the greatest place to bring a vegetarian perhaps, even if the meat is fake, but Alfie's been raving about it ever since it opened.

I can immediately tell that inside it'll be one of those intimidatingly hyper-trendy places — all converted-warehouse chic, floor-to-ceiling mirrors, garish neon lighting and great slabs of wood and concrete everywhere. There's a bouncer on the door: a big, scary-looking, shaven-headed guy in a black suit so tight he can hardly breathe. He's giving off a really threatening vibe, and I worry he's going to stop me entering. But he barely even glances up as I pass inside.

I wasn't wrong about the décor in here. If anything, it's even more concretier than I'd imagined. I hadn't expected it to be quite so rammed this early in the evening, though. I'm surrounded by squads of skinny-jeaned lads in tight shirts flexing their muscles and showing off tattoos to sleek-haired girls sipping neon-coloured cocktails through pink straws. The walls ring with raucous laughter and the sharp chinking of glasses, while beneath it all comes the unnerving wobbly whub-whub throb of bassline music. I have the unsettling feeling of gate-crashing a party where everyone knows everyone else, and no-one knows me.

I take a deep breath and force my way through the throng to the bar, resisting the urge to clap my hands over my ears and run for the exit. It takes a good five minutes for me to get served, and when I've finally got my drink, I clamber up onto a stool — no mean feat in this dress — and wait for Alfie.

Whenever I'm meeting someone in a place like this, I like to arrive early, to let them find me. The problem is, Alfie's always really late, and by the time he eventually arrives, I'm swivelling my head like a crazed meerkat every time a man enters the bar, wondering if it's him.

My life would be so much easier if people wore name tags and wristbands, like they do at work. But in lieu of name tags, what I look out for when I'm waiting for a friend is this special look of recognition people have when they see someone they know. I call it the *I-know-you face*. It's an involuntary reaction — a look of mild surprise — where their eyebrows will raise a few millimetres, and their mouth will give a little twitch, as if they're about to speak.

So, I'm sitting self-consciously on my stool, scanning the room and sipping at my vodka lime soda, when I become vaguely aware that someone's staring at me.

It's a young woman, about my age, with a pale, angular face, wearing a brazen scowl. I turn away with a fluster of irritation. Why is she looking at me like that? Does she know me? Perhaps my make-up's smudged? Probably it's this stupid dress — it's far too revealing and I'm regretting wearing it now. I put my glass down to hoik up the bodice, sneaking a surreptitious glance to check if the girl's still watching me.

She is! But as our eyes lock together, I experience an

unnerving jolt of surprise because I realise I'm staring at my own reflection in the mirror above the bar. My cheeks burn with discomfort. I get caught out like this all the time. You'd think I'd be used to it by now but it's still really messes with my head when it happens.

I study my reflection and try to lodge the information in my brain, even though I know it won't stick. Large brown eyes, lank can't-do-anything-with-it blonde hair, an unhealthily pale complexion, and that deep-set frown between my eyes which invites all those helpful *cheer up* comments.

My *resting bitch face* — that horribly sexist phrase which has probably been said to me even more times than I've been offered *pennies for my thoughts.*

I force my mouth into a cheery grin. Is this any better? No, now I look deranged. People are going to think I've lost the plot, perched up here on my stool, gurning at myself in the mirror.

'Is this seat free?'

A handsome man with a foreign accent startles me out of my thoughts. And before I can tell him I'm waiting for someone, he flashes me a broad smile and sits himself down.

The shiny gold Rolex on his wrist, as orange as his tan and as fake as his smile, flashes in the light as he holds out his hand and says, 'Luca.'

I stare at his hand unenthusiastically, like I've never seen one before. I hate being chatted up in a bar. It's all this dress's fault — it's far too revealing. You show the tiniest bit of skin and immediately men are swarming all around you, gawping open-mouthed like goldfish nibbling at a lump of stale bread floating on the water.

'My name. Luca. From Romania,' he explains in an accent so thick it's hard understanding him. Although he looks quite presentable — smartly dressed in a buttoned-up pale pink polo shirt with a thin blue stripe, neatly cut hair, clean fingernails (a thing I always check) — there's something about him I instinctively don't trust. But because I'm trapped up here on this dumb stool, I don't have any choice except to take his hand.

'Please, what is your name?' he asks earnestly, leaning in a little closer.

'Phoebe,' I say reluctantly as I retrieve my hand from his overly firm grasp.

'Ah! Phoebe. What a beautiful name. Feeee-beeee.'

The soft breathy way he says it, like he's teasing apart a ball of cotton wool, sets my teeth on edge. I glance anxiously across to the door, desperately hoping Alfie will rescue me soon.

'You are very beautiful, Fee-bee,' he continues, dropping his gaze from my face down to my breasts in a really obvious manner, like he doesn't even care that I know he's doing it. I have the uncomfortable feeling he's choosing a joint of meat at the butcher's.

'Actually, I'm waiting for someone,' I explain, drawing my arm across my chest to scratch at a non-existent itch on my shoulder.

He gives a nonchalant shrug. 'Is okay. I buy you a drink while you wait. No?'

'I'm all right thank you.'

'Aww, won't you have a drink with me Feeee-beeee? Plee-ease?' He places his hand on my knee. 'Don't you trust me?'

Clang-alang-alang. An alarm bell is going off in my head. *No, I don't trust you actually, and I think it's time to get out of here*. I need to be as far away as possible from this arsehole, from the noise of this bar, from the sea of faceless jabbering strangers that surround me.

'I'm sorry, I have to go,' I tell him, but as I dismount

from the stool he grabs hold of my arm and forces me to look into his eyes.

'Phoebs! It's me!' he says, dropping the phony accent.

'Alfie?' I stare at his grinning face as it undergoes its sudden transition from unknown to known. Eyes, nose, mouth — nothing actually changes, except for the knowledge that this is Alfie, my boyfriend, the man I think I love, the man I was going to ask to move in with me. The man who, unfortunately, is uncannily good with accents.

He lets out a hoot of laughter. 'You should see your face!'

My eyes are welling up with tears — a mixture of relief and anger, in equal measure. 'Why did you *do* that to me?'

He looks at me incredulously. 'What's the matter? You aren't *cross,* are you?'

'Of course I'm cross,' I snap. 'You know how hard it is not being able to recognise people.'

'Aw, c'mon Phoebs, there's no need to vex. You have to learn to chill when we're out. You're always so uptight. Where's your sense of humour?'

'It wasn't very funny.'

'*I* thought it was.'

'If you think that being chatted up by some slimy Romanian is funny, then there's something wrong with you.'

'Hey, who you call *slimy*?' he asks, putting on the accent again.

I scowl at him and give an angry, non-plussed *hmmn* through pursed lips, wondering whether Claire and Beth were right about him after all. Is everything he does just fake?

He holds up his hands in surrender. 'Too soon? Okay, okay. I'm sorry. I didn't mean to make you upset. Forgive me?' He tilts his head to one side and makes mournful eyes at me. 'Please?'

He knows I'm a sucker for his puppy-dog act, and even though I'm still angry with him for acting like such a dick, I decide to leave it. I hate it when we argue and, after all, this is supposed to be our special anniversary.

I poke at the melting ice in my glass with my straw and can't help thinking he's right about one thing though: I should learn to loosen up more when we're out. What's wrong with me? This is the second time this evening I've been accused of not having a sense of humour. I let out a long breath and say: 'Okay, I forgive you.'

'Thanks babes.' He takes my hand and kisses my knuckles one by one, so softly and delicately that the contact of his lips on my skin sends little flutters up my arm.

'Can I get you another drink?' he asks, cocking a finger at my glass. 'Vodka lime soda?'

'Okay. Thanks.'

I study his face while he's being served. I may not be able to recognise a face, but that doesn't stop me from being able to tell if someone's good looking. And Alfie is very good looking. *Too* good looking for me really. Good looking people always have very symmetrical features, which makes it much harder to recognise them. I often wish he was a more goofy-looking guy, with maybe a squint in his eye, a beaky nose or a lopsided smile. But nobody's perfect — it's not his fault he's so handsome, poor thing. Luckily for him I don't care about appearances. I judge people by what's on the inside, not the outside.

When he's got the drinks, I decide it's time to lighten the mood with presents. I fish my little package out of my handbag, and can't stop beaming with anticipation as I hand it over.

'What's this?' he asks.

I study him closely. Has he forgotten or is he pretending again? 'It's a present, silly. Happy anniversary.'

He opens the little jewellery box and takes out the pair of gold cufflinks I've bought him. Real gold, mind, not fake like that Rolex he's wearing. He makes a show of studying them, twisting the little hexagons between his fingers so that the highly polished metal throws off bright little sparkles of light.

'I had your initials engraved on them.'

'Oh? Thanks.'

He doesn't seem very impressed, and slowly it dawns on me what a ridiculous present I've bought him. What on earth was I thinking? I'm not sure he actually owns a shirt with a proper collar, let alone one that needs cufflinks. I should just have bought him that pair of trainers he's been dropping hints about. But I'm always buying him clothes and I wanted to get him something more meaningful and lasting for our anniversary.

'You hate them don't you,' I say in a deflated voice.

'No, I think they're great. Thanks babe.' He gives me a little kiss, slips the cufflinks back into the box, and pops it into his pocket.

I flash him a little smile to hide my disappointment. This evening isn't working out at all how I'd hoped.

As he gulps down a couple of mouthfuls of lager, he studies me across the top of his pint, then sets his glass down on the bar. 'What's wrong?' he asks.

'Nothing.'

'You think I forgot it was our anniversary?'

'No.'

'Yes you do. I *have* got you a present, but I left it at home.'

'Oh, okay. Thanks, you can give it to me some other time.'

He narrows his eyes suspiciously. 'You don't believe me, do you.'

'Of course I do,' I say brightly.

'You think I'm lying.'

'No, I believe you. Honestly.'

'We can leave now to get it if you like,' he says, becoming agitated.

'Shhh! Don't be so silly. It can wait.' I try putting a placatory hand on his arm, but he shrugs free and won't calm down.

'How do you think it makes me feel? Knowing my girlfriend doesn't trust me?'

'I do. *Please*. I'm sorry.' I wish he wouldn't get so tetchy. He often gets worked up like this and I'm not very good at calming him down.

Despite my protests he stands up, prises his phone from the pocket of his tight jeans, and orders an Uber.

As we move slowly through the London traffic, I try to figure out what triggered his bad mood. Was it just because I didn't find his Luca the Romanian act funny? Or maybe he *really* hates those cufflinks? He thinks I don't believe he's bought me a present, but I've no reason to doubt him. Or at least, I didn't. But now I'm beginning to wonder why he's making such a big deal of it.

Whatever the reason, he's acting really pissed off. He raps his knuckles against the window and does that irritating joggling thing with his leg he always does when he's annoyed.

We pull up outside a tall, bay-windowed Victorian building, which stands on its own, all Bates Motel-like, on the corner.

'Wait here,' Alfie tells me, hopping out of the taxi.

'Can't I come in?' I ask, unbuckling my seatbelt.

'It's all right, I won't be long,' he calls in a casual voice, and hurries away down a set of white-washed steps.

It's crazy. He's been living in Lewisham for over a month now, yet this is the first time I've seen his place. If I suggest coming back here after we've been out, he comes up with all these excuses and we always end up back at mine.

I wait in the taxi until he returns. He gets into the cab with a jubilant gleam in his eyes, and, with a theatrical flourish, hands me a package.

'Here you go. Happy anniversary. Sorry I didn't have time to wrap it.'

It's a plain cardboard Amazon package, the size and shape of a medium-sized book.

'Ooh! What can it be?' I turn it over in my hands and make a big fuss so he can see how delighted I am with it. Then I notice an unfamiliar name and address printed on the label. 'Who's Nisha Harlan?' I ask.

'Just a girl at work. I got her to order it for me on her Amazon Prime account. Go on, open it,' he adds, in an excited voice.

When I tear off the cardboard strip, a crisp white box smoothly slides out of the package. I give a little gasp of surprise because I was wrong: it isn't a book, it's an iPad Pro.

'It's the new model. It wasn't cheap,' he tells me proudly.

'Thank you!' I exclaim. Not because I especially need or even want a new tablet, but because I'm so relieved he was telling the truth about the present. I throw my arms around his neck and give him a kiss. Maybe he isn't the total mooch that some people would have me believe. And perhaps the evening isn't a total bust after all.

Chapter 3

WHEN I WAKE the next morning, I find that Alfie's already gone. He must have snuck out when I was still asleep, which is annoying because I was going to sound him out about moving in together. I didn't broach the subject last night because the moment never felt right, and after we got back to the flat, we had a take-away, and then went to bed for some very athletic make-up sex.

I'm surprised I didn't hear him leaving though. Doing night shifts really messes with my sleep patterns and the tiniest of noises will usually wake me. It's another reason why I'll be glad to move out of here. Although Claire and Beth try to be considerate, my room's right next to the sitting room, and they're not very good at keeping the noise down during the day when I'm trying to sleep.

Luckily they're not up yet, so I roll over and close my eyes, and when I wake again it's nearly midday.

The bedroom's stiflingly hot because someone — and by someone, I mean Claire — has whacked the heating up to the max. She complains about being cold in the middle of summer and isn't happy unless the radiators are hot enough to fry eggs on.

I find them both lolling on the sofas in their pyjamas, with that fragile, glazed-over, not-yet-quite-sober look in their eyes from too much alcohol and not enough sleep. There's a Saturday morning cookery-and-chat show on TV. A shiny slab of meat oozing purplish blood is being dipped in egg yolk and rolled in breadcrumbs.

'Uugh, gross!' Claire grunts, blowing out her cheeks

as if she's going to be sick. She grabs the remote, and switches channels, but it's another cookery show. Swirls of some kind of creamy, yellowy gloop is being piped into vol-au-vent cases.

'This is even worse!' Beth complains, shielding her eyes.

'Heavy session last night?' I ask, with a little laugh.

'I may have had a couple of drinks,' Beth admits.

Claire playfully throws a cushion at her. 'A couple? You were ruined!'

'What time did you get in? It must have been very late cos Alfie and I didn't hear you.'

'We couldn't help hearing *you* though,' Claire says, with a little raise of her left eyebrow. 'The walls aren't very thick you know.'

I feel my cheeks burn with embarrassment, and try to come up with a witty retort, but am too distracted by the thought of Alfie's sweaty, out-of-focus face straining with pleasure, which has popped into my head.

We watch TV in silence. Claire massages her eyelids with the tips of her fingers and lets out a low moan. Beth raises her head up off the cushions to announce she's never touching alcohol ever again. But she's not fooling anyone because we all know she'll be out on the lash again this evening. And since it's clear that nobody's in the mood for talking, I go and fetch my new iPad from my bedroom.

I make a big show of taking it out of the box, holding it up conspicuously with the Apple logo showing, then fiddling about with the plug and the charging cable, in the hope that they'll ask me about it and I'll be able to prove to them that Alfie isn't as inconsiderate as they think. But they're too hung-over to pay much attention to what I'm up to, so I end up having to tell them: 'Look what Alfie bought me.'

They both turn blearily to look at me.

'An iPad. It's an anniversary present,' I say.

'Nice,' Claire says, in a flat tone of voice which implies the very opposite. Just because Alfie bought it.

I thought she'd be impressed. She's always flexing about the fact that she has the latest iPhone, and how much better it is than the older model Beth owns, and how all Apple phones are superior to the old Android phone I've got.

'It's the latest model,' I say in a bright tone, trying to compensate for her lack of enthusiasm.

She just wrinkles her nose: 'He likes to flash his cash, doesn't he.'

I give up. I can't win. First she complains that he's mooching off me and now she's complaining because he's bought me something nice. I get on with the task of setting it up, but although it's supposed to be child's play, my head's soon throbbing with the effort of concentration and eventually I give up. I'll get Alfie to do it for me. He's a genius with any kind of technology. I send him a WhatsApp:

Message: *Hi Alfie, I'm having trouble setting up the iPad. Will you do it for me if I bring it this evening? Thanks. PB xxxx*

Message: BTW d*on't forget we're going to Suzi's tonight for dinner. We have to be there at sever thirsty. xxxx*

Message: **Seven thirty*

I know he's not keen on going to Suzi's. I don't really want to go to Suzi's either, but at least she would get to meet him at last, and I'd be able to prove to my big sister that I can actually hold down a relationship, and just because I don't have a flashy house in Dulwich and a partner who earns a fortune in banking or whatever it is that Alistair does, my life isn't the total f-up she tells me it is.

It wasn't always like this. Growing up we were really close. She's four years older and would look out for me at school because she knew how hard I found it. At lunchtime and break times she'd let me hang out with her friends. Then, after school, I'd wait nervously by the drinking fountain, until I saw someone waving to me across the playground. She'd give me a little double nod so I'd know it was her, and we'd walk home together. I was her little shadow and she was my mother hen.

Everything changed when our parents separated. Suzi left to live with Mum, leaving me behind with Dad, and she was far too busy going out every night and being popular to spare time for her babyish little sister.

These days we only see each other very occasionally, and when we do it's a pretty awkward affair. At least Alfie will be there this evening so there won't be any of those tricky moments when the conversation dries up and I can't think of what to say because my mind's gnawing away on the same unanswered bone of a question: *why did you choose to move out with Mum and drop out of my life?* She's never given me any sort of explanation and after all these years I'm still struggling to find closure.

Alfie's not replying to my messages, so I put my phone on the coffee table and slump back into the chair. Outside it's dank, overcast and keeps threatening to rain. Inside, the heat pumping out of the radiators is sending us all to sleep. It's one of those stale, languid, waste-of-time Saturday afternoons when the hours drift past in a haze and no-one has the energy to do anything more energetic than look up from their phones from time to time to ask *anyone want another cup of tea?*

At four o'clock the drowsy fug is pierced by the shrill ringing of the doorbell. No one stirs, but it keeps ringing, until eventually Beth raises her head off the cushion and wearily asks: 'Is anyone going to get that?'

I would go, but I hate the embarrassment of not recognising someone I ought to know, so I give a non-committal shrug and let her answer it.

A woman's voice, shrill and accusatory, reverberates down the hallway. 'Are you Phoebe?'

'I'm sorry, what do you want?' Beth answers defensively.

'I'm looking for Phoebe. Is she here?'

I'm already on my feet, hurrying to the front door. A short girl in her twenties, with dark hair and dark skin, stands on the steps. Her hands are on her hips and she's all puffed up and ready for confrontation.

'You Phoebe?' she asks.

'Yes.'

She looks me up and down, then gives a disdainful snort, like I've failed a test I didn't know I'd entered. 'I want a word with you.'

'Okay,' I say uncertainly.

'In private,' she hisses.

I give Beth a little nod to let her know it's okay, and when she's gone, I ask the girl: 'I'm sorry, do I know you?'

'I'm Nisha,' she declares.

Nisha Harlan? The girl who bought the iPad for Alfie? Why on earth would she come here looking for me?

'Oh, so you know who I am, then,' she states, reading my expression.

'You work with Alfie.'

She rolls her eyes like I'm a complete idiot. 'I don't *work* with Alfie. I'm his *girlfriend*.'

I blink at her in confusion, my brain racing a hundred miles an hour, trying to figure out what she's talking about. Is this some twisted practical joke? Is Alfie waiting round the corner with a smirk on his lips? I wouldn't put it past him. I can just picture him laughing about it afterwards: *Phoebe, you should have seen the look on your face!*

'Girlfriend?' I ask feebly.

'*Girlfriend*,' she repeats in a snidey, childish, sing-song voice. Then her face hardens and the dark skin at the corners of her mouth whiten with anger. 'Don't act dumb with me. I'm not an idiot. I know *exactly* what's been going on behind my back. I'm warning you: stay away from my boyfriend.'

My stomach's giving a panicky flutter as she jabs her finger aggressively at me. She has long manicured fingernails, painted the same fuchsia pink as her lipstick. Her whole outfit is very put-together, very smart, and not Alfie's type at all. But what if she's telling the truth? Could Alfie be carrying on with someone behind my back?

No. I decide the girl must be delusional, and my nurse instincts finally kick in. I have to deal with crazy stuff like this all the time at work — violent patients who spit in your face and threaten to stab you when you're trying to administer a shot of lorazapam; psychotic patients who run up and down the ward shouting in everyone's face until they've tired themselves out — and through it all you have to be professional, keep calm, and try not to take any of it personally.

With delusional patients, the most important thing is to avoid challenging them because you can never predict how they'll react. 'Okay. No problem,' I say, in a calm, measured voice. 'I'll stay away from him.'

She stares at me open-mouthed, stumped by my unexpected response. Obviously she was looking for a fight and now doesn't know what to do. Although her hard eyes simmer at me, her mouth snaps shut.

I say nothing and present her with my most neutral expression, hoping I don't look too resting-bitch-facey.

It's working. She backs off and steps down onto the pavement. 'Just keep the fuck away from him! Or else I won't be responsible for my actions.' Her voice is wavering, her confidence faltering, like she's gone off script and isn't comfortable with having to improvise.

I nod my head empathetically and tell her *okay*.

'I mean it! Stay away!' she yells one last time, before turning and walking off.

I hurry inside, shut the door, and heave a sigh of relief.

'You okay?' Beth asks solicitously.

'I'm fine,' I reply, although now that I can afford to relax, my legs are going to jelly.

Claire's at the window, her nose pressed to the glass, peering up the street. She motions for me to come over. 'Was it that girl who's crossing the road?'

'No, the black girl in the lime green coat who keeps glancing round.'

'Black girl?' Beth says, puzzled. 'You mean *Asian*.'

'Yes, sorry. Asian.'

I often get caught out like this. I think being face blind makes me race blind too. It's a complete minefield and I try to avoid the topic for fear of causing offence.

'So, what was that all about?' Claire asks.

'She's under a delusion that she's Alfie's girlfriend!'

Saying it out loud makes it seem ridiculous rather than threatening. This is the sort of thing that happens on *TOWIE*, not to someone leading such a boring, mundane life as me.

'His girlfriend!' Claire's face brightens with excitement and her nostrils flare as though she can actually smell gossip in the air. 'So, Alfie's been cheating on you? I'm not surprised.'

'He's not been cheating,' I protest. 'The girl's delusional.'

'She doesn't *look* delusional.'

I give an annoyed snort. 'You can tell that she's delusional just by looking at the back of her head?'

'There's no smoke without fire.'

'Look,' I say, getting riled, 'I know Alfie. He'd never

cheat on me.'

Claire arches an eyebrow and in a condescending voice says: 'You sure? He's always seemed like the type to me.'

The type? What does she even know about men? She's never had a relationship that lasted longer than three months. She's probably just jealous, I decide, as I strop off to the kitchen. But, as I fill the kettle, I start to wonder whether this girl really does work with Alfie. And how did she get hold of my address? And who the actual hell is she, anyway? I'm sure there's a simple explanation for it all, but when I ring Alfie to ask him about it, he doesn't pick up.

I spend the rest of the afternoon trying his number and sending messages, but he doesn't respond. Beth faffs about, oohing and aahing at everything I say, while Claire sits there with a big fat smug look on her face, convinced Alfie really is having an affair. And all the while a little alarm bell's clanging away in the back of my head, warning me something isn't adding up.

Eventually I can't take any more. I get to my feet and announce: 'I'm going to Alfie's!'

I'm sure he'll be able to clear everything up. And when he has, we'll go on to Suzi's for the dinner we're both so looking forward to.

Chapter 4

EVEN THOUGH IT'S only a few miles from Tooting to Lewisham as the crow flies, to get there you have to take a tube into central London and then it's a long, tedious bus ride all the way back out again.

It's dark by the time I'm nearing my stop. The idling vibrations of the bus make my teeth chatter as we inch our way, stop-start, past fried chicken shops, minicab offices, mobile phone repair kiosks, and off-licences. Alfie's always slagging off Tooting for being a dive — which to be fair, it is, in a culturally diverse, cheerfully run-down kind of way — but everything here seems grittier and somehow more threatening. It's probably just because I don't know this part of London very well, but the longer this journey goes on, the more my confidence in Alfie wavers.

As I walk from the bus stop, a chilly wind whips up the litter around my feet. I clutch at my coat, wishing I'd worn jeans rather than this thin flowery green dress. But the last time I wore jeans to Suzi's, she gave me one of her sniffily disdainful *oh-you-decided-not-to-bother* looks, which left me fuming all evening. She may only be four years older than me, but the way she acts you'd think she was my mother.

Darkness pools at the bottom of the steps leading to Alfie's front door and I hesitate for a moment before going down and ringing the bell. When no-one comes, I cup my hands on the frosted glass and peer into the dark hallway. There are no lights on; there's no sign of anyone at all. Where *is* he? Have I travelled all this way for nothing?

I hear a noise coming from round the back and,

ignoring the clang-alanging in my head, go to investigate. I find a cramped little garden, all overgrown with brambles, but no sign of Alfie. It was probably just a fox I heard.

It's pretty grim back here. The garden's filled with heaps of junk and piles of gluey, rotting leaves; the grey pebble-dashed walls of the house are streaked with marks from the leaky gutter; the paintwork's all peeling and the panes of glass in the back door are cracked. It could definitely do with a bit of TLC and I'm surprised Alfie would choose to live in a run-down place like this. Perhaps it's why he's not been keen on me visiting?

I can't help giving the back door handle a little rattle before I leave though, and to my surprise find it's unlocked. I push the door open and stick my head inside.

'Alfie?'

My feeble voice barely seems to penetrate the darkness. My pulse quickens as I grope for the light switch and an old-fashioned florescent tube on the ceiling winks into life.

If I thought the garden was a mess, it's nothing compared with this kitchen. Dirty plates and mugs are piled up in the sink, there are stacks of greasy pizza boxes on the floor, and dirty ashtrays heaped with cigarette butts on the countertop. It's the same in the hallway: the wallpaper's peeling off, the carpet's covered in stains, and pervading everything is the caustic odour of stale cat pee. Alfie surely can't live here, can he?

An uneasy panic overtakes me. I must be in the wrong house. I need to get out before someone catches me snooping. But as I turn to leave, I spot a red rucksack lying on the floor of a bedroom off the hallway. My inner-alarm bell's going into overdrive, but some instinct makes me check it out.

It's filled with clothes. There's a pair of jeans, some underwear, a shirt, a jumper. I hold up the jumper and examine it in the dim, gruelly light that seeps in through the thin curtains, trying to decide if it's one of Alfie's. And then I notice a little bag of white powder in the jumble of clothes. A prickling sense of unease races over my scalp.

I tip the contents of the rucksack onto the floor and rummage through them. Hiding among the clothes are twenty or thirty small plastic baggies of white powder. I stare at the little pile with my mouth hanging open like a drooling idiot, my brain spinning in confusion. Is Alfie dealing drugs?

A sudden noise makes me jump. It's the back door slamming shut. Then a man's voice: 'You understand what ah'm sayin' fam?'

There's a pause, then laughter.

'Ex-*act*-lee! I'm laike, I can't be bovvered with this shit no more!'

The thick south-London accent and aggressively cocky swagger fills me with dread. I'm on my knees, frantically trying to shove everything back into the rucksack, but before I'm done, a guy in a hoodie and skinny jeans is standing in the doorway, fixing me with a cold, steely, unwavering gaze.

'Hold on bruv, something's com up. Gotta go. Yeah, call you later bro.'

As he puts his phone away, I notice that under the hoodie he's wearing a pale pink polo shirt with a thin blue stripe. A massive sense of relief floods into my bones. 'Alfie! I've been trying to get hold of you all day —'

'What the fuck're you doing here?' His face contorts with rage as he strides towards me, and now he's in my face and my back's against the wall and I'm clutching the empty rucksack against my stomach like some sort of shield.

'The back door was open and I —'

My voice tails off as I watch him clench his fingers, draw back his arm, and then drive his fist into my stomach.

The impact sends me reeling backwards. I strike my shin on the edge of the bed and fall onto the mattress, my breath coming in noisy, shallow gasps because all the air's been knocked from my lungs.

Now he's kneeling astride me, grabbing my arms and shaking me, yelling at me to stop. But I can't help it. The more I panic, the less oxygen I'm drawing into my lungs. My voice scratches in my throat and I let out a guttural scream, like an animal in a slaughterhouse.

'Shut the *fuck* up!' he bellows.

But I can't help it. I'm gasping for air, and I feel like I'm drowning.

He puts his hand over my mouth and places his knee on my chest, forcing a long, dizzying breath from my lungs. I think: *this is it; I'm going to die.*

But by expelling the air from my body, he stops me hyperventilating, and oxygen enters my lungs again. Slowly my breathing steadies.

'That's better,' he says, removing his hand. I think he's going to let me get up, but when I see the crazed shimmer of excitement that dances in his eyes, I know it's only just beginning.

When he tugs at my dress, I give a tiny gasp of surprise but make no attempt to resist. All my strength's drained away and I'm too stunned, too scared and too confused to move. I lie completely motionless, screwing my eyes shut, letting him paw at my knickers, willing him to get this over with as quickly as possible.

I try to zone out and ignore the weight of his body as he drops down on top of me. I try to disconnect myself from the painful feeling between my legs as he pushes himself inside me. I try to close my ears to the sound of his grunts as he begins thrusting. I try to convince myself that this is all happening to someone else, as if my real self is hiding in the corner of the room, watching dispassionately as a pale piece of size 16 flesh with a flimsy dress all rucked up around her waist is being energetically skewered.

He's hurting me, but I know I've no choice except lie here and wait until he's done. *But please please please please let it be over soon. Concentrate on the ceiling. Think about something else. Oh god, oh god oh god, I'm going to die!*

And then, burning through the pain, like a searing flash of lightning, is a burst of something different. I can't stop myself from letting out a gasping squeal.

'Oh, you like that, do you?' he snarls, thrusting harder and harder into me, his face a twisted mask of desire.

I'm horrified by what's happening to me. Disturbing waves of pain, pleasure and shame surge uncontrollably through my system. Tears are running down my cheeks.

When it's finally all over he rolls off and lies panting and sweaty by my side. Then he turns with a smug smile on his face, propping himself up on an elbow to plant a sloppy kiss on my lips, and says: 'That was fuckin' amazing.'

I'm so dumbfounded by the banality of his words that the hazy, blurry, suddenness of what has just happened jerks into sharp focus. The touch of his clammy arm against mine makes me blench in disgust. I think I'm going to be sick.

'I'm going to the bathroom,' I say, attempting to sound normal, but my voice comes out strained and unnatural.

I slide off the bed and, as I cross the room, I gather up my knickers, my shoes and my bag. When I reach the door, he calls out *hey!* and I freeze in my tracks. For a moment I think he's going to try to stop me, but instead he gives a self-satisfied smile and says: 'Thanks babes!'

He looks so relaxed lying there with his hands behind his head and his trousers around his ankles. My gaze is drawn unwillingly down his half-naked torso, to his flaccid cock. It lies as innocuously as a baby bird in the shadowy nest of his crotch, but it glistens with the sticky metallic menace of a gun that's just been fired.

When he catches me looking, he gives a conspiratorial wink, and I hurry off to the bathroom and slide the lock. My heart's pounding like crazy and my legs tremble so violently I can barely stand.

I examine my face in the mirror — eyes convulsed with fear, lips twisting in confusion. There's a glowering patch of red on my cheek and for the first time in my life I'm able to recognise my face. It's familiar because I've seen this kind of face at work: it's the face of a victim of domestic violence.

I splash my face with cold water and vigorously rub at my skin, as if I could rid myself of the mark on my cheek. But even if I could erase it, there's nothing I could do about the dirty, guilty feeling of shame that crouches foetus-like in the pit of my stomach.

A dull thump on the bathroom door sets my heart racing again. 'Are you gonna be much longer? I need a piss.'

I can't face him. I stand motionless, unable to reply.

He bangs on the door again, harder this time, making the door rattle on its hinges. 'Hurry up! I'm bursting.'

I notice that the bathroom window's open and quickly clamber up onto the ledge. I perch there for a few moments with my knees up by my ears, like a frightened sparrow, staring down into the darkness. And then I jump.

Other than grazing my knee when I land, I'm unharmed. I keep my head down as I scurry along the passageway, and when I reach the street, I slip on my shoes and begin to run.

My breath trails behind me in foggy clouds as I race along the pavement. It's cold and I regret having to leave my coat behind, but at least I've got my phone and my handbag and — still balled up in my right hand — the pair of knickers I fished up from the bedroom floor. I quickly shove them away in my bag before anyone notices the crazy girl running through the night in a summer dress and waving her underwear like a flag of shame.

Even though Alfie doesn't appear to be following, I don't allow myself to slow down. My eyes are blurry from tears and I can't think straight. Unfocused thoughts spiral wildly in every direction, like showers of sparks from a Catherine wheel. I just can't understand why I didn't do anything to stop him. I didn't tell him no, I just lay there and let him do his thing. Perhaps I like violent sex? Perhaps I like being scared? Perhaps I wanted him to rough me up, to force himself onto me, to force himself into me. *Oh, you like that, do you?* I can't help picturing his self-congratulatory expression afterwards, acting as if everything was normal. *Thanks babes!*

My phone's ringing. That'll be him. I wonder how long he was banging on the door before he twigged I wasn't in there. I let the phone go to voicemail, but he's persistent. Again and again he rings, until the sound of the phone is really messing with my mind. I take it out of my bag, to switch it off, and see that it isn't Alfie calling; it's Suzi.

I answer: 'Hello.'

'Phoebe? Where *are* you? You were supposed to be here half an hour ago.'

I'd forgotten all about our dinner date. 'Look Suzi,' I begin, 'd'you think we could —'

'You'd better not be trying to cancel on me?' she says in a menacing tone. 'We've rearranged this twice already because of you, and I've gone to a lot of effort.'

I've not got the strength in me to fight, so I tell her: 'I wasn't cancelling. I just wanted to know what I should bring.'

'Just bring yourselves. Wait a minute, have you even left yet?'

'I'm in Lewisham —'

'Lewisham? God Phoebe, how long are you going to be?'

'Fifteen minutes, maybe twenty, tops.'

'Twenty minutes! Okay, but *please*, don't be any later.'

I book an Uber. According to the app, it'll be ten minutes before the driver even arrives, so there's no way I'll be in Dulwich in twenty minutes. Suzi's going to kill me.

The driver catches my eye in the mirror when I get in the car. His nostrils flare, as if he can detect the smell of sex on me. Like he knows. I look away and stare numbly out of the window.

A gang of gangly, hoodie-wearing youths are loping along the pavement. As they cross the road in front of the car, they all turn in my direction. Like they know too.

A burning sense of shame seeps from the crown of my head to the curling tips of my toes. I shut my eyes and bury my face in my hands.

Chapter 5

I WAIT ON the steps, anxiously tapping my foot, until the door's opened by a slim blonde-haired woman. She's wearing a clingy, low-cut wrap dress with a bold, peacocky print, and a lime-green pin-striped shrug. It has to be Suzi, because who else would wear such garishly clashing fabrics, but I wait for her to give me the curt little double nod, just to be sure.

In the old days, when we were close, before our parents' divorce, before Suzi moved out and everything turned sour between us, this nod would be delivered with a big-sisterly grin of encouragement. This evening she's angry with me for being late and there's barely a hint of a smile.

'You're here,' she states flatly. 'No coat?' She may be colour-blind when it comes to fashion, but you can't fault her powers of observation.

'I forgot to bring one!' I say with a bright little laugh.

But the laugh is a mistake. It's too soon for light-heartedness because my emotions are too raw. The laugh rasps painfully in my throat as an image of Alfie lying on the bed flashes into my mind — a sinister half-naked figure, half-man half-beast, like a centaur. What am I doing here? I shouldn't have come. I should have gone home, crept into bed and curled up into a ball under the duvet. I feel like crying.

Suzi hugs me and gives me a mwhah mwhah kiss on each cheek, and even though there's something passive-aggressive about the way that the bones of her skinny body poke into me, I have an urge to confide in her.

But before I can, she asks: 'Where's Alfie?' and peers

over my shoulder, as if she might spot him lurking in the bushes.

'He couldn't make it.'

'What? Again?' She studies me with a sceptically raised eyebrow.

What can I say? *Sorry, but I discovered a stash of drugs in his bag, so he viciously attacked me, and after it was over I escaped through a window, and then you rang and I couldn't tell you what happened, so here I am.* Instead, I say: 'Something came up.'

'Really?' she says, unimpressed by my feeble explanation.

I shrug.

'How long have you two been together now?'

'A year —' I tell her, bracing myself for the chastisements which are sure to follow.

'A year and I still haven't met him!' she complains. 'Are you ashamed of me? Is that it? Well, I'm sorry, but, aside from our wonderful father, I'm the only family you've got.'

She breaks off with a dramatic, martyred sigh. She loves stirring up painful memories, and then uses them to make me feel bad. I'm sure she's not finished yet, but before she can get back up onto her high horse, I notice her eyes flicking up to my cheek, and with genuine concern she asks: 'What've you done?'

'Nothing.' I turn away but she takes my chin and steers my face to the light.

'Your cheek's all red.'

I gently touch my fingers to the tender spot where Alfie slapped me. 'Oh that. I did it at the gym yesterday. Walked right into one of the weight machines. What an idiot! Ha ha!'

My laugh is more fake than Alfie's watch, but thankfully Suzi doesn't seem to notice. She's more interested in my keep-fit regimen. She's always nagging at me to take up running or yoga or Pilates or something.

'You've joined a gym? That's great. Is it close to the hospital?'

'Yes,' I reply, desperately trying to think where my nearest gym actually is.

'Come on inside, it's cold out here. You must be freezing. Are you doing mainly cardio or weights? Do they have lots of classes?'

Peow peow, peow! She fires questions at me like bullets, but I duck them all with an evasive shrug and head for the kitchen.

Suzi stops me with an amused chuckle: 'Where are you going Phoebs? We're in the dining room. I'm afraid you've missed the starter. I couldn't keep them all waiting any longer.'

'Wait a minute, what d'you mean *them all?* I thought it was just you, me, and Alistair?'

It turns out that she has a dozen or so guests sitting round the table in the dining room, who all turn expectantly when I enter, as if I'm their entertainment, come to perform close-up magic between courses or something. I smile awkwardly.

'Everybody, this is my sister Phoebe.'

My eyes flit from face to face like some sort of crazed bee trying to gather pollen. I give a feeble little *hi.*

A tall, heavyset man with a receding hairline and thick-rimmed glasses makes a big show of getting to his feet. It's at moments like this that I could do with Suzi by my side to whisper people's names in my ear, like she used to do at family gatherings. *The girl wearing the hideously ugly green top and jeans that don't fit her is our cousin Gillian. That boy over by the door — no, the one with the ginger hair and the snotty nose — is Matthew from next door. I think he fancies you!*

The man comes over and gives me a big bearish hug.

'You made it! We were beginning to wonder if you were coming!'

It must be Alistair; husband number three. In his early forties, though he could be mistaken for fifty; an earnest, kindly man possessing the relaxed self-assuredness and the monied sense of entitlement that comes from a private education.

All Suzi's husbands have been cast in the same mould: posh, rich and a lot older than her. She definitely has a type, though finding someone who's her type doesn't mean she sticks with them for long. Her first marriage only lasted one year; the second two. Maybe she'll make it to three with Alistair? I hope so. Of her three posh, rich, older husbands, he's definitely my favourite.

'Where's *Alfie*?' Alistair asks, saying Alfie's name in air-quotes as though he might just be a figment of my imagination.

'He couldn't come. Sorry. He sends his apologies.'

Suzi makes a show of clearing away the table setting that was meant for Alfie, and I take my place next to a fleshy-faced man with crinkly, salt-and-pepper hair whipped up candy-floss style on the top of his head. I quickly flip through my mental *Guess Who?* cards but draw a blank.

'Hello, I'm Phoebe,' I say, holding out my hand.

The man gives a childish pout of disappointment. 'You don't remember me?'

I peer into his face for a second and then do a little double take, as though I've just recognised him. 'Oh yes, sorry! Of course I do. Hello again.'

'This is Francesca,' he says, introducing the narrow-faced, dark-haired woman by his side. 'Phoebe was on at our table at Alistair's wedding last year,' he explains, and now I remember him: Charles Fairleigh-Granger, the eldest of Alistair's three brothers; a sweaty-palmed mansplainer in love with money and the sound of his own voice.

I'm poured a large glass of red wine and try not to grimace as I sip at it. I try to avoid wine if I can, especially red, because it goes straight to my head, and I get the most vicious, brain-rottingly headachy hangovers the next day. It's not as if I even like the taste, so I don't know why I drink it.

I glance around the table with a grinding sense of despondency. What on earth was Suzi thinking when she invited me? She knows how I struggle on these sorts of occasions. I'm sure her friends are all very nice people, but I know I'll have absolutely nothing in common with any of them. They all seem to be bankers and lawyers and owners of internet start-up companies, and I can just picture the way they'd look down their noses at me if they found out that I'm only a lowly nurse. While they were signing off on a high-finance deal, or making an executive presentation at a Board meeting, I was sat in a tiny cubicle beside an elderly patient, stroking her hair until she fell asleep.

I take another swig of my drink. Despite my aversion to red wine, I've somehow nearly emptied my glass.

'More wine?' Charles asks, re-filling my glass before I can stop him. 'This is a 2006 Rioja. A very fine year.'

'It's very nice,' I tell him, examining the rich, dusty-blood coloured liquid with a sage nod, as though of course I knew that 2006 was a fantastic year, and didn't everyone?

Charles lectures me about the blend of grapes they use to make the wine; the tannin content; the oak barrels they store it in, while I sip away at it — I'm supposed to be getting notes of vanilla, toasted coconut, nutmeg and tobacco (really?) — and wait for an opportunity to change the subject. But he's one of those people who stretches his words out longer than necessary to paper over the natural pauses in the conversation, making it impossible to get a word in.

My attention's drifting and I can't stop my thoughts

from returning to Alfie. Over and over it replays in my mind, but already the details are growing fuzzy. Did he hit me once, or was it twice? Did I really make no attempt to stop him even though every atom of my body was crying out NO? And — oh God — did I really climax in the middle of the most horrific incident of my life? That's the worst part: the horrified shock I experienced when I realised I was coming, and the smug look on his face when he saw me. That was the moment he knew he'd won: *you enjoyed that, didn't you.*

But I didn't. I hated it more than anything I've ever experienced in my life. Why would my body betray me like that? Am I really one of those women who finds sexual pleasure in dangerous situations? Maybe this sick thing has lain dormant in me until now? Maybe I wanted it to happen? Oh God, there must be something seriously wrong with me. But it makes no sense. I abhor violence, I hate getting drunk, and I'm the least promiscuous person I know. I cross my legs, and wince in pain from the bruising.

'I'm sure Phoebe's heard enough about Rioja for one evening,' Francesca says, making Charles put down the glass he's swirling under my nose.

'I'm not boring you, am I?' he asks.

'No.'

'See. Phoebe's not bored.'

'Well, maybe you could change the subject anyway. For my sake.'

'All right,' Charles replies tetchily, and turns to me with a bright smile: 'So Phoebe, what did you say your boyfriend does for a living?'

'I didn't,' I reply bluntly, wondering how he's managed to pick on the only subject in the entire world I want to talk about less than red wine.

Charles laughs, thinking I'm trying to be funny, and I tell him Alfie works in sales, which thankfully isn't interesting enough to provoke any further questions. I wouldn't be able to answer them anyway because Alfie has always been so vague about what he actually does for a living. Is that because he makes his money dealing drugs? Is everything I thought I knew about him wrong? Romantic, caring, attentive Alfie? Alfie, who takes me to the cinema, who buys me presents, who loves me? Alfie, who lies, who's probably cheating on me with that girl Nisha, who stole her iPad and gave it to me as a present, who slapped me across the face and pushed me onto the bed —

My phone buzzes again. It's been buzzing on and off since I sat down, but I've been ignoring it. Charles leans to me conspiratorially, so close that I can smell the red wine on his breath. 'Aren't you going to answer that?'

I tell him *no*, but he goes on about it, like he's making a hilarious joke: 'You're obviously a very popular girl! Ha ha! Shall I answer it for you? Ha ha ha! Someone's *really* desperate to get hold of you! Ha ha ha ha!'

Ha ha ha ha. I get my phone out just to make him be quiet. There are ten missed calls from Alfie. As I switch the phone off, I catch Suzi staring at me across the table, and I'm struck again by the desperate urge to talk to her. What she told me earlier was true. She's the only family I've got, the only person in the world who really knows me, the only person I could consider opening up to about what happened. Perhaps I can grab a few minutes alone with her?

She's mouthing something at me.

What? I mouth back silently.

Put that away! she mouths, jerking her head angrily at the phone in my hand.

Thanks a lot Sis! I put it away. Charles has topped up my glass again so I knock it back, hoping the syrupy wine might deaden the pain. So far it isn't working though — the alcohol's just making me more woozily confused than ever.

I try not to think about Alfie, and to focus instead on the conversation going on around the table. But it's as incomprehensible to me as the cluckings and gobblings of a barnful of turkeys flapping their wings and shaking their wattles at each other.

When it's time to clear the dinner plates I get up to help, but Suzi shoos me away and I can see I'm not going to get any time alone with her tonight.

When the table's ready, Suzi returns from the kitchen with the pudding — some sort of wobbly retro-style mousse or syllabub, decorated with piped cream and little pieces of candied fruit. Everyone oohs and aahs appreciatively, but the gelatinous sheen on it just makes me feel nauseous.

I've had enough. I can't bear any more of Charles, of my sister, of all these lovely, terrible people. As I get to my feet, the chair scrapes across the floor with a horrendous grating screech, making everyone look up from their dessert.

'I'm sorry,' I mumble, to no-one in particular, 'I have to go.'

I hook my bag over my shoulder, hurry out of the dining room, and let myself out of the house. Half-way down the gravel path I catch my foot on something that sends me sprawling onto my knees. Just when I thought this disaster of a day couldn't get any worse! It's like this is all some massive joke at my expense. I should be laughing. I can hear Charles' voice in my head: *ha ha ha ha!*

Suzi finds me sitting on the path, gingerly picking gravelly little fragments out of the torn skin on my knee. She peers over me with her hands on her thighs. 'So, are you going to tell me what's going on?'

'What d'you mean?' I ask innocently.

'This —' She gestures at her pathetic little sister sitting in a pathetic crumpled heap on the pathetic dirty ground.

I want to tell her everything, but my brain's so befogged with 2006 Rioja that I can't think where to start.

She sighs impatiently. 'Look, I've got a houseful of guests in there wondering where I've got to. If you don't want to talk, that's fine by me. I'm not going to force you.'

I catch sight of her expression in the shifting shadows: it's as hard as glass and it skewers my heart. It's the same defiant, closed-down mask she wore eighteen years ago when our parents announced they were separating and asked us to choose who we wanted to live with. The day Suzi chose to walk away from me. Horrible, stingy tears of self-pity well up in my eyes.

She gives another sigh. 'It always has to be a drama with you, doesn't it. How can anyone help you if you turn everything into a performance?'

'Help me? Isn't it a bit late for you to start playing the supportive big sister after all these years?'

'Oh, not *this* again.'

'Never mind, forget it,' I say, wondering how we ended up on this topic. I didn't mean to bring it up.

'Phoebe, you weren't the only one who had a hard time when Mum and Dad split, you know. And it was much harder for me.'

I glower up at her through the gloom, but don't reply.

A figure appears in the doorway behind her, and Suzi turns to see what's caught my attention. 'Oh, hi darling!' she calls.

It must be Alistair. 'Is everything okay out here?' he asks.

'Everything's fine.' Suzi reaches out her hand and pulls me to my feet.

'How much longer will you be?' He sounds quite annoyed. And more than a little bit tipsy.

'I'm just talking with Phoebe.'

'Okay, that's very nice. But don't forget whose idea it was to host this dinner party. And who it was that insisted we needed a new tablecloth, new glasses, new table mats and — what else was it? Oh yes that's right, a new coffee table, because our old one is just *so last year.*'

'I think I should be going,' I mutter to Suzi under my breath, but she grabs onto my sleeve and tells Alistair:

'Let's not talk about this now darling. I'll just be two minutes and then I'll come, I promise.'

'Fine!' he says in the tone of a moody teenager, meaning *it's not fine*, and strops back to his guests who must be wondering what all the drama's about.

Suzi's still holding onto my arm and although I'm itching to snatch it away, a part of me is desperate to tell her what happened. I want her to hug me tight and tell me everything will be all right. But that's not how our relationship works.

Instead, she says: 'It's Mum's anniversary in two weeks,' and my jaw becomes taut and my shoulders tense up, because I know where this is going.

'Can you believe it?' she continues. 'She's been gone ten years!'

'Uh-huh.'

She eyes me sharply, and in a reproving tone says: 'Don't you think we ought to do something to mark the occasion?'

'Maybe.'

'Ten years! Surely we have to do *something*!'

I can't stand this bullying, self-righteous, holier-than-thou tone she uses with me. 'Why? Why do we have to do something.'

'If we don't mark the occasion, who else will?'

'Geoff?'

Suzi pulls a sour face at the mention of the man Mum

was living with at the time she died.

'Dad then?' I respond, regretting it as soon as the words have escaped my lips.

'Oh yeah, right! I doubt he'll be sober enough to know what day of the week it is, let alone remember that it's Mum's anniversary.'

An image of Dad shading his blood-shot eyes from the dazzling sunshine as he staggered drunkenly out of a Spanish bar flashes into my mind. He moved to Spain the summer I graduated. I flew out to stay with him for a week in his tiny one-room apartment in Estepona, and basically spent the time following him from bar to bar, watching him cadge drinks off rich ex-pats until he passed out.

Suzi gives an exasperated sigh. 'Won't you at least come with me to visit Mum's grave this year?'

'I don't understand why you have to turn every occasion into a big show of mourning?'

'It's just one day a year, for Christ sakes! It's a chance for us to show that we haven't forgotten her.'

Except it isn't just one day. I get mawkish messages from Suzi all the time. On Mum's birthday, at Christmas time, at Easter:

Feeling melancholy :(Hard to believe Mum would be sixty today.

Another Christmas without Mum :(Missing her more every year xxx.

I wouldn't be surprised if she starts sending sad-face emoticon messages on National Cheese Day or National Wear a Hat Day:

So sad, you know how much Mum loved hats <:(

If only Suzi realised how upsetting I find her messages. Pretending we were one big happy family, when the truth is that after the divorce, Christmases and Easters were the most miserable times of the year.

'I don't need to visit Mum's grave in order to remember her. All the memories are in here,' I tell her, tapping the side of my head.

She persists: 'One afternoon, that's all I'm asking of you.'

'I really don't want to, Suzi.' The thought of raking over the coals of my memories of Mum is starting to freak me out.

'If you won't do it for our poor mother, then do it for me. It's the *least* you could do.'

I'm about to ask her what exactly she means by that, but I realise there's no point. I learnt a long time ago that it's impossible reasoning with Suzi, so, I tell her:

'Okay, okay, I'll come.'

Chapter 6

I HEAD OFF up the road towards the station, struggling to process everything. I was a fool to think I could confide in Suzi. And now, because she caught me when my guard was down, I've no choice but to go along with her to the cemetery. I know she only wants me on hand with a packet of Kleenex because she needs an audience. After all, what's the merit in shedding tears if there's no-one there to see it?

I glance back at the house. She's watching me from the front door with a pained expression on her face, rubbing at her temples with her fingers. She always has to play the martyr and make out that it was easier for me than her when Mum and Dad split. The truth is though, that until tonight, it was by far the most traumatic thing that had ever happened to me.

My life can be divided into two halves as cleanly as you might cut open a piece of fruit. There was the time before Mum left and the time after. And the hard, unbreakable stone at the centre of the fruit is the day my parents announced they were separating.

August 2004. I was eleven, and the long summer holiday between junior school and senior school was drawing to a soggy close. It had been the wettest summer for fifty years, a miserable, stuck-indoors, can't wait for it to be over kind of summer.

Suzi was fifteen, practically a grown-up in my eyes, while I was a particularly immature and no doubt very annoying eleven-year-old. We shared a poky bedroom at the front of the house and although we had always got along well when we were younger, that summer we were really getting on each other's nerves.

I was upstairs in the bedroom reading *The Princess Diaries* or playing *The Sims* or whatever it was that a particularly immature and annoying eleven-year-old was doing in 2004. Everyone else — Mum, Dad, Suzi — was downstairs.

'Phoebe, can you come down here!'

'In a moment.'

'Now Phoebe!'

'All right!' I shouted irritably, and stropped downstairs.

The instant I entered the room I could tell something was up. They turned to me with tight-lipped expectation, standing with their arms hanging awkwardly by their sides, like actors on stage waiting for the cue for the scene to begin. The tension in the air was palpable, like the build-up of a static electric charge in the atmosphere before a storm. The scene is imprinted so forcibly onto my mind that, all these years later, I can examine it like it's a painting, or a still from a movie. That old stripy sofa we had with the removable cover which, despite repeated washing, couldn't shift the felt-tip pen stains; the ugly wooden coffee table in the middle of the room we'd always catch our shins on; the 32" TV in the corner which seemed so colossal when Dad proudly brought it home. But as hard as I try, I can't make out their faces.

No-one spoke. 'What's going on?' I asked innocently, trying to catch Suzi's eye. I always relied on my big sister to make sense of the world for me, but she just turned away without speaking. Judas!

Mum said: 'Perhaps we should all sit down first.'

I sat on the chair by the door, Suzi and Mum were on the sofa, but Dad stayed on his feet. The bright sunshine streaming in from the window behind gave him the golden halo of a mediaeval saint.

Mum cleared her throat nervously. 'As you know, Dad and I have been having difficulties for a while now —'

Difficulties? I remember thinking. *What difficulties?* Yes, they had their arguments, but didn't all parents argue?

'So we've decided it would be best if we spent some time apart. I've found a flat. It's only fifteen minutes from here, so you wouldn't be far from Dad and your old school friends.'

Her mouth was moving and words were coming out, but I couldn't make sense of them. I turned to Dad in confusion.

There were tears in his eyes and in a flat, pinched voice he told me: 'Mum's moving out.'

Those three words, as sharp as a scalpel blade, cleaved my heart. Mum was leaving us. Mum was ripping the family in two.

I turned to her for reassurance, but she just gave me a thin-lipped silvery smile, which made me shiver because I'd seen that smile on the cinema screen only a few weeks before. It was exactly the same chilling smile that Dolores Umbridge gives Harry Potter in *The Order of the Phoenix* as she tells him that the bloody lines he's scratching out on his skin are for his own good.

Even though I can't bring Mum's features to mind, that Dolores Umbridge smile of hers is stamped indelibly on my memory. And after she smiled, she told me in a condescending voice that *it's for the best.*

For her best maybe, but for my best? For Suzi's best? For Dad's? It chokes me up to think about it because, of course, every woman should be free to leave an unhappy relationship. But I just can't help the bitterness, anger and sense of abandonment from resurfacing whenever I think about that day.

Mum exchanged a look with Dad before continuing: 'Your father and I have discussed it — at length — and agreed that you girls are old enough to choose where you'd like to live. Suzi's decided to come and live with me, but you have to make your own decision.'

I looked to Suzi for help again, but she was staring fixedly at the furniture now, refusing to look me in the eye. *Et tu Brute!* Except we hadn't done *Julius Caesar* at school yet, so I was probably just thinking *you mean cow!*

Everyone was waiting for my answer, but my mind was all a whirl. I had no idea what to say. Mum was doing that Dolores Umbridge smile thing again and Suzi was having a staring contest with the coffee table, but when I looked at Dad, he gave me such a helpless, pitiable shrug that I impulsively jumped up, grabbed hold of his arm, pulled it tightly to my chest, and announced: 'I'm staying with Dad.'

I don't think anyone was expecting me to make that choice, and looking back on it I'm not even sure Dad wanted me to stay with him. But once my mind was made up, I refused to budge, no matter how much Suzi and Mum tried to reason with me.

They moved out a week later. Dad helped ferry their things round to the new place in that battered old red Ford Ka we used to have. I was waiting in the hallway when he returned home from the final trip. He shut the front door and just stared into space for the longest time, with the most fearfully bleak look in his eyes. When he finally noticed me standing there he softly muttered: 'I didn't want any of this to happen.' I took hold of his hand, and we stood together in the hallway, jerky little sobs racking his body.

Initially I was able to console myself with the thought that at least I had the bedroom all to myself now. But I missed having Suzi around, especially at night-time. When I had trouble getting to sleep, I used to make her talk to me. I'd lie all curled up under the duvet taking comfort in the quiet breathy sound of her voice, drifting in and out of consciousness, with one foot in the real world and one in the world of dreams, until I nodded off. After she moved out, I developed a fear of the dark, and couldn't get to sleep unless the light was left on.

Then there was Dad's drinking. After Mum left, he just fell apart. *My medicine*, he'd call it. *Medicine for a broken heart*. Each week before Mum brought Suzi over, I'd help him clear up the empty bottles that had accumulated on the kitchen worktop, and down beside his armchair and under his bed. He'd make a game of it. It was our little secret, something to strengthen the bond between us. Of course, even at the age of eleven I knew that his drinking wasn't a game. It was deadly serious.

But it wasn't Dad's drinking that I found hardest to cope with; it was the feeling of being abandoned by my own mother. I can't think about those days without becoming emotional. It's funny how some things stay with you all your life. I'd always hoped that one day we might be reconciled, but by the time I was ready to forgive her, she was already dying of pancreatic cancer, and three months later she was dead.

I sniff back the tears as I cross the busy main road and follow as it elbows round towards West Dulwich station. There's a park on one side, and on the other side I can see the baleful "H" of rugby posts looming up out of the dark, empty expanse of a sports ground. Blaring traffic races along the street in between, painting red and white trails of light in the cold air. I screw up my eyes to the smarting lights, block my ears to the noise, and hurry on.

I can't stop thinking about Mum. If only she were still alive. But I've no one in my life to look after me. No one to take me in their arms and hug me and stroke my hair and tell me it's going to be all right. No one to let me know that I'm safe and that nobody will be able to hurt me anymore.

Chapter 7

THREE A.M. AND I'm at home, in bed, unable to sleep. Every time I try to clear my mind, the memories of Alfie come crashing through the fragile surface of my thoughts. And then my brain begins worming away at the same list of questions: *Why did he do it to me? Why didn't I try to stop him? Why did I squeal with pleasure when it was the most hideous thing I've experienced? Why do I feel so empty and dead inside?*

On and on it goes, an endless train of thoughts that circle around inside my brain like a serpent trying to catch its tail. Why, why, why? It's driving me insane.

I end up having to throw off all the covers because I'm burning up from repulsion, anger and self-loathing. Then all at once I find myself crying — proper crying, with sobs and tears and body-shuddering jerks. I bury my face in my pillow so the others won't hear. Where did these tears come from with no warning at all? And when will they stop? It's like my body's sprung a leak and I've no idea how to fix it.

By the time morning comes I'm more tired and confused than I was when I went to bed. I switch on my phone and find a dozen unread messages from Alfie. What does he want? To apologise? To gloat? To remind me how much I enjoyed it and ask if I want to do it again? I shudder with disgust, and even though I know it's the wrong thing to do, I can't help reading his messages.

Message: *Hi Phoebs, what you doing today? Xxx*
Message: *Trying out the new cufflinks. Looking fine!!*
Message: *Wanna hook up later? Let me know. Xxx*

The sheer mundanity of his words takes me aback. It's like nothing whatsoever happened last night.

Message: *Hey Phoebs, don't leave me on read.*
Message: *Can you tell me what I'm supposed to have done?*
Message: *Are you actually ghosting me?*
Message: *I miss U Phoebe xxx*

The messages continue all day, alternating between declarations of love and increasingly angry accusations that I'm being unreasonable. Then he gives up on WhatsApp and bombards me with phone calls instead. It's unrelenting. He must be sitting there with his finger on the redial button. I can't imagine what state of mind he must be in.

Little slivers of doubt begin to infiltrate my thoughts. Although it happened less than twenty-four hours ago, the memories are already starting to fray and become fuzzy. I think it was Alfie, but maybe it wasn't him? There was the pink shirt and the jumper in the rucksack which I think were his, but that's just circumstantial evidence, not the sort of evidence which would hold up in court.

You'd think I'd have been able to tell it was him when he got close to me, when he laid on top of me, but it all happened so fast and with such violence that I'm not certain of anything. The man didn't sound like Alfie and he certainly didn't act like Alfie. The Alfie I know would never hurt me. Would he? Perhaps he really is innocent?

But if it wasn't Alfie, then who was it? A total stranger? The notion makes me shudder from head to toe and I think I might be sick.

By seven p.m., when I leave for work, I've had thirty-six missed calls and I don't know what to believe anymore. I've slid from the black and white world of certainty into a misty realm where everything is an indeterminate shade of grey.

The waiting room's already heaving, and on top of that two nurses called in sick tonight and the supply nurses haven't shown up. But it's actually a relief to be forced to switch off from my problems and deal with the aggro and chaos of a busy A&E department instead.

I take bloods, administer meds, and handle the frustrations of waiting patients with my usual calm efficiency. But as the night wears on, everyone's getting fractious, tempers are fraying, and I'm struggling to cope because of a lack of sleep and the emotional trauma of the last 24 hours.

There are no empty beds anywhere in the hospital, so we can't move patients out of A&E, and it's left to us front-line staff to deal with it all. It's like a war zone. The resuscitation bays are full; the cubicles have had to be doubled up; we're having to treat people on chairs; and there are patients on trolleys in the corridors, some of whom have been waiting 48 hours for a bed — mostly elderly patients who call out in confusion every time you squeeze your way past. Meanwhile, the average waiting time keeps getting longer and longer and we're having to turn away ambulances.

The daughter of a dementia patient shrieks at me hysterically for discharging her father, even though I've explained that there's no reason for him to be admitted to hospital.

A very elderly lady with thinning white hair and sallow, papery skin is dying. Her breath comes in raspy shallow gasps and she's fallen into unconsciousness. The relatives are in two minds about resuscitation, but there's nothing much we can do anyway. As I tell them I don't think she'll make it through the night, my voice chokes up and I have to hurry out of the room before I lose it.

As I pass through the waiting room, a woman grabs

my arm, and demands to be seen because she's been waiting for over ten hours. When I explain that we have to deal with the most urgent cases first, so I'm afraid she'll have to wait her turn, she pinches my arm, shouts '*You fucking slut!*' right in my ear, and then spits in my face. The woman sitting beside her cheers as I hurry away to wipe it off.

The police bring in a man high on heroin and methadone, then leave him with us, even though there's nothing medically wrong with him. He tells me to *fuck off* when I try to check his pulse and becomes so violent that I have to call security. I watch from the corner of the cubicle with tears in my eyes as he hurls obscene racial abuse at the security guard, and my colleagues ask if I'm okay, concerned about me because out of all of us, I'm usually the one who doesn't let things get to me at work.

Eight hours into my shift I get a needle stick injury while taking bloods. Partly it was the fault of my patient, a twenty-six stone, forty-one-year-old man who kept wincing and jerking his arm away like a big baby whenever I brought the needle near him, but mainly it was my fault because my tiredness is making it hard to concentrate. And now I'm going to have to go and get my own blood tested.

I manage to grab half an hour's sleep on my break, but if anything, it's left me feeling more tired. By five a.m. the exhaustion's really kicking in and I have to rub my eyes to stay awake. I'm trying to work out a gentamicin dose for a septic patient, but every time I check the calculation I arrive at a different answer. I tell myself to pull it together; *only another three hours to go.*

Finally, after more than twelve hours, the shift is over and I emerge from the building, blinking and yawning in the crisp morning air. I make my weary way home along Tooting High Street just as everyone else is starting their day, so shattered that I don't notice the good-looking young man in a blue jacket waiting on the pavement ahead of me, until he speaks:

'Why haven't you been answering your phone?' he asks, with the light-heartedly reproachful look an indulgent parent might give a naughty child.

Alfie! I'm so taken aback by his cheerful manner that I can't speak. It's like my tongue has been frozen by anaesthetic.

'It's all right. I forgive you,' he says, giving me a little peck on my cheek and taking my hand. 'I'll even treat you to breakfast if you like. C'mon.'

Before I can react, he's leading me inside *Crema Crema*, a Mexican-vegetarian café by the tube we've been to before, which serves expensive artisan coffees and all-day brunch. As we weave a path through the mishmash of vibrantly painted tables, wooden chairs and plastic stools, the rich smell of spicy, fatty food turns my stomach.

Every cell in my body is telling me to get out of here, but my brain's too addled from tiredness to think straight. Is this the man who attacked me on Saturday, or is he innocent? I just don't know. I'm still wandering in that foggy no-man's-land lying between two versions of the truth. In one version it was Alfie who found me in his bedroom, and in the other it was a complete stranger. But I have no idea which version is correct, and my memories have become so fragmented that it's impossible now to piece everything back together.

'Are you hungry? I'm starving,' he says, handing me a menu.

The words come into focus and I read them automatically: *Smashed avocado toast. Battered cauli and bean goujons. Skewered vegetables doused with virgin-pressed rape seed oil.* Every item conjures up a fresh image of brutality. I didn't know vegetarian food could be so violent. I snap the menu shut and place it on the table.

'D'you fancy going to *The Bedford* tomorrow?' Alfie

asks. 'This guy I know is friends with one of the bands who're playing and says he can get us free tickets.'

I stare at him in a numbed silence, unable to reply.

'You okay?' He tries to take hold of my hands, but I pull them away.

'What's the matter? You seem mad about something.'

I still can't speak. I wish I wasn't here. I want to go home, take a shower, climb into bed and forget about everything.

'You're not still hacked off with me because I forgot our anniversary, are you?'

I shake my head.

'Well, what are you so upset about?'

I close my eyes, trying not to think about *it*, but the images flash through my mind with a queasy rapidity.

'Phoebe!' Alfie demands.

'It's about what happened in your flat!' I blurt out in a despairing, choked up voice.

He gives me a puzzled frown. 'You've never been in my flat?'

I can hardly process what he's saying. 'Please Alfie, don't mess with me.'

'I'm not messing. Seriously, trust me. I don't know what you're talking about.'

He seems so genuine. Surely he's telling the truth?

'Are you ready to order?' a handsome, darkly-bearded waiter asks.

'I'll have the Crema All-day Breakfast. And can I have it with extra mushrooms and refried beans?' Alfie hands back his menu and turns to me with an expectant smile. 'Phoebe?'

The handsome waiter's waiting with the nib of his pen pressed to his pad, but my brain's working overtime. My relief that it *wasn't* Alfie who attacked me is tainted by sickening disgust at the realisation that I was abused by a stranger.

'Are you going to order?' Alfie asks, becoming irritated.

'I can come back later if you like,' the waiter says helpfully.

'No, it's okay. Phoebe?' Alfie gives me an impatient smile and I quickly order a coffee.

'I'm not hungry,' I explain when the waiter has gone.

When his food arrives, Alfie tucks into his breakfast, and tells me about his latest scheme for making money — something about reconditioning old office furniture.

My coffee sits untouched as I try to come to terms with everything, only half-listening to Alfie's plans. Everything's still a grisly haze. The only things that are crystal clear are the memories of the tears running down my face; the clammy fingers pressed over my mouth; the sharp knee digging into my thigh —

'Phoebe?'

'Uh?'

'What d'you think?' Alfie's waiting eager-faced for me to say something.

The muscles of my mouth are so tense that I struggle to speak, and when I do my voice sounds choked and all mushed up: 'Great!' I tell him.

'You finished then?' he asks, wiping his plate with the last of his toast.

'Yes,' I reply, though I've barely touched my coffee.

He signals to the waiter. 'What d'you want to do now? I was thinking we could — oh, hang on.' His phone's ringing. 'Sorry, I've got to take this. Could you get the bill? Ta.'

He answers his phone, then reaches under the table to retrieve his bag. He swings it over his shoulder and I watch as he weaves a zig-zag path through the diners towards the door. It's only when he reaches it that I realise what he's carrying: a rucksack. A red rucksack. The same red rucksack with white stitching around the pocket that I found stuffed full of drugs. The room seems to lurch vertiginously as my world spins 180 degrees back to the certainty that it *was* Alfie that night after all.

I pay the bill in a daze, make my way to the door with trepidation, then push it open and step out into the bright sunshine. Alfie's talking on the phone by the edge of the pavement, with one foot up on a bicycle rack. He throws back his head and laughs, combing his fingers rakishly through his hair. I don't think I've ever seen him looking more handsome, or more dangerous. But even though he appears to be laughing, I notice that his eyes aren't smiling at all. It's all a performance. I stare at him with revulsion, asking myself: *What sort of man are you really?*

Before I can come up with an answer, Alfie's finished his call. 'You ready then?' he asks. 'D'you fancy going down to Garratt Park?'

He knows it's one of my favourite local spots. There's a stretch of water banked by scrubby trees on the far side of the park, and a narrow little footpath which follows the river all the way down to the Thames at Wandsworth. Even though you're in a busy part of south-west London, it's quiet and secluded and there's usually never anyone else around: it's the very last place I'd want to be alone with him right now.

'I'm really tired. It was a tough shift last night.'

'Oh. Okay,' he says with a shrug and an insouciant smile.

But I don't trust this handsome smile he's giving me. Who knows what secret intent lurks unseen in the crinkled corners of his eyes. I turn and quickly march across the road at the lights, but before they've changed, he's hurrying after me, telling me he'll walk with me.

All the way back to the flat I tell him I'm tired and need to get some sleep, but my breathy protestations count for nothing. I can't shake him off and the nearer we get to home, the greater my anxiety. Claire and Beth will already have left for work. What if he tries to come inside?

Soon we're standing on the pavement outside the building. My palms are sweaty and I'm breathing heavily. I scan up and down the street, but there's no-one around to come to my aid if I need it.

'Aren't you going to invite me in?' he asks.

I can't look him in the eye. I stare up into the sky, wincing with uncertainty, panic-levels rising.

'Phoebe?' A note of confusion has entered his voice.

I glance nervously over to the flat and see a face at the window. Someone's home after all! It's as if my silent prayer has been answered. Emboldened, I turn and tell him: 'You're not coming in.'

He studies my expression for a few moments, and when he realises I'm being serious, starts to get angry. 'Jesus, Phoebe. What're you playing at?'

'You're not coming in,' I repeat emphatically, taking a quick look up to the flat to reassure myself that there's definitely someone there.

'I'm your boyfriend!' he says, like it's a threat.

'I don't want to see you anymore.'

'You're breaking up with me?' he scoffs, as though the idea is implausible.

I don't know what to tell him. I just want to get inside where I'll be safe. I tell him: 'Yes.'

'Just like that? For no reason?' It still doesn't seem to have sunk in.

'I'm serious Alfie. This is goodbye.'

I hasten up the steps to the front door. He follows,

grabbing hold of my arm, but lets go when he sees that he's being watched from the house.

'Fucking hell Phoebe —'

The front door opens. Claire's standing in the doorway beckoning me to come inside. I scuttle past and she slams the door smartly behind me.

'Are you okay?' she asks.

Before I can answer, Beth has joined us in the hallway, her face crimson with excitement. 'What was all that about?'

'Oh! You're here too,' I say.

'We're both working from home today,' Beth explains.

When she says "working", she actually means they'll maybe have a couple of *Teams* meetings or *Zoom* calls, and the rest of the day will be spent chatting and drinking coffee and wiggling their mice every so often to make it look like they're busy, and I'm going to have to accept that I'm not likely to be getting any sleep today.

'I'm going to have a shower,' I tell them, heading for my room to get changed.

'Not so fast,' Claire instructs me, grabbing my arm. 'First you've got to tell us what's going on? She steers me into the sitting-room and makes me sit beside her on the sofa.

I look from her expectant face to Beth's, experiencing the feeling that I'm a suspect in an interrogation scene from *The Line of Duty*. I'd rather not say anything, but I know they won't let up until I do, so I tell them: 'We had a row.'

'About that girl who turned up here on Saturday?' Beth asks, pulling her chair a little nearer.

What do I say? I tell them what they want to hear. 'Yes,' I lie.

'Did he admit that anything was going on between them?' Claire asks.

'No.'

She rolls her eyes scornfully. 'You didn't believe him though, did you?'

'No.'

'So, you two've split up then?' Beth asks.

I nod. That, at least, is true.

Beth claps her hands together and beams. Claire leans closer and places her hand on my leg, like we're bessie mates all of a sudden.

'Can I be honest with you?' she says.

No, I think, *please don't*, but I know she's desperate to get it all off her chest. 'What?'

'I've never actually liked Alfie. Neither of us do.'

'Really?'

She gives my hand a sympathetic little squeeze. 'Obviously I'd never have said anything while you were dating. But now you've finished with him —' She breaks off to study my expression. 'You don't mind me telling you this do you?'

Yes! I think, *I do mind*, I really don't want to talk about this now. But I just give a non-committal shrug and let her continue.

'Good. Because I've always felt there was something a bit — I don't know — a bit off about him. I never could quite put my finger on it, but you know what I mean, don't you?'

I say: 'Not really.'

Beth joins in: 'It's that thing he does with his eyebrows when he's looking at you.'

'Like he's scoping you out.' Claire narrows her eyebrows, cocks her head to one side, and squints down her nose.

Beth bursts into laughter. 'Yes! Just like that!'

They don't seem to have noticed I'm not finding this funny.

Claire flicks her hair back behind her shoulders and continues with her list of complaints. 'He's always bragging about how much money he earns, and yet he's always broke. Funny that.'

'He borrowed fifty quid off me three weeks ago and he's never paid me back,' Beth adds.

'He's borrowed lots of money from me too,' Claire says quickly, but I'm not sure whether to believe her. She's probably only saying it because she doesn't want to be out-Alfie'd by Beth. I can't imagine how they'd react if they knew what he was really like.

Claire notices I've gone quiet and does her goofy eyebrow impression again to try and raise a laugh, but I'm not amused.

'Oh come on. You weren't taken in by his act, were you? That's all it was, an act.'

When I still don't reply she peers at me with curiosity. 'Wait a minute — you still have feelings for him, don't you?'

Feelings? I definitely have feelings. Shock, fear, revulsion, confusion. It's only that I don't want to talk about them. I look to Beth for help, but she just gives me an insipid smile.

Claire continues: 'You do! He's so not worth it. You can do so much better.'

I think back to the heady, heart-fluttering excitement I experienced when Alfie and I first started dating. I'm not sure I'll ever be able to recapture those feelings with anyone again.

'Listen to me Phoebe. He cheated on you. And you can never trust him again. Once a cheater, always a cheater.'

Ironically, I don't even know if Alfie actually has been cheating on me, because I never got to ask him.

My phone rings. It's him! But before I can reject his call, Claire snatches the phone right out of my hand. She tucks her hair behind her ear and waits a few seconds before speaking in a composed, business-like voice, as though she's my PA.

'Phoebe knows you've been cheating on her. And she doesn't want to see you. Ever. So please don't ring her again. Thank you. Goodbye.'

Her eyes gleam with exhilaration and her mouth breaks into a wide, triumphant grin as she drops the phone into my hands and cheerily tells me: 'You're welcome!'

Chapter 8

SO, AS FAR as Claire and Beth are concerned, everything's sorted. Alfie cheated on me, we've split up, and nothing could be simpler.

They take me under their wing and welcome me into the bosom of their friendship group. Not only am I part of their gang now, I'm treated with extra-special attention because I've been wronged by the *two-timing bastard.*

They take me to meet their friends at a karaoke bar in Soho where we all get drunk and murder some Beyoncé, Taylor Swift and Spice Girls anthems. Yay, Girl Power! They tell me to *Be strong.* They tell me *We're here for you.* They tell me *We've got your back!*

Having so many female friends is a brand new experience for me. I've always struggled to make friends, and those rare times when I have been able to establish a friendship, it's usually with a guy rather than a girl because I find men easier to talk to.

Later that week the girls take me to the cinema, and we watch a romantic comedy, which they rip apart afterwards for being heteronormative and reinforcing patriarchal stereotypes. Which makes me feel guilty because I quite enjoyed it.

They drag me along to hot yoga at their gym, and I feel hopelessly out of my depth and worry about how awful I look in the sweaty ill-fitting leggings I've borrowed.

They tell me that I seem so much happier since I split up with Alfie — *and don't I wish I'd finished with him ages ago?*

I might appear to be happier, but it's all an act. My

cheeks ache from the effort of presenting them with a grateful smile every time they ask if I'm enjoying myself. I'm touched that they're including me in their social activities — after all, this is exactly what I'd hoped for when I moved in — but the truth is that I'm becoming more confused with every day that passes. I feel guilty whenever they bring up the *two-timing bastard* because I haven't told them the truth.

I desperately want to get on with my life and make things normal again. My problem is that Alfie was my normal, and without him my life seems empty. To be honest, even though I don't want to admit it, a big part of me really misses being with him.

It would be easier if I could occasionally put him out of my mind, but unfortunately Claire's bossy phone manner wasn't enough to dissuade him from contacting me. If anything, it's made things worse. I'm bombarded with messages, phone calls and voicemails. And when these don't provoke a response, he comes round to the flat and makes angry scenes on the doorstep when we won't let him in.

At first Claire seems to relish these encounters. As soon as the doorbell goes, she's on her feet, eyes blazing with excitement, mentally rolling up her sleeves for a big fight. It's *Drama* with a capital *D* and she's loving it.

I'm not allowed to speak to him, of course. I have to wait in the sitting-room and listen as their raised voices echo down the hallway while they bicker back and forth like a couple of Year Seven kids in the playground.

'I just want to *see* her.'

'She doesn't want to see you.'

'Two minutes, that's all —'

'I've told you; she won't see you.'

'Why don't you let her come and tell me to my face?'

While Claire dukes it out with him on the doorstep, I experience the same sense of dispiritedness I had as a child listening to Mum and Dad arguing in the kitchen when I was in bed trying to get to sleep.

But Claire refuses to budge. She's both a rock and a hard place. She's Gandalf confronting the Balrog in the mines of Moria and making sure that he *SHALL NOT PASS!* She marches into the sitting-room wearing the determined scowl of a boxer returning to their corner after a successful round and slaps her hands together: 'There!'

But of course Alfie doesn't give in that easily. He comes round again the next day, and the next, and with each visit he becomes more vitriolic, shouting and calling her names.

Eventually even Claire begins to tire of it, and when she refuses to answer the door, Alfie thumps his fists on it and bellows my name through the letter box like a wounded animal.

Claire and Beth tell me: *You've got to do something.* But how d'you end a relationship with someone who won't let it end?

Their patience has worn thin, and their girls-together solidarity has all evaporated now that they've realised this is real life, and not a game. They stop inviting me out with their friends, and they become naggy, picky and pass-aggy about the tiniest of little things.

Are you going to wash up these pans? they ask *w*hen I'm still in the middle of eating my dinner.

D'you think we could all try to keep the bath clean after it's been used? they moan, as if I'm the one responsible for scumming up the bathtub, when I only ever use the shower.

We're out of loo roll they inform me briskly, like it's my job to keep the cupboard stocked, even though I bought an Andrex sixteen-pack on Monday and I've no idea what on earth they're doing with all the toilet paper.

They start muttering about involving the police. But

if I went to the police, I'd be forced to explain what happened at Alfie's flat that night, and the thought of having to relive the experience makes me feel sick inside.

The only time I've ever had dealings with the police was after being mugged outside the tube station a couple of years ago. The mugging itself wasn't so bad — I wasn't hurt or anything — but at the police station afterwards I got all tied up in knots trying to describe my assailant. They made me paw through folders containing pictures of weasely-faced young men scowling at the camera, and all I could do was shrug blankly until they got fed up with me for wasting their time.

If I reported Alfie for attacking me, the questioning would be one hundred times more intense. They'd ask what I did to try and stop him, and I'd have to admit I did nothing. Maybe they'd conclude that, *well it's not rape then.* Worse still, I imagine that if it actually did go to trial, the defence lawyer would inform everyone that I climaxed. *How can it be rape if she enjoyed it, m'lud?*

So, I keep my head down, stay in my room, and try to avoid my flatmates by working as many extra night shifts as I can, never able to shake the fear that Alfie may try and accost me on the way to or from work.

Chapter 9

QUARTER PAST EIGHT, on a cold, overcast Sunday morning at the end of October, and I'm returning home after my third night shift in a row. The clocks went back during the night, so we had a thirteen-hour shift instead of twelve, and that extra hour has left me dead on my feet. They don't even pay us for that extra hour either, which doesn't seem fair.

I slide my key into the lock and open the front door as quietly as possible, hoping Claire and Beth will still be in bed. They're not. They're waiting for me in the living room with fixed, solemn, Easter-island statue expressions on their faces.

Claire says: 'We need to talk.'

'Sure.'

'About Alfie,' she adds.

'Okay,' I say guardedly.

I sit in the chair by the door with my bag on my lap, feeling like an addict whose friends are staging an intervention. You see these things on TV dramas all the time. It never ends well.

Claire tosses her hair back and begins. 'Last night we spotted someone lurking in the bushes at the back of the house.'

'And you think it was Alfie?'

'Oh, come on,' she scoffs impatiently, 'it wasn't the bloody postman!'

I'm taken aback by her sudden aggression. I look from Claire's pissed off face to Beth's pissed off face and don't know what to say. I say: 'I'm sorry.'

Claire narrows her eyes into a glower. 'We never know when he's going to turn up on our doorstep and create a scene.'

'We don't feel safe in our own house anymore,' Beth adds through pursed lips.

'I'm really sorry.'

Claire's voice rises with indignation. 'Being sorry isn't enough. *You* might be okay with this situation, but why do *we* have to put up with it? You've got to *do* something.'

'You want me to speak to him?'

Claire stares at me with disbelief. 'After all the effort we've spent keeping him away from you? You're not going to be able to stop him with one little conversation.'

'What else can I do?'

'You can go to the police,' Beth replies firmly.

I give a sharp intake of breath. 'I can't!'

'Why not?'

'I — I just can't,' I mutter feebly, looking helplessly around the room, suddenly feeling close to tears. I don't know what to do. I don't want to be the kind of selfish girl who lets her personal problems impact on everyone else. But going to the police is not an option.

'You have to call them,' Claire says in a flat, forceful tone, 'or —'

She breaks off to let the word *or* hang threateningly in the air and exchanges an uncomfortable look with Beth. It suddenly dawns on me that this isn't an intervention. It's an ultimatum.

'Or what?' I ask.

'Or else we'll have to ask you to look for somewhere else to live,' she says bluntly.

It's my turn to be incredulous. 'You'd do that?'

She avoids my eyes. 'What choice do we have? We have to put our own safety first.'

'Beth?'

Beth stares at me with an unexpected coldness and nods.

Sharp tears spring into my eyes. 'Okay. I'll do it.'

As soon as I've agreed, they're all smiling and friendly and we're best pals once more. But I've no intention of contacting the police. I can't. I only said it to keep them off my back. I go to my room and dump my bag on the floor. I can't believe they'd gang up on me like that. It's at times like this that you find out who your real friends are. That's two more people to cross off my massive list of friends, leaving me with — how many again? I know — none. I'm not even exaggerating. I'm on friendly terms with most of the girls at work of course, but I don't feel I could turn to any of them in a crisis. I've never been any good at making friends. When it comes down to it the only people I've got in my life are an overbearing sister and an alcoholic father. Estepona's a bit of a commute, but perhaps Suzi will let me hide out at her house for a while until this has all blown over?

I dry my eyes, blow my nose, and compose myself before picking up the phone.

'Hiya,' I say breezily when Suzi answers.

'Phoebe!' She seems surprised and pleased that I've rung. As we exchange pleasantries, I experience an upwelling of feelings for her. But there's a growing note of suspicion in her voice, and finally she asks:

'Are you ringing for any particular reason?'

'Well, I do have a favour I'd like to ask you?'

'I *knew* you couldn't just be ringing for a chat!' Her voice purrs with smugness and it's like a bucket of cold water has been thrown onto my little familial fantasy. I worry that she's going to turn me down.

'So? What is it?' she demands.

'Could I come and stay with you for a while?'

'How long's a while?'

'A week or two. Maybe longer? I don't really know. But something's happened and I really can't stay here.'

There's a little pause before she answers. 'To be honest, it's not great timing —'

`'Fine!' I say, cutting her off before she embarrasses both of us with her flimsy excuses. 'Don't bother. I knew I shouldn't have asked.'

'Wait —'

'It's quite all right. I understand. There's not enough room in your five-bedroomed Dulwich mansion for your little sister.'

'It's not a mansion. And we've actually only got four bedrooms. But if you'd let me speak, I was going to suggest that you could stay in the flat. It would be a lot easier for you to commute to work from Clapham rather than schlepping all the way from here.'

'Oh! Sorry.' Now I feel bad for jumping to conclusions.

'That's all right. I mean, it's not like you leapt down my throat when I was just trying to do something nice for you — oh wait, you did!'

' I'm sorry! But what about your tenants?'

'The flat's empty at the moment because we're in the process of refurbing it.'

'Refurbing?'

'Oh, it's nothing too drastic. There are a couple of rotten windows which need replacing. There's some minor electrical work. We're putting in a new shower, getting new carpets, and everything needs a fresh lick of paint.'

'So you need someone to be on site to let the workmen in?'

'I'm not forcing you. You sounded desperate.'

'You're right. I'm sorry. It would really help me out,

big time.'

I feel guilty for being so touchy and ungrateful. This whole business with Alfie has rattled my nerves. Staying in Suzi's Clapham flat would actually be the perfect solution.

'How soon could I move in?' I ask.

'You can move in whenever you like.'

PART TWO

Chapter 10

I STAND ON the pavement outside Suzi's one-bedroom, first-floor flat, with my bags at my feet, squinting up into the bright sky. Neat rows of silvery clouds are sailing from east to west above the pointed gables of the Victorian terraced house that will be my refuge for the next few weeks. I take a deep breath and savour this glorious feeling of sanctuary and escape.

The flat originally belonged to the first of Suzi's posh, rich, older husbands, and she acquired it as part of her divorce settlement. It keeps going up and up in value and is now worth half a million pounds, or something. For a one-bedroom flat? It's crazy.

I stayed here with them for a few weeks between my second and third years at uni, sleeping on the couch, getting under their feet and no doubt making them regret ever having agreed to put me up. I wasn't the world's most gracious house guest — no doubt that's one reason why Suzi doesn't want me staying with her in Dulwich — though in my defence, Dad had just emigrated to Spain leaving me with nowhere else to go.

Laithwaite Road is exactly as I remember it. Tall, narrow houses painted in turquoisy greens, rusty pinks and sandy yellows, as though a row of beach huts had been washed up in the middle of London. Regimented strings of Audis, BMWs and Mercs are parked nose to tail along both sides of the street. Everything reeks of money and of good taste.

Everything, that is, except the gaudy, kitschy menagerie of gnomes frolicking in the front garden. They must belong to the ground-floor flat, because Suzi most definitely wouldn't have purchased them. At least, not unless *Liberty* is stocking them these days.

In addition to regular-style garden gnomes — the ones with fishing rods or holding rakes or pushing wheelbarrows — there are all sorts of unusual ones. There's a Rasta gnome in an over-sized knitted hat, a punk gnome with a blue Mohican giving passers-by the finger, and a gnome wearing brightly-coloured Doc Martens, waving a flag with the extinction rebellion hour-glass logo on it. There's even a Beyoncé gnome in a black leotard doing the fingers-pointing-to-the-ground *Single Ladies* dance. The neighbours must hate them, but there's something about them I find appealing — perhaps it's the thought that my life would be so much easier if everyone was as distinctively attired.

I dump my things in the kitchen-cum-lounge-cum-dining-room and have a look around. Suzi warned me it might be a bit grim. Normally she'd have had the place deep-cleaned between tenants, but there was no point because of the building work. Unfortunately, the last tenant didn't do any cleaning throughout the entire time that he — it was a man, surprise, surprise — lived here. He claimed he was scared to go near the cupboard where the cleaning things were stored because he had a phobia of faces. He told Suzi that whenever he opened the cupboard door, he'd have a freak out because the Henry vacuum cleaner was grinning back at him. Hmm, seems like a very convenient excuse to me.

It takes all of five seconds to complete the tour of the flat, but it's not actually as dirty as I feared. I've certainly lived in worse places, and when you flat-share with strangers you quickly learn to suppress your inner Monica-from-*Friends* or you'll soon be falling out over housework and cleaning rotas.

I open the windows to blow away the stale air; I wipe down all the surfaces in the kitchen; I get out the scary hoover and give the place a quick once-over.

As I'm making the bed, I notice that the big sash window has no curtains, which is a bit weird seeing as the bedroom's right at the front of the house. Either the Henry-phobe was an exhibitionist, or he took them with him when he left.

I take down the kitchen curtains and re-hang them in the bedroom. Although they're neither wide enough nor long enough to quite cover the whole window, they'll make do for now.

I fall back onto the bed, exhausted but contented, and stretch out my arms and legs like a starfish. I feel safe here in this old Victorian building, with its high ceilings and its thick brick walls which have stood solid for over a hundred years. For the first time in weeks, I can allow myself to relax. The muddy browns and foggy greys of my indecision and uncertainty begin to fade. I start to feel myself again.

The ringing of the doorbell startles me out of my thoughts. Who can it be? No-one except Suzi knows I'm here. I didn't even tell Claire and Beth my new address. I go down the stairs with rising apprehension, imagining all sorts of worst-case scenarios whereby Alfie has somehow found me.

I open the door to a large woman wearing a yellow figure-hugging kimono and paisley-print low-cut trainers. She has very short electric pink hair, which looks really good against her dark skin, and a pair of gold, hooped earrings. I breathe a sigh of relief.

'I'm Denise,' she tells me with a broad smile, holding out her hand. 'I live in the flat beneath you.'

So, she's the gnome lady. I'm instantly drawn to her

because of her distinctive appearance. I explain that I'm Suzi's sister and am only here on a temporary basis while the flat's being refurbished.

'Isn't it going to be rather inconvenient if there's work going on?' she asks.

I give her an *it's complicated* look which she accepts without further probing, making me like her even more.

'I would ask you up for a cup of tea,' I tell her, 'but I've got no kettle and no cups. And no tea bags either, for that matter.'

'Then you'll have to come to mine.'

Denise's flat is as eccentric as her dress. It's overflowing with up-cycled furniture painted in pinks and minty greens; there are piles of over-stuffed cushions in clashing prints; feathery dream catchers hanging from the bookshelves; and pervading everything is the faint musty smell of antiques and patchouli oil.

Although the furnishings may be soft, the hundreds of books crammed into the bookcases and balanced in irregular heaps on the floor certainly aren't: *Who's killing the Earth and what we can do about It? Race, identity and societal responses to inequality; Toxic masculinity: the hidden rapist inside every man.*

I've always felt intimidated by people who own a lot of books. I've only owned nine books in my entire life — the first five *Harry Potters* and the four books in the *Twilight* Series. I don't think Denise would be very impressed with them.

'Bernard, off!' she shoos an enormous fluffy ginger cat from the chair. He seems reluctant to give up his seat, and when I sit down he won't stop staring. It's hard to tell whether he's just being inquisitive or if he's really pissed-off with me.

To be fair, I'm more of a dog person because you

always know where you are with them. Their expressions are easy to read, and if not, their wagging tails will soon give them away. But you can never quite tell what a cat might be thinking.

I hold out my fingers for him to sniff, and in a calm, friendly voice say: 'Hello puss.'

In reply he gives an irritated hiss and swipes at me with his claws out. I only just manage to snatch my hand away in time.

Denise finds this hilarious. 'Don't worry! He can be a bit temperamental sometimes, but he doesn't bite.'

'It's not the biting, it's the scratching I'm worried about.'

'Oh, it's not his fault, poor thing,' Denise says, going all gooey. 'He's a rescue cat. When I first got him, he scratched like hell.' She rolls up the sleeve of her kimono to show me the red tramlines running up the inside of her arm. 'It's why I named him Bernard Hermann. Because he's a bit of a psycho. Ha ha!'

I don't get it — Bernard Hermann? — but I laugh anyway to be polite.

'Would you like some wine?' Denise asks, producing a bottle and two glasses. 'You okay with red?'

She pours the wine then raises her glass. 'Welcome to Clapham.'

'Cheers.' I take a sip of my drink. It tastes foul. Although I manage to stop myself from spitting it out, I can't help pulling a face.

Denise laughs again. 'Sorry, I should have said: it's beetroot wine. It's organic and vegan.'

I try it again. It has a very peculiar taste: sweet, earthy and basically very beetrooty.

Denise is studying my face expectantly. 'What d'you think?'

'It's — distinctive.'

She gives a warm chuckle. 'It grows on you. By the end of the bottle you won't even remember it came from a vegetable.'

She knocks back her wine and starts telling me about herself. She's a Human Resources manager for a large manufacturing company. She's originally from Dudley, but moved down to London twenty-five years ago, which means she must be a lot older than I thought. I was guessing early to mid-thirties, but she must be in her forties at least.

'Are you okay with the gnomes?' she asks.

'Sure.'

'They don't bother you?'

I shake my head. 'I quite like them actually.'

'I only ask because the guy who used to rent your flat had a problem with them.'

'He didn't like gnomes?'

'He had a phobia of them. Anything with a face on it freaked him out. Have you ever heard of such a thing?'

'Actually, Suzi did mention it, but I didn't believe her.'

'There's a name for it. Po— Pu—' She pops her lips like a guppy. 'It's on the tip of my tongue. Damn, what was it? It's going to really bug me now. Pugophobia? Hold on —'

She fetches a heavy-looking book from the shelf. *The New Encyclopaedia of Fears, Phobias and Anxiety Disorders*. 'Any kind of phobia worth its salt will be in here.'

She flicks efficiently through the pages. 'Here it is. Prosopophobia — a fear of faces. Not pugophobia — apparently that's a fear of buttocks!'

I can't help laughing: 'Buttocks?'

'He may have suffered from that too for all I know. There was something a bit odd about him. Mind you, all of us have our peculiar quirks and problems. There's no such thing as normal really, is there.'

'Hmm,' I say in wholehearted agreement, and I'm wondering whether to tell Denise about my face blindness when my phone rings. It's Alfie. I reject the call with a scowl.

'Boyfriend troubles?' she asks.

How did she know? 'Ex-boyfriend,' I tell her. 'He keeps hassling me. In fact, he's the reason I'm staying here.'

'D'you want to talk about it?'

Maybe it's the sweet beetroot wine, maybe it's the cosy pat-clash furnishings, or maybe it's Denise's grounded, motherly manner, but I find myself opening up about Alfie. I tell her almost everything, just glossing over exactly what happened in his flat, and when I've finished, she leans forward and gives my hand a gentle pat.

'I went through a similar thing when I was your age, so I know how awful it can be,' she tells me with the meditative air of someone used to dispensing advice.

'This woman I'd been seeing went psycho on me when I finished the relationship. It was *awful*. And because I was young and naive, I tried to be nice by letting her down gently. But it only made things worse. She'd pick up on the tiniest crumb of comfort I was giving her and blow it out of all proportion. The best piece of advice I received was this: *No Contact Ever*. You have to cut these kind of people out of your life. Block their calls. Get a new phone number. And, even when you're feeling low and might be tempted to see them, never, never, never drop your guard.'

I nod gravely, thinking back to the breakfast I had with Alfie at *Crema Crema* when we came close to getting back together.

Denise tops up our glasses again. 'Being stalked can ruin your life. My ex used to send me faxes —'

Faxes? How old actually are you, I wonder, my estimate getting nudged upwards by another ten years.

'She'd draw these graphic pictures of what she planned to do to me. Scared the shit out of me. And yet despite all that I still had feelings for her. I despised her and loved her at the same time. Does that make sense?'

'Yes,' I admit. 'A part of me still cares about Alfie, even though I know I shouldn't.'

'It's only natural. The human brain is wired to look for love. You can love someone even when they're toxic for you. It can be a real head-fuck, believe me, but you have to learn to accept it and move on. And never allow him to talk you into taking him back.'

'I won't, don't worry, I can promise you!'

'Amen to that!' Denise says, raising her glass. She has more to tell me about relationships, and while she talks, I let the subdued, mussy atmosphere of the room envelop me like a warm, woolly blanket.

Chapter 11

WHEN I WAKE the next morning, my head's pounding and my stomach's churning from the beetroot wine, which isn't fair because I didn't even really have that much to drink. I just sipped from my glass and watched Denise polish off the bottle on her own. I never used to be this bad with alcohol. It must be because I'm getting old. I can't sleep it off though because the builders are due in half an hour.

Once I've let them in, I leave them to it and go for a walk on Clapham Common to clear my head. It's a gloriously crisp autumnal morning and the fallen leaves give a satisfying crunch underfoot. I walk with a lightness of step I haven't felt in a long while, and because I don't have to worry about not recognising anyone around here, I even raise my eyes and smile at passers-by.

After a quiet breakfast in the café near the bandstand I head down to the shops to get some things for the flat. I also pop into the Vodafone shop to see about getting a new phone number. I assumed it would be a real hassle, but it's very straight-forward and the curtain-haired assistant doesn't even ask why I want a new number. I guess it's a more common request than I thought.

Halfway down Battersea Rise there's a shop selling over-priced home and garden nick-nacks. A gnome in the window catches my eye. Although it has the traditional long white beard and red, pointed hat, it's wearing high heels and a short green dress stretched tightly over an impressive pair of breasts. On an impulse I buy it for Denise.

I've always liked giving presents. I was that kid who'd

spend hours copying the stuff they made on *Blue Peter* and *Art Attack* to give as Christmas presents. My long-suffering family would be forced to *ooh* and *aah* indulgently over the pencil case made from a washing-up liquid bottle, or the bird feeder made from an old pair of tights. When I was a bit older, I'd save up my pocket money to buy little gifts for the girls in my class. I'd get them gel pens, snap bracelets, those ugly gonk things that go on the end of pencils. I never expected anything in return, I just gave for the pleasure of giving, until Suzi told me I should stop, because it was a bit weird.

Hopefully Denise won't think it's weird. She'd better like it, because her present actually cost more than my new kettle, mugs, frying pan and cutlery-set combined.

Luckily it seems to go down well. 'Thank you!' she gushes, with a hoot of delight. 'We need to come up with a name.'

She thinks about it for a moment and then, with a shriek of laughter announces: 'I know. Norma Snockers!'

'Okay.' That's a bit weird, but, whatever. Maybe it's a generational thing?

'D'you get it?' she asks, nodding eagerly.

I don't want to admit that I don't, so I give a sudden *ahh!* of comprehension and then that groaning laugh everyone does when cracker jokes are read out at Christmas.

We go outside and she positions Norma in a prominent spot on top of the little grassy hump, overlooking the fish pond.

I find the gnome's presence strangely comforting. When I leave for work, I give a cheery nod, and when I return, shattered after a twelve-hour shift, the sight of Norma always makes me smile. My life falls into a comfortable routine. I have a longer commute to work, which is actually a good thing because it allows me time to start reading novels again. Two or three times a week Denise and I will have dinner together, and we always end up talking into the early hours of the morning over a bottle or two of her vegetable-based wine.

Living on my own has the big advantage that I can sleep during the day without fear of being woken by inconsiderate flatmates. But more importantly, I feel safe here in Suzi's flat. Although Alfie knows where I work, and there's always the chance he'll ambush me there, he doesn't know where I live. And now that I've changed my phone number, he has no way of contacting me.

I come off the Socials too, and feel so much better. It's only when you step away that you realise it has very little to do with connecting with people. It's really just about showing off and making out your life is better than it really is.

I decide to enrol in kick-boxing classes, and it turns out I've got a real talent for it. It's great for developing physical strength, but it's fantastic too for mental health. You're training your brain to act quickly as it responds to punches, masters sharp reflexes and memorises combos. It's also a great way of releasing stress and gaining a feeling of empowerment.

Even more importantly, I'm slowly starting to address what happened when Alfie attacked me. Not the attack itself; the orgasm thing. It was really weirding me out. My cheeks would burn with shame and I feared that there was something seriously wrong with me. Finally I google *women who orgasm while being raped* and learn that it's not actually an uncommon response. The discovery sends me reeling. All the guilt and disgust I've been carrying around, thinking I was some sort of damaged person who got off on abusive sex, when maybe I'm not such a freak after all. It doesn't make everything better of course, but hopefully I can stop blaming myself when I know I did nothing wrong.

Chapter 12

WEDNESDAY. I'VE GOT a mandatory study day today, and don't have to be at the hospital until eight. Which is lucky because I'm feeling a bit ropey again this morning, after a little too much of Denise's nettle and ginger wine. I wasn't planning to stay so late or drink so much, but two of her Zumba friends were over and they were hilarious.

I pour myself a glass of home-made kefir, made from coconut water, which Denise gave me to clear up my thrush when nothing from the chemist's was working. Maybe it will clear up my hangover too? I need my brain to be firing on all cylinders to pass the drug calculation test today. They make you take it every couple of years, and although it's not difficult, my brain just turns to jelly in exam situations.

As I'm shutting the front door, a man carrying a holdall comes up the garden path and calls out a breezy: '*Good morning*! I'm here to sort out your electrics.'

'Oh? I wasn't expecting anyone today.'

'This *is* 26 Laithwaite Road, isn't it?'

'Yes. I suppose you'd better come in.'

I try not to let my irritation show, but I'm going to be late if I don't leave soon. I wish Suzi wouldn't do this to me. She promised she'd let me know well in advance when her builders were coming because she knows how much I hate having strangers turn up unannounced.

But because, after all, it's not the electrician's fault, I feel the need to overcompensate by making him a cup of tea and telling him to help himself to the biscuits in the tin by the microwave, and save my anger for the terse message I leave on Suzi's voicemail.

We have the drug calculation test first, and then there's a lecture on medication management, and one on naso-gastric tubes. After lunch there's a session on palliative care, and then we have Moving and Handling, which is how to roll people around the bed without doing your back in. We've all heard it a hundred times before and the session is really dragging. I keep yawning, having to fight the urge to sleep. It's like sitting through a GCSE maths lesson all over again, except that instead of drawing hearts and flowers with boys' names in them on my pencil case, I'm fantasising about coffee. The moment this is over I'm going straight down to the coffee shop for a caffeine fix, even though I'm supposed to be cutting down. I read this article which explained that the headaches you get from caffeine withdrawal are actually caused by your brain swelling up and pressing against your skull. Now, that surely can't be good for you, can it? Plus, at £3 a cup, times four a day, times seven days a week, times 52 weeks a year, it really adds up — but don't ask me to do the maths.

When I finally get away from the lecture-room, and am standing in the queue at the coffee shop waiting to be served, I can't help rattling my fingernails restlessly against the screen of my phone. The guy in front of me turns round. He gives me the *I Know You* face and I quickly check his features against my mental *Guess Who?* database, figuring he's most likely to be a nurse, a junior doctor or one of the therapists from work. Late twenties or early thirties. Brown hair and a short beard. Average height and average build. Handsome, but not model-handsome. I draw a blank, but smile and pretend to recognise him anyway: 'Hello!'

'Hello,' he replies uncertainly, a puzzled frown creasing his forehead, and I realise I've made a mistake.

'Sorry, my bad. I thought you were someone I knew.'

'No probs,' he says with a friendly smile.

I feel my cheeks redden as he watches me jangling from foot to foot with caffeine-dependency nerves. He probably thought I was trying to chat him up. Awkward!

Luckily the barista's ready to serve him and I'm spared further embarrassment. He orders a medium flat white to go, and when asked for his name, tells her *Tom*.

Tom — I store his name away in my mental filing cabinet alongside the thousands of names of people I'll never recognise again. My faux pas convinces me that I really should give up caffeine, so I study the board to see what else they've got. There's way too much choice though, and when the barista asks what I'd like, in a panic I ask for a salted caramel and Belgian chocolate latteccino, even though I'm not really a fan of salted caramel. Or hot chocolate either, to be honest.

I wait at the collection point, busying myself with my phone, trying not to look in Tom's direction, but when our drinks are ready I can't avoid catching his eye. The corners of his mouth give a cute little quizzical twitch. 'After you,' he says, gesturing for me to go ahead of him.

'Thanks.' I take my drink and head for the tube, thinking how weird it feels to be going home when it's only just getting dark. As I pass through the station's entrance, I hear someone shouting my name, and jerk round to find a man in a black jacket brandishing a takeaway cup of coffee at me.

'Phobe! Wait!'

I narrow my eyes suspiciously: 'How d'you know my name?'

He holds up the cup, and in a slow voice like he's teaching a toddler to read, traces the two syllables with his finger: 'Phoe-be.'

I glance down at the cup in my hand and find it has *Tom* written on it. I give a sigh of relief: it's the cute guy from the coffee shop. Which explains why my drink didn't taste as chocolatey or as salted caramely as I was expecting too.

I hand over his drink with an apology: 'Sorry. I've had a couple of sips. I'll buy you another if you like?'

'No, it's okay, don't worry about it,' He says, passing me my latteccino, and we start chatting.

He's easy to talk to; softly spoken, with a lilting sing-song north-east accent, which I've always been drawn to. He's from South Shields mind, not Newcastle, and he sounds exactly how the comedian Sarah Millican would sound if she were a handsome, but not model-handsome, bearded man of average height, with a deep, resonant voice and a twinkle in his eyes.

When I tell him I'm a nurse, he seems genuinely impressed, and I warm to him even more. His office is right next to the coffee shop, and he's an even bigger coffee addict than I am.

'No doubt I'll be bumping into you again sometime?' he states hopefully.

'Maybe. But usually I'm working shifts, so I don't get off until much later.'

He seems disappointed. 'In that case —' he clears his throat — 'perhaps we could meet up sometime? For a drink? Or a meal? Or just a latteccino?'

His gauche spluttering makes me smile. So different to Alfie's smooth confidence. I'm charmed, and I haven't been charmed in a long while. But it's way too early to start dating again, and I really don't need a man in my life at the moment. But before I can tell him *no*, he groans and bites disappointedly on his bottom lip.

'You're seeing someone? Of course you are. I'm sorry.'

'No, it's not that.'

'So you're single?' His expression suddenly brightens.

'Yes, but —'

'But you don't date men?'

'No, it's not that. I'm just not looking for a relationship at the moment.'

'That's okay. It doesn't need to be a date. Just friends.'

'Well —'

I pause a moment, thinking about my lack of friends and the long hours I spend on my own in the flat, and despite my better judgement I tell him:

'Okay. That would be nice.'

'Excellent!' he exclaims with a grin. 'When are you free?'

We agree on a day and exchange phone numbers. As I'm saving *Tom Coffeeshop* to my contacts, my phone starts to ring. It's Suzi. Finally calling to apologise, I hope.

'Sorry, d'you mind if I get this?'

Tom Coffeeshop motions me a polite *go ahead, be my guest* gesture with the palm of his hand.

'Phoebe hi, it's Suzi. Look, I'm sorry about the mess up this morning. I wasn't expecting anyone today though. There's nothing booked in the diary.'

'Really?' I say, maintaining a pleasant, measured tone, conscious that Tom's listening.

'Yes, really. Was it the plasterer?'

'The electrician.'

'That's odd. The electrician's not due back until the twenty-fourth. I'll have a word with him.'

'Thanks. Suzi, would you mind if I rang you back? I'm in the middle of something.'

'Oh, okay. Sorry. Actually I've just got one little thing to tell you: change of plan.'

I give a groan. 'You're not having second thoughts about paint colours, are you?' Only yesterday she made me pop in to B&Q on my way home from work to get their largest tin of Farrow & Ball chicken-feed-yellow paint because she decided it would go better in the lounge than the batshit-green, or whatever it was, that she had me lugging home for her last week.

'No, it's not paint, it's about tomorrow. Can we meet at the cemetery at twelve instead of two? I thought we might go for a meal together afterwards?'

'Oh!' I say in surprise.

'You hadn't forgotten about tomorrow had you?'

'No. Of course not,' I tell her, hoping my indignant tone is convincing.

'You remember where her grave's located?'

'Yes.'

'Are you sure? It's a big cemetery.'

'I know. Don't worry, I'll find it.'

'Okay, I'll see you tomorrow then. And Phoebe?'

'What?' I ask warily, because I know she can never resist delivering a parting shot. And in a prim, school-teachery voice she tells me: *Please don't be late*, as if I'm an irresponsible child who's incapable of telling the time, rather than a twenty-nine-year-old woman who has life-or-death responsibility for patients.

'I'll be there,' I reply.

'Great. Oh, by the way, I almost forgot —'

'What?' I say exasperatedly, rolling my eyes for Tom's benefit. I mouth *Sorry* to him and he smiles, making a yackety-yak gesture with his fingers and thumb, and mouths back: *It's okay.*

'Did you like the flowers?' Suzi asks.

'What flowers?'

'The flowers from Alfie.'

I stop mugging at Tom and freeze. 'Alfie?'

'Oh! Maybe I shouldn't have said anything. Don't let

on that I told you. He rang yesterday to see if I knew the postcode for your new address. He couldn't ask you because he wanted the flowers to be a surprise. He seemed terribly upset about something. Did you two have a row? To be honest, I'm surprised he had my number.'

I feel my face go ashen. 'Suzi! Oh my God! Why did you have to do that?'

'What? What did I do?'

I can't believe it. Just when I'm finally feeling safe, and now Alfie knows where I live. Then it occurs to me that maybe it was Alfie who turned up at the flat this morning and not an electrician.

'Suzi, I've got to go,' I say in a quavery voice and hang up. My head's spinning and my legs suddenly feel shaky.

Tom eyes me with concern. 'Is everything all right?'

'Yes. Well, actually, no, not really.'

'Anything I can do?'

'No, I've got a bit of a domestic emergency.'

'I'd better let you go then. But I'll see you next week?'

'Yes. Thanks. Looking forward to it.'

I stand in the front garden staring up at my window. It's dark and there doesn't appear to be anyone there. I know I'm probably fretting over nothing, but what if Alfie's lurking inside, waiting for me to come home?

I can't think why I rushed back in such a hurry to tackle this bogus electrician on my own, with only a half-drunk salted caramel and Belgian chocolate latteccino to defend myself with. I give a grim, derisory snort at my own ridiculousness. What was I going to do? Throw it in his face and hope he's lactose intolerant?

There's no answer when I ring Denise's bell. I've a vague recollection that this is her Community Choir night, in which case she won't be back before eight. But I'm too scared to go up there on my own, so I'll just have to sit it out on the grassy knoll with Norma and the other gnomes until she gets home.

After twenty, maybe twenty-five minutes — long enough for my backside to go numb — a man emerges from the house opposite and crosses the road.

'Can I help you?' he calls over the garden fence, his voice dripping with suspicion.

'It's all right, thanks. I live here,' I explain, hoping my reassuring smile will be enough to persuade him I'm not planning on creating trouble.

He eyes me mistrustfully. 'With Denise?'

'No, I live in the flat above.'

He doesn't seem convinced. 'And you're doing a spot of late-night gardening?'

I give a nervous fluttery laugh. 'No.'

'You've lost your key?'

'No, I've got the key.' I take it out of my purse and wave it around to prove it. 'I know it's sounds silly, but I'm too scared to go up.'

He frowns at me uncertainly, not sure if I'm being serious, but says nothing.

'I think there might be someone inside the flat.'

'You should ring the police then,' he advises, his voice low and earnest now.

'I don't want to involve them. It's probably all in my head. But —' I shrug helplessly.

'But you're scared.'

I nod idiotically.

'Would you like me to go up and check for you?' he suggests.

'Would you?'

'Sure.'

'Thank you! That would be great!' I gush with relief.

I wait down by the front door while he heads up the stairs to the flat. My pulse is racing and, my ears strain for sounds of conflict, but I don't hear anything.

After a few moments he appears at the top of the stairs. 'It's okay, you can come up. There's no-one here.'

In the hallway he hands me back my key with a jaunty two-fingered salute. 'All safe ma'am. Every room's checked.'

'Thanks. I feel so silly.'

'You shouldn't. It's better to be safe than sorry.'

There's a calm authority about his manner which makes me feel safe in his presence. When he turns to leave, I'm suddenly afraid to be left on my own.

'D'you want a drink?' I blurt out.

I make him a cup of tea and we sit side by side on the sofa. His name's Robbie and he lives in the tall house directly across the street. He seems nice. Quite tall, good-looking, and bearded of course. He's a Yorkshireman, and from what I can glean, single. I feel so much better knowing there's someone just over the street who I can call on in an emergency. Who knows what Alfie might do now that he's discovered where I live.

'I can't thank you enough,' I say, even though I've thanked him a hundred times already.

'I really didn't do anything.'

'Except give me peace of mind. And what's that worth?'

'I don't know?' He thinks about it for a while, and then a broad smile spreads across his lips: 'Is it worth a date?'

Another invitation? I must be giving out some powerful date-me pheromones this evening. I explain that I'm not looking for a relationship at the moment, but he says that's okay, it doesn't have to be a date, it can just be a chance for neighbours to get to know one another. And partly because I'm feeling vulnerable, and partly because I already said yes to Tom earlier, I find myself saying yes to Robbie as well.

When he's gone I can't help from checking the bathroom and the bedroom, just to reassure myself that there really is no-one else here, and then I have a shower and grab something to eat.

I try to settle down in front of the TV, but I just can't shake the feeling that the sanctity of my haven has been compromised. Why did Suzi have to go and give out my address? I know it's not really her fault, because how was she to know when I never told her about Alfie, but why couldn't she have been more circumspect? I can't help feeling angry, and it's easier to be angry with her rather than with myself.

Chapter 13

I WAKE REALLY early the next morning and can't fall back to sleep, which is so annoying. On days when I don't have to work, I can guarantee that I'll be wide-awake before it's even light, no matter how sleep-deprived I feel.

I stayed up late last night, waiting for Denise to come home because I really needed to talk to someone. But when I finally messaged her to find out where she was, I discovered that she was out with her Zumba friends and wasn't going to be home for ages (apparently Wednesdays are Zumba; Community Choir rehearsals are on Thursdays).

So now I'm wide awake and I've got hours to kill before I need to leave for the train. After breakfast I decide to give the flat a thorough top-to-bottom clean, even though it doesn't really need it. Every now and then I go to the bedroom window and peep out onto the street, just to check that no-one's there. And finally, at eleven, after checking once again that the coast is clear, I set off for the station.

It's a clear, sunny day. There's an invigorating wind blowing from the north, but all the way down Battersea Rise I experience an unpleasant feeling of being followed. I know I'll freak myself out if I start rubbernecking, so I don't look round until I'm queuing up at the machine in the ticket hall at Clapham Junction.

A young man's standing behind me, and I do a double-take, thinking for a moment it's Alfie. But the man looks right through me, without the slightest glint of recognition in his eyes. Obviously it isn't him; it's just a trick that's being played on me by my increasing paranoia.

The train pulling into the station is almost empty. I sit by the window, dump my bag on the seat beside me and lean back with a sigh. It's half an hour to Brookwood, so I've plenty of time to recover my composure.

Just as the train departs a man in a red jacket comes and sits diagonally opposite me, which weirds me out when there's virtually the whole carriage to choose from.

I steal a glance at him: youngish, slimmish, brownish hair, a shortish beard. Sort of nondescript in an attractive-ish way. I drop my gaze before he spots me staring, and wonder: could it be Alfie?

I examine his shoes: white Nike trainers with multicoloured flashes. I don't recognise them — it's definitely not one of the pairs I bought him, but that doesn't mean anything. If I were braver, I'd say his name out loud and see how he responds. But most likely he's just some random guy.

I keep my head down, fiddling with my phone and trying to ignore the fact that someone's sitting there. But the constant, unnerving feeling that his eyes are burning into the top of my head is making my scalp prickle.

It's only when the train approaches Woking, and the man stands up and walks down the carriage, that I'm able to relax. I crane my head against the window as the train pulls out of the station, trying to get a better look at him, but the platform's already deserted.

Brookwood's the next stop. I linger for a little while in the ticket hall pretending to study the timetable, until I'm certain I've not been tailed, and then follow the signs. I pass along a foot tunnel under the tracks to a metal gate where I press a buzzer to be let through, and then, suddenly, I'm in the cemetery.

Wide tarmac paths wind through a heathy landscape of giant redwood trees and sprawling rhododendron bushes. Dotted haphazardly in between are headstones, statues of angels, and some very grand marble mausoleums. Squirrels scamper about on the ground, birds are cheeping in the trees, and from somewhere in the distance I can even hear the hammering of a woodpecker. It's all very bucolic.

I'd forgotten quite how big this site was. According to Geoff, Mum's grey-haired boyfriend who lectured me about it at the funeral, when it opened in 1854 this was the largest cemetery on earth. It's weird how ten years later I can still remember the date it opened, whereas the funeral itself is just a hazy blur.

It was Geoff's idea to bury Mum out here at Brookwood. He forked out the money for the plot, he hired the caterers, he selected all the hymns and readings and basically organised everything. I couldn't help feeling side-lined, and on the day of the funeral it was as if I was just a family friend who'd been asked along to beef up the numbers, rather than the daughter of the deceased.

I'd never particularly warmed to Geoff. Which was probably a bit unfair of me seeing as it wasn't his fault that Mum hooked up with him with unseemly haste after separating from Dad. She always claimed they only met after she'd already moved out, but I've often wondered whether Geoff might have been the reason she left.

I meander through the shady spaces under the broad spreading cedar boughs for twenty minutes or so before I finally find Mum's grave: a simple stone with an inscription in black letters.

In loving memory
Angela Gallagher
3rd April 1961 - 10th November 2012
Always in our thoughts
Rest in peace

Gallagher, not Drummond, because she'd reverted to her maiden name after the divorce. I remember thinking that it didn't seem like my mother had actually died because the name on the order of service wasn't one I was familiar with. Sitting in the row of purple chairs in the little funeral chapel, I couldn't take my eyes off the coffin. I couldn't come to terms with the fact that the corpse inside had been a flesh-and-blood human only two weeks earlier.

Whereas I was numbed by grief, Suzi was a weepy mess. She wore this black floaty dress with bat-wing sleeves and had a lacy shawl draped across her shoulders, giving off a strong bohemian, Stevie Nicks vibe — which might have been intentional because Fleetwood Mac's *Rumours* was Mum's favourite album and *Go Your Own Way* was played at the end of the service.

Suzi gave a teary eulogy, and the rustling of her shawl against the microphone every time she waved her arms around filled the chapel with eerie muffled beyond-the-grave-like sounds. She talked about what a wonderful person Mum was, how kind-hearted and generous, and how much she loved us, and I felt conflicted because this wasn't quite the mother I knew.

I couldn't stop feeling resentful. Why didn't she love me like she loved Suzi? Why did she desert me when I was eleven? And why did she have to go and desert me again by dying? And worst of all, now that she was dead, I knew that we'd never have a chance to mend our relationship.

I'm surprised to find tears tickling down my cheeks. I didn't cry at the funeral ten years ago, so why am I crying now?

'Phoebe!' A woman wearing a floral trench coat, running tippy-toe in high heels across the grass, is waving. When she gets close enough, she gives me the *it's me* nod and I wave back.

'Sorry I'm late. The traffic was *awful*, and then I

couldn't find anywhere to park. I booked the table for one o'clock, at an authentic-looking Italian place in Woking. I hope Italian's okay for you?'

She breaks off and studies me with a quizzical tilt of her head. 'Have you been *crying*?'

'Maybe,' I reply defiantly, and then, more sheepishly, admit: 'A little.'

'I thought you didn't go in for all this weepy stuff. Didn't you tell me that visiting mum's grave was maudlin?'

'I said it was mawkish.'

'Maudlin, mawkish, whatever. It shows you do care, after all!' She rummages around in the handbag hanging in the crook of her arm, pulls out a little pack of tissues, and passes them to me. 'Here.'

'Of course I care,' I say taking a tissue from the packet and blowing my nose.

'You didn't shed a single tear at the funeral.'

'I'm surprised you noticed with all your moaning and wailing.'

'My mother had just died!' Suzi replies indignantly.

'My mother had just died too.'

'Ice maiden.'

'Drama queen.'

'*Elsa*,' she says, with the self-satisfied smile of a tennis player sending a winning passing shot over the net.

But I get the *Frozen* reference immediately. 'Anna!' I shoot back.

We stand there grinning at each other for a few moments, and then Suzi says: 'Shall we have a minute's silence?' And without waiting for a reply, she closes her eyes and reaches out for my hand.

I surrender it to her warm grasp, but as I bow my head, my attention's caught by a movement near the cedar trees to our right. A man in a red jacket is watching us. It must be the same guy from the train. A frightened little yelp escapes my lips.

Suzi opens her eyes and appraises me with an air of irritation. 'What now?'

'Look,' I hiss, prising my fingers from her hand and pointing in the direction of the trees.

'What?'

'Behind you.'

But by the time Suzi finally turns, the man has already disappeared behind bushes.

'What am I supposed to be looking at?' she asks.

'There was a man there.'

'A man,' she says flatly. She doesn't seem impressed.

'He was watching us.'

'A man. In a public space. Was watching us. And?'

'I'm sure it was the same guy I saw on the train. He followed me here.'

She throws up her arms in exasperation. 'Where else d'you think he'd be going if he got off the train at Brookwood? There's not a whole lot else here apart from the cemetery. I know what you're trying to do.'

'What d'you mean?'

'Conjuring up phantom figures in the undergrowth because you can't bring yourself to give up sixty seconds of your precious time to honour Mum's memory.'

'Oh, come on, that's not fair,' I protest, glancing anxiously around in case the man has returned.

'So where were you on the ninth anniversary of her death? Or the eighth? Or the seventh, the sixth, the fifth? Where were you when she was dying?'

'What?' I ask sharply.

'I said —'

'I heard what you said. I'm asking what you meant by it.'

'You didn't visit once while she was in hospital.'

'I was away at university.'

'You couldn't have missed one day of lectures for your dying mother?'

'It wasn't like that. I was in the middle of a work placement, and it's a long journey down to Hampshire from York, especially as no-one actually told me she was going to die. Anyway, why would she want me there when she had you and Geoff to look after her?'

Suzi sighs impatiently. She just doesn't get it. She's never tried to understand how difficult that time was for me. Her eyes flick skyward momentarily, and then bore into me. 'Even if you're not prepared to do it for Mum, surely you could play along for my sake? After everything I've done for you.'

'Hold on a minute, what d'you mean everything you've done?' I don't know why she's getting so angry with me.

'Where to begin? How about giving you a place to live rent-free for a start.'

'But you offered! And it's not like you're losing out on any rent. I thought you appreciated having someone there to let in the builders and check up on the work? And what about all the tins of paint you've got me lugging home?'

'Paint?'

'They're really heavy you know. I've still got marks across my fingers where the handle was digging in. Look —' I hold my hand out, knowing how petty this must be coming across.

Suzi peers at my fingers blankly.

'Okay it doesn't look much, but it was nearly a week ago and it's still a bit red.'

Suzi's staring at me again, her eyes taut with aggression, her cheeks flushed with anger. 'I don't need you there to let the builders in, you know. Things were progressing quite happily before you arrived.'

'I may be stupid, but I can take a hint. I'll move out.'

'What?' She pretends to look surprised.

'I'll move out. I'll go back to Tooting,' I say trying to sound martyred, but unable to keep the self-pity out of my voice.

'You really don't have to.' She sounds almost convincing, but it's too late to take it back now.

'You obviously don't want me there, and that's fine. It suits me better anyway. It takes a lot longer getting to work from Clapham.'

I quickly turn to leave so she won't see that I'm starting to choke up. What's wrong with me? Every little thing at the moment has me breaking down in tears.

'Phoebe, wait!'

'Don't worry, I'll be out first thing in the morning,' I say, weaving a path through the gravestones.

'Please don't. What about lunch?' she calls, but I pretend not to hear.

'Sorry. Got to go. I've got a train to catch,' I shout, and hurry away before she can stop me.

All the way home I'm so mad at Suzi that I don't pay any attention to the other passengers on the train. I just sit there fuming, with metaphorical steam spouting from my ears. Even when I'm trudging back up the hill to the flat, I don't once look over my shoulder to see if I'm being followed.

There's a name for this: Ukhtomsky's Dominance Principle. We studied it in a module on pain management at university. Basically, if you're experiencing multiple pain stimuli, you're usually only aware of the most painful of them.

So, for instance, sticking a drawing pin into your

thumb can make you forget about your toothache. And thinking how annoying your big sister is can make you forget that perhaps you're being followed.

She's always been annoying. I don't know what her problem is. All my life she's bossed me about, and can't stand it when things don't go her own way. It's the control freak in her. Everything in her life has to be perfect. She's got her perfect home, her perfect husband, her perfect job — and she can't stomach the fact that her sister's just a hot mess.

I try ringing Beth, to let her know I'll be moving back to the old flat, and when Beth doesn't answer, I ring Claire. There's a long silence after I've told her the news. 'What's the problem?' I ask.

'We weren't sure whether you were coming back. I told my cousin she could have your room.'

'Oh. Well can't you tell her that the room isn't empty after all?'

There's another long pause and I can almost hear Claire squirming down the phone line, before she finally admits: 'She's already moved in.'

'What? When were you planning on letting me know?'

'She's come down from Edinburgh and doesn't know a soul in London. She's only nineteen. I told my aunt we'd look after her.'

'So you're saying I can't have my room back?'

'We'll cover your share of the rent so you wouldn't be out of pocket.'

'What about all my stuff!'

'Relax. It's all packed away.'

'Oh. Thanks,' I say, in a flat, despondent tone.

'You're welcome,' Claire answers, choosing to ignore how upset I am. I've got no choice: It would be worse than awkward if I had to insist on kicking out Claire's cousin to move back in with them. I'm going to have to swallow my pride and give Suzi a call.

Chapter 14

THE PROBLEM WITH Ukhtomsky's Dominance Principle is that as soon as you've removed the drawing pin from your thumb, the pain in your tooth immediately returns. So, as soon as I've sorted out things with Suzi (I left a grovelling apology on her voicemail and told her I'd like to stay on in the flat after all, if that was okay with her), my anxieties over the fact that Alfie's got my address immediately resurface.

Whenever I go out, I have the unnerving feeling that I'm being watched; a vague sense of someone just outside the periphery of my vision. But when I turn to look, no-one's there. It's as though I'm playing a real-life game of Grandmother's Footsteps.

Travelling to work on the tube, I cast furtive glances at the men lined up along the row of seats opposite, wondering if one of them might be Alfie. The being-watched feeling doesn't leave me when I'm at work, either. In a busy hospital people are coming and going all the time — that young guy who's been sitting in the waiting room for an hour without checking-in seems suspicious, doesn't he? Even that porter pushing an empty wheelchair along the corridor — maybe Alfie's sneaked in and got hold of a uniform?

Heading home along the High Street I can't help glancing behind to check if I'm being followed. Perhaps that guy waiting outside Sainsbury's, eating a sandwich under the streetlamp is Alfie? Or the guy who accidentally brushes against my arm as I wait to cross the road?

Because of my preoccupation with whether I'm being followed, I don't at first connect together the odd, seemingly random things that start turning up at the flat.

Firstly, an old Freeman's catalogue is posted through my letterbox — which someone has been through to gouge out the eyes of the female models and scribble beards and moustaches on the men.

The next day I get a Scientology leaflet inviting me to a psychology assessment centre for a free, no-strings-attached personality test that will help me identify the things in my life which hold me back from reaching my true potential.

Stranger still is the bird's nest, complete with two pale blue birds' eggs, which someone leaves in a box on my doorstep.

Initially I assumed these things were meant for the Henry-phobic previous tenant — who knows, maybe he was into home shopping, Scientology and ornithology? But when I receive a copy of *Nursing Times* with a picture of a frazzled-looking female nurse on the cover, and the headline *Struggling For Recognition?* it's clear that someone is deliberately trying to unnerve me. And that someone must surely be Alfie.

Tuesday. A normal mid-week day shift, but I didn't check the weather forecast before I left for work and as I walk home from the tube it starts to rain. It's a proper full-on storm, with heavy rain, gusty winds, and bright flashes of lightening that set the sky alight, followed by deafening cracks of thunder. By the time I get home I'm utterly soaked.

In my hurry to get in out of the rain I fumble with the key in the lock — *more haste, less speed* Dad would have chided. And then the door won't open. I give it a wary shove, expecting the worst, and am relieved to find that the door's just blocked by a pile of post lying in the hallway.

As I bend down to gather up the bulky envelopes, there's a blinding burst of lightening behind me, and for a brief moment the whole garden lights up as bright as day. It's like a scene from a horror movie: the gnomes are stationed

Wicker Man-style in a ring around the grassy mound, and standing in the middle are the shattered remains of the Beyoncé gnome. Her head is missing, her neck's just a jagged stump, and she's pointing demoniacally at the sky.

I hold the wad of envelopes over my head and hurry out into the garden to take a closer look. Did Alfie do this as a warning to me? He knows I like Beyoncé, and I'm a Single Lady. Or am I reading way too much into it?

A sudden roar of thunder in the distance makes me blench in fear and I spin round to find Denise tapping on her kitchen window, motioning me to come in out of the rain.

'What on earth are you doing out there?' she asks as I stand dripping in her hallway.

'Someone's been messing with your gnomes. I'm afraid Beyoncé's had her head smashed off.'

'Beyoncé? I don't have a Beyoncé gnome.'

'Yes you do. You know — *Beyoncé*.' I assume the *Single Ladies* pump-walk pose, but Denise stares blankly back at me, like I've completely lost the plot.

'In her black leotard. *You* know. *Uh oh-oh, oh-uh oh-oh-oh,*' I start singing *Single Ladies,* pumping my arms like pistons and marching up and down the kitchen.

'I know who Beyoncé is. But I promise you, I don't own a Beyoncé gnome.'

'But you do!' This is so frustrating! I dash outside and retrieve the gnome from the gruesome tableau.

When Denise sees it she gives a gusty laugh: 'That's not Beyoncé. That's Usain Bolt!'

'It is?' When I examine the gnome more closely, I see that what I took for a leotard is actually a black running vest, and Beyoncé's long hair is a flag draped across Usain Bolt's shoulders.

Denise takes Usain from me with a sorrowful shake of her head. 'I bet it was those kids that hang out on the corner after school eating burgers and smoking dope. Those little bastards!'

'It might not have been them?' I suggest.

'No, it was those bloody school kids. I'll give them hell if I catch them.'

I should tell her that I'm pretty sure Alfie was responsible for Wicker-Manning her gnomes, but I'm too tired to face one of her lectures.

'We need a drink,' she decides. I follow her into the kitchen and drop the soggy envelopes onto the table.

'What've you got there?' she says, pouring us a glass of prune and dandelion wine.

'Brochures, I'm guessing. They all came in the post today.'

'Aren't you going to open them?'

'It's just junk mail,' I say light-heartedly, picking up one of the envelopes. But as I tear it open, I have an uneasy feeling. It's got my name and address on it, and aside from Suzi and Denise, there's only one person who knows I'm living here.

It's a catalogue. *LustBunnies.co.uk*. The cover has a close-up of a discretely naked couple locked in a loving embrace. *Everything you'll ever need for a toe-curling finish*. The pages are filled with pictures of vibrators, love eggs, cock rings and all manner of strange-looking plasticky things I didn't even know existed.

Denise grins.

'*I* didn't order it,' I protest.

'No, of course not!'

'Honest!'

She cocks a disbelieving eyebrow at me and takes another damp envelope from the table. 'Well well well, what do we have here? *SugarLoving*. Super-sexy bargains and plus-size bangers. Now that sounds exciting —'

She stops when she sees me squirming in my chair. 'Wait — are you telling me you don't own any toys? Oh my child! There's a whole world of fun waiting for you to explore. You can borrow some of mine if you like. I've built up quite an extensive collection over the years.'

I feel myself blushing furiously and am too embarrassed to look her in the eye. Alfie was always teasing me about my prudishness. He'd take great delight in embarrassing me in public by talking loudly about sex. Surely he must be responsible for ordering these brochures?

'You don't need to be coy. A bit of self-love might be just what the doctor ordered.'

I bite my tongue and let her tell me all about vibrators and love balls and dildos made of texturised rubber that have the exact same feel as skin. When she's finally finished, she pours another drink and asks: 'Are you around tomorrow night? The Zumba girls will be coming over after class.'

'Sorry, I'm busy,' I say.

'Working?'

I shake my head.

'Wait? What is it? I can tell by the look on your face that you've done something you shouldn't have.'

I try to deny it, but she forces it out of me, and I tell her all about Robbie and Tom.

'So you've got *two* dates!'

'They're not dates,' I protest. That's why I haven't mentioned it before now. I knew she wouldn't be impressed.

She starts lecturing me: 'You're still emotionally fragile from your last relationship. You need to give yourself time to re-centre yourself.'

'They're not dates!'

'Trust me, I know what I'm talking about. Relationships formed on the rebound are never going to be healthy.'

'I'm not planning on starting a relationship. Honest. And anyway, they both seem really nice.'

Denise eyes me thoughtfully. 'I'm sure your last boyfriend seemed really nice when you first met him too. They always do. It means nothing. You have to listen to your gut instincts and stop paying attention to your heart.'

I can't deny that she's right about Alfie. When I first started dating him, he was charming, generous and kind. And then he wasn't.

Denise is waggling her finger at me. 'I mean it Phoebe. It's really easy to move too fast when you're coming off a bad relationship. What's the hurry? You're still young.'

'I'll be thirty next year,' I protest.

'Thirty!' Denise snorts, 'Ooo, that's so old! Now listen to me, I'm being serious. I think you should cool it, even if it's just for a few months. It would be wrong for you to climb back up onto the dating horse.'

'Okay, okay, I'll cancel the *dates*. Even though they aren't dates.'

'Really? That's great!' Denise seems surprised, and rewards me by topping up my drink, which I sip at guiltily because I've no intention of cancelling at this late notice.

Chapter 15

WHAT'S THE BEST sort of venue for a non-date? Tom suggested a bar and Robbie suggested a pub, but because I hate the noise and clatter of those sorts of places, I asked if we could go to a restaurant instead. And as I'm new to the area, I left it to them to choose where to eat. Weirdly, they both chose the same restaurant: *Anonymous*, in Stockwell, which according to its enigmatic website, serves "Contemporary English cuisine with a Mediterranean twist".

The website doesn't give much else away, so I'm not quite sure what to expect. It turns out to be one of those ultra-stylish places with green-grey walls, gold leafed fixtures and fittings, boldly patterned cushions and smart leather dining chairs. When I push open the door my ears are assaulted by noisy, clattery, chattery restaurant sounds, and I have to grit my teeth and suppress the impulse to flee. I scan the room for a man with an *I-know-you* look of recognition on his face, hoping to catch sight of it before it turns into an *I'm-standing-in-front-of-you-and-still-you-haven't-seen-me* look of incredulity.

'Phoebe!'

'Phoebe!'

On both evenings I'm spotted before it gets embarrassing. But whereas Robbie jumps to his feet and waves, Tom just gives a shy smile and a little nod of greeting which I almost miss. He does eventually get up to help me with my coat, and then pushes my chair in behind me when I sit down, but it's a bit formal, a bit awkward, a bit *Teen First Dates.*

The same waiter serves me on both evenings. I'm able to recognise him by the huge, feathered tattoo wrapping around the back of his neck, and I can't help staring at it as he goes to fetch the menus.

'Not a fan of tats?' Robbie asks, when the waiter's gone.

'You don't like tattoos?' Tom enquires in a guarded whisper.

The problem with tattoos is that they remind me of Alfie. He had a full sleeve of tattoos on one arm — there was a spooky-looking skull, some sort of tiger or lion, a half-naked lady, and I can't recall what else because they all merged together, and I don't really want to think about it.

'I like *some* tattoos,' I say diplomatically.

'That's lucky then,' Robbie says with a relieved grin.

'You've got tattoos?'

'A few. Not too many.'

And Tom has tattoos as well, but I don't ask to see them.

'Shall we have wine?' he says, holding up the wine list.

'Red or white?' Robbie asks.

'You choose,' I reply.

Tom scratches his beard.

Robbie scratches his beard.

'Is white okay?' Tom asks.

'We'll have the house red,' Robbie tells the waiter.

I'm not really fussed about wine, though I generally prefer white, so Tom comes out slightly better for drinks ordering.

I can't help comparing my two new friends. It's weird to be sat here in the same restaurant on two nights in a row, at the same table, wearing the same dress, being served by the same waiter, and, due to the lack of vegetarian options on the menu, even ordering the same food. Everything's the same, except the company. It's like I've set up some sort of controlled trial to determine who I like the best.

'So, what d'you do for work?' I ask over my grilled halloumi and artichoke salad, with lemon aioli dipping sauce.

'I'm a trainee accountant,' Robbie answers.

'I work in PR,' Tom replies.

Both times I raise my eyebrows in surprise. I'd have thought it would be the other way round. I can see Robbie working in PR because he's got that warm confidence you need to put people at ease, whereas Tom seems more hesitant, with a slow, measured way of talking that seems more suited to discussing numbers, or whatever accountants do.

The halloumi starter is okay the first time, but rubbery and over-cooked the next day and I struggle to finish it. The only vegetarian main on the menu is goat's cheese tart. I've never liked that strange vomity tang that goat's cheese has, and would far rather have a nice cheddar, but restaurants seem to think it's some special kind of delicacy, and when you decide to become a vegetarian you very quickly get used to eating things in restaurants you don't like.

Robbie orders the rib-eye steak — *the connoisseurs cut of choice because the fattier steaks are always the tastiest.* I smile, even though fat in meat has always grossed me out. The enthusiastic way he attacks his steak reminds me a little of Alfie, except Alfie would never have brought me to this kind of restaurant or engaged in this type of conversation or smiled at me over his steak and asked me to tell him all about myself.

Tom orders the fish but seems to regret it after spending the first five minutes picking out all the bones and dropping them in an unsightly pile on the edge of his plate before he can start eating. 'How's the tart?' he asks.

'Mmn, good,' I reply, forcing down another mouthful.

'At least there's no bones in goat's cheese,' he replies from behind his hand, trying to unobtrusively pick a fish bone out of his mouth.

He tells me he's from a big family. Three older sisters and a younger brother, plus four cats and two dogs. And a budgie. I don't think he's trying to be funny, but there's something faintly comical about the way he says this that makes me smile. He's not like the guys I've dated before and I can't quite make him out.

Robbie on the other hand, with his gruff Yorkshire accent and his blunt way of talking, seems more straightforward. He tells me he's doing his accountancy exams, and that it takes five years to qualify — which is a bloody age and he's going to have a bloody great party when he's finished to celebrate the fact that finally, at the age of thirty, he'll be able to drop the word *trainee* from his bloody job title.

Tom asks me about my family, and I tell him I have a sister in Dulwich, a Dad who lives near Marbella, and that my Mum died ten years ago this week. I tell him about my job (fulfilling but tiring), whether I like living in Tooting or Clapham best (Clapham) and how long I've been a vegetarian (nine years, and no, I don't miss bacon).

Robbie asks if I watch *Love Island* (no — which surprises him, like there's a law which says all twenty-something women must watch it) or *Gogglebox* (yes — and we agree that the best Goggleboxers are the two sisters from Leeds, and the woman with the gay best friend who lives in a caravan in Hull. All from Yorkshire, btw, Robbie points out proudly).

I'm having a good time, except for the fact that I keep hearing Denise's voice in my head: *it's too early to date.* But it's not a date!

Robbie tells me amusing anecdotes about his boss,

who's a bit of a David Brent, and thinks they're all one big happy team when in truth everyone's bitching about him behind his back. Robbie's obviously a funny guy, even if he does have too much product in his hair.

Tom's a funny guy too, but I'm not entirely sure it's deliberate. When he drops his knife and bends down to retrieve it from under the table, he pulls such a goofy, clumsy-me face, that I can't help laughing.

But Alfie used to make me laugh too, and I hear Denise's voice in my head again: *if you're still comparing people to your old boyfriend then you haven't moved on. Simple as.*

I wish voice-in-the-head-Denise would pipe down for a bit, because these aren't dates, and the desserts have arrived and I'm finally getting to eat something that's not made from cheese.

Chapter 16

PHOEBE'S SITTING ACROSS the table from me and doesn't have a fucking clue who I am. Not a Scoobie. Although I've played this trick on her before, I've never carried it on for so long. I still find it hard to believe she can't recognise me. I'm not gonna lie, waiting for her to arrive at the restaurant I was convinced she was playing a crazy game of double bluff. But then, when her eyes scanned my face blankly without even the slightest flicker of recognition, like a wonky nut spinning on a screw and never catching the thread, I knew she wasn't faking it. She couldn't recognise Gordon Ramsey, Ed Sheeran, or Adolph fucking Hitler, even if he walked into the restaurant, marched up to our table, and gave her a Nazi salute. She'd think he was just some random guy with a comedy moustache.

It's funny really. When we were a couple, that vacant, bovine look which clouded her face when she couldn't recognise me really pissed me off. But now I love spotting it. It makes her so vulnerable. It reminds me that I can get away with anything. Turn up to her house with a holdall full of electrical bits to "fix" her wiring: she's clueless. Grow a beard, put on an accent and engineer a "date": she's completely in the dark.

Having this power of knowledge over her is a massive turn-on for me. In fact, fabricating a life for myself is giving me a raging hard-on. I tell her about my family, my job, the story about the time the neighbours' cat got stuck up a tree and I ended up in hospital after trying to rescue it; the story about travelling down to London for Princess Diana's funeral and waving at Prince William and Prince Harry and they waved back. In reality there's no job, no cat, no tree, and no fucking Princess Diana story, because she died before I was born and the poor little princes had already marched along behind the hearse and the whole country had already cried its heart out, boo-hoo-hoo.

Lying has always come easily to me. Ever since I can remember I've known that life is easier if you lie. I lie to people to make them feel better. I lie to get them to give me stuff. I lie to get them into bed.

It's all so easy. The only things you need to be a successful liar are a good memory and a fearless don't-give-a-shit attitude to life. And luckily, I have an amazing memory and the only shit I give is to make sure that it's me shitting on other people.

The thing that's best about lying though, is that it's fuck-king exhilarating! Because, when you think about it, life is basically pretty tedious most of the time. I get bored really easily and if I didn't lie, the empty pointless nothingness of life would eat away at me like a disease. Lying and acting on my impulses supplies me with the injection of adrenaline I need to survive.

Lying to Phoebe is almost *too* easy because I know her so well. I know what her favourite drink is, her favourite film, her favourite TV programmes. I know how to make her laugh, I know how to make her feel compassion, I know exactly how to make her like me.

I'm like an evil scientist conducting experiments on an unwitting subject. I used to do this all the time as a kid. Like pulling legs off spiders to see how many they could lose before they couldn't walk anymore. Or putting wasps into a jar of bleach to see how long they'd survive. Once I found a severely injured squirrel in the park and brought it home in a plastic bag. I skinned it alive and planned to remove its internal organs one by one — a sort of body-part roulette —

to see when it would die. But my horrified parents discovered me behind the garage, knife in hand, covered in blood, before I could complete my experiment.

Phoebe's the subject of this particular experiment, and luckily my parents aren't around to intervene.

Actually, scrub that. This meal isn't an experiment. It's more like the film *Groundhog Day*, when Bill Murray lives the same day over and over again, and tries to find out as much as he can about Andie MacDowell so that he can get into her knickers. I fucking *love* that movie. It's a mind-controllers wet dream. Phoebe is my Andie MacDowell, except without that annoying simpering smile. And I'm Bill Murray, but twenty years younger and much, much better looking.

I have to be careful though. I almost blew it when she asked me to guess her favourite drink. I was going to say *vodka lime soda*, but that would have been far too on the nose and might have aroused her suspicions. I'm playing a delicate game here. I must have patience if I'm to drive her back into my arms, or all this subterfuge will have been a waste of time.

Though it doesn't really matter even if I do fuck this up. She's so gullible that I can always arrange another chance meeting, put on another sexy northern accent, and get myself another date. It's just a game for me.

When you think about it, all of life is just a game really. It took me a good few years to learn this lesson. When I was really little, like at primary school, I had a really hard time making friends. I didn't like them, they didn't like me, and they always saw through my lies and manipulations.

But when I was about ten years old, I realised that if you pretend to be the person someone wants you to be, you can get away with anything. I created a different personality for everyone I interacted with, and everything just clicked into place. Suddenly I was the most popular boy in the class.

I acquired a "best friend" who I could manipulate into doing whatever I wanted. I was the first boy in my year to lose my virginity, and by the time I left school I'd slept with most of the girls in my class, and quite a few of the boys.

Of course, I have primal urges which need satisfying like everyone else, but for me the sexual act is all about power and the excitement of having a woman submit to me completely. The moment it's over I feel exactly the same way I feel after eating a Big Mac: it'll be a while before I fancy another one.

What I really don't like is having to deal with messy after-sex emotions. There's nothing worse than clingy woman who want to spoon and cuddle up after they been fucked. They cover my neck with little kisses and speak in quiet whispers about how we're meant to be together and how much they love me. When that starts to happen, I know it's time for me to move on. Which isn't a problem because finding sexual partners is very easy. Most women like a confident man. You just have to be careful not to be *too* confident. In order to be successful, you need to monitor the person you're talking to, adjust what you say, and very soon you'll have them eating out of your hands. I stare at the way Phoebe is holding her spoon, and imagine her hand wrapped around my cock, wanking me off.

'— ever be possible for a woman?' she asks, the pitch of her voice rising expectantly at the end of her sentence.

What the fuck? I've not been paying attention to what she's been saying. But, no sweat, it doesn't matter because I can read her expression like a book. The little twist of her mouth, the tension just above her eyebrows, the way the muscles of her neck have tightened as she prepares to nod, they all tell me she wants me to agree with her.

I tell her earnestly: 'Yes.'

She rewards me with a smile. I smile back, making sure I don't come across too cocky. I know that although

Phoebe likes confidence in a man, she's also attracted to vulnerability. So, I've been showing a bit of swagger and some tongue-tied hesitancy. It's a delicate balance. If I push too hard, I might scare her off, but if I'm too soft I risk being friend-zoned.

And that, I reflect as I reach under the table to scratch at the inside of my thigh so that the back of my hand rubs against my aching cock, is the last thing I want tonight.

Chapter 17

THE WAITER TAKES away our dessert bowls and we order coffee. Tom has a flat white, Robbie has a double espresso, and because I'm still off the caffeine, both nights I order a decaf Americano.

When the bill comes they both offer to get it, but I insist on paying my share. I'd have insisted on paying even if we were on a date. I don't understand why some women — Claire for example — consider it a deal-breaker if the guy doesn't pick up the tab on a first date. I wouldn't want that because I'd hate to feel like I owed him anything.

The waiter fetches our coats and then we're standing on the pavement outside the restaurant.

'So —' Robbie says expectantly.

'Well —' Tom begins, hesitantly.

On both evenings it's like an unspoken *what next?* is left hanging in the chilly evening air between us. To pre-empt any awkward uncertainty, I whip out my phone and exclaim in surprise: 'Is that the time? I didn't realise it was so late!'

We exchange hurried *goodbyes*, *that-was-funs*, and *yes-we-must-do-it-agains*, and then I rush off to catch the tube before either of them can point out that it would have made more sense to get a cab home together since we're going in the same direction.

Chapter 18

FUCK IT! I jab the palm of my hand into the back of the passenger seat. *Fuck! Fuck! Fuck!* The driver looks round anxiously to see what's going on, but I ignore him.

Okay, okay, so it's not the end of the world. But according to my plan Phoebe should be sitting here beside me on our way back to her flat for some prime first date sex. Instead, I'm all on my lonesome, adrenaline surging through my system, with a bad case of blue balls.

Where did I go wrong? What could I have done differently? Before our meal I worried I was laying it on too thickly with the smashed gnomes, the magazines and those sex catalogues, but obviously I've not spooked her enough. I'll have to ramp it up a notch if I'm going to win her back.

But what about tonight? After all the effort I've put in I should be bumping uglies with Phoebe, instead of heading back to an empty flat to jizz into a crumpled tissue.

I check my phone. It's only half-past ten, for fuck's sake. That settles it. I'm not going home. It's time to drop the phony accent, fish out one of my duplicate keys, and pay a certain lucky lady a visit. She's in for the surprise of her fucking life when she gets home. Just so long as I get there before her.

I rap my knuckles on the glass partition and give the driver the address. 'And can you put your foot down mate? I'm in a hurry.'

Chapter 19

ASIDE FROM THE awkwardness when it came to say goodbye, I had a really good time tonight. Which makes two nice evenings out in two days with two really nice guys. Perhaps things are finally turning around for me?

I trot up the path to the front door with a real bounce in my step — partly because of my good mood and partly because I'm buzzing from the alcohol — and give a cheery wave to Norma and the other gnomes. Then out of the corner of my eye catch sight of something which makes me stop in my tracks: a shadow flits across the curtains of the first-floor window.

My heart's pounding in my chest and I feel an uneasy contraction in the pit of my stomach as my mind conjures up all sorts of scary scenarios. *There's someone in the flat. A burglar? A murderer? Alfie?*

I stand rooted to the spot, my eyes fixed on the ill-fitting bedroom curtains, but there's no sign of anything now. Perhaps I imagined it?

Pull yourself together and stop being so melodramatic I tell myself. *You've been in this situation before, and your fears amounted to nothing.* I've got to stop acting like a scaredy child all the time. I should confront my fears head on.

But, just in case I'm wrong, I'm not risking going up there unarmed. I look around for a weapon: Denise's gnomes. I select the ugliest-looking one, which I figure she'll miss the least if it gets damaged. Then I carefully unlock the front door and creep up the stairs as silently as I can with the ugly gnome raised above my head.

Chapter 20

I HEAR THE front door click shut. She's home! And I only just made it in time. I'm crouching behind the sofa, drumming my fingers restively on the carpet, the blood pounding in my ears. I'm in a state of heightened excitement, pumped up by sexual frustration and by the little toot of coke I had in the back of the cab.

I savour the delicious anticipation of imminent chaos that thrums through my body. Moments like these are the only times I actually feel alive! Everything in between is just a stultifying emptiness which would kill me if I did nothing about it. I'm like a shark that has to keep the water flowing through its gills or else it will drown.

I concentrate on slowing my breathing so as not to give myself away, but my excitement is mounting. I picture the confusion, surprise and fear on her face when I jump out. I think ahead to the sexual act, to the point when I'll penetrate her body and finally submerse myself wholly in the moment. That delicious split-second of time when everything that's happened in the past is forgotten, when everything that may happen in the future is of no consequence, that moment when I can become one with my thoughts, when I can drop the fake personas and just be the real me.

Footsteps are approaching. I hold completely still, like a cat waiting to pounce on its prey, counting under my breath: *one, two, three —*

Chapter 21

'PHOEBE!'

A WOMAN barks my name in surprise. She's wearing a striped jumpsuit and is sitting on a Moroccan-styled coffee table that's blocking the door to the lounge.

'Suzi? Thank God it's you!' I lower the gnome and put it onto the coffee table with a sigh of relief.

'What a welcome! We're you going to hit me over the head with — what on earth *is* that?' She frowns at the ugly, egg-shaped gnome with its mop of blond hair. 'Is it supposed to be Boris Johnson?'

I shrug my shoulders. 'I suppose so. Denise must have bought it as some kind of ironic political statement.'

'So your plan was to brain me with Boris Johnson?'

'I thought you were an intruder. Why didn't you let me know you were coming?'

'I didn't know you were going to be here! If you remember, the last words you said to me were that you were moving out.'

'Didn't you get my voicemail?'

'No.'

'I left it last week. You didn't get it?'

She shakes her head. 'What did it say?'

'It said that I was sorry and I didn't mean to fly off the handle with you. And would it be okay if I stayed on in the flat.'

She gives me a magnanimous smile: 'I forgive you.'

'And I can stay here?'

'On one condition.'

'Which is?'

'You have to give me a hand with this,' she says, slapping the coffee table with the palm of her hand.

I don't think I've ever seen such a strikingly ugly piece of furniture. It has a glass top that's etched with circles and triangles, and a bulbous, gold-coloured base. It must weigh a ton. I can't imagine how she managed to get it up here on her own. All those hours spent toning her arms in the gym have finally paid off.

'Where did it come from?' I ask, imagining it was a junk shop impulse purchase.

She tucks a loose strand of hair behind her ear with a bitter-sounding sigh. 'It's from *Heels*. Guess how much it cost?'

'I've no idea.'

'Go on, guess.'

'I don't know what new coffee tables cost. Four hundred pounds?'

She gives a derisive snort. 'I wish!'

'Eight hundred?'

She shakes her head. 'One thousand three hundred and fifty pounds.'

'Ouch!'

'And it's ghastly isn't it.'

'It's — unusual.'

'You don't have to lie.'

'Okay, it is ghastly.'

'That's what Alistair thinks too! When it arrived, he went ape-shit-crazy. *Why d'you keep buying all this furniture? Don't we have enough already? Every day there's another bloody delivery man at the door. The house is full of stuff we don't need.* Blah blah blah. Moan moan moan. On and on and on. We had a big row about it, and I said that if the sight of it was so offensive to his eyes, I'd take it round to the flat so he wouldn't have to look at it any more. It nearly killed me carrying it up those bloody stairs. Look, I've crushed my thumb.'

She thrusts it under my nose, and I give it a squinty-eyed examination. It's a little red and swollen, but nothing serious. Some impulse makes me take hold of her hand, plant two little kisses on her thumb, and as I return it to her lap, I say *Iddy widdy better now*, which is how Mum would comfort us when we came to her with our little scrapes and bruises.

Suzi gives me a sideways glance: 'Are you drunk?'

'No. Yes. Maybe a little.'

Her eyes light up. 'Ooh, where've you been?'

'Nowhere,' I reply airily, getting up. 'C'mon.' I pull her to her feet. 'We can't leave this ugly old thing here. Or the coffee table either!'

Chapter 22

'GUESS WHO!' I shout, jumping out from behind the sofa.

Nisha's eyes widen in fear, and she lets loose a piercing shriek.

'It's only me!' I tell her.

She stares at me uncomprehendingly for a second or two, then bursts into tears. I take her in my arms and stroke her hair. 'Poor baby. Did you get scared? I'm sorry.'

When her sobs have subsided, she tries to twist round and look up at me, but I hold her in a tight embrace to make sure that she won't catch sight of the big grin on my face. Her histrionics are always entertaining. If she breaks a nail or if a tiny little insect gets anywhere near her, she'll scream like someone's trying to murder her. Just say *boo!* and she'll jump right out of her skin. I don't understand why everyone seems to have so little control of their emotions. You turn on the TV and there's some reality show where they're all shouting and screaming and acting fucking *extra* over the tiniest little thing.

I never let my emotions get the better of me. The last time it happened I was about nine years old. An older boy had threatened me with a hammer because I'd been mouthing off at him and I was so scared that I wet myself and burst into tears. The shame and humiliation made me vow I'd never show weakness like that again. If you came at me with a hammer, I wouldn't flinch. I'd look you in the eye and say *go on, fucking do it* and you'd back down. Or maybe you wouldn't back down, but I still wouldn't care. Broken bones mend, bruises fade, but I'd have learnt something about you to use against you later. Oh, don't worry about that — I always get my own back.

'You gave me such a fright,' Nisha complains.

'I know. I'm *sowwy*. Paw 'ickle baby.' She loves this sickly baby talk crap. I feel her body slacken in my arms and I pull her even tighter to my chest. I kiss the soft delicate exposed skin on the back of her neck, only gently at first, and then more fiercely. A re-awakening sexual desire surges like electricity through my body.

'Not now Alfie,' she says.

Something about the casual, condescending way she says this makes me angry. Why should she always be the one to decide when we have sex? The more I think about it, the more angry I become, until something finally snaps. My mouth fills with a bitter, metallic taste and a thrilling image of Nisha being fucked senseless springs into my mind. My jaw becomes rigid with purpose and I grab hold of her wrists.

'Please, not now. I don't want to.'

Her strained voice is an annoying whine. She squirms in my arms, trying to escape my grasp, but her muffled protests only make me want her more. She looks up at me with questioning eyes that are flecked with fear, her expression turning to shock as I raise my hand and slap her across her face.

Chapter 23

AFTER WE'VE CARRIED the coffee table into the flat, Suzi tells me she's got more things in the car which need to be carried up.

'What is all this?' I ask with surprise when she opens up the boot of her BMW. It's rammed full of cardboard boxes.

'Just stuff I've accumulated over the years. Alistair forced me to have a big clear out because he said there was no room in the house anymore. I couldn't bring myself to throw it away, so it's been sitting in the boot for weeks.'

'Where's it going?'

'I'm hoping it will all fit in the attic.'

I didn't know Suzi's flat even had an attic. The boxes are heavier than they look, and it takes us forever to lug them upstairs. And it turns out that the attic's already full of Suzi's junk, so we have to stack everything in a big pile in the corner of the lounge.

As we're carrying the last of the boxes, its bottom gives way, and everything falls out. There are old magazines, cards, bundles of letters held together with half perished rubber-bands, jigsaw puzzles and board games. Among them I spot a flattened lid.

'So you did take it!' I say with a sharp intake of breath.

'What?'

I grab the lid and wave it in front of her face accusingly. '*Guess Who?* I can't believe it! You told me you didn't know where it was.'

It takes only a second for Suzi to realise I'm referring to a conversation from years ago. She slips right back into it, like it's 2004 again. 'No I didn't. Anyway, it was mine.'

'I don't think so. I got it for my tenth birthday.'

'You agreed I could take it when Mum and I moved out. Don't you remember?'

'I did not!' I reply indignantly. All the anger I felt eighteen years ago comes flooding back, which is ridiculous, I know. Apparently, rattling around at the bottom of the grab-bag of slights and resentments I've been carrying with me since childhood, were these unresolved feelings about a silly board game.

'Look, I'd love to stand here arguing but I've got to get back.'

'You aren't staying? What about your big fight with Alistair?'

'It's late and he'll be worrying where I've got to. I'll call you.'

She gives a perfunctory wave and hurries off down the stairs.

That's just so typical of her — walking away when things get uncomfortable. I'm left clutching the lid of the *Guess Who?* box, which is held together by old Sellotape that the years have made flaky and discoloured.

Suzi is wrong though. I never said she could have it. She was fifteen when they moved out, far too old for toys. But for some reason she insisted on having the board games.

It makes sense, she explained, *because you haven't got any friends and you can't play them on your own, can you?* But I didn't want her to take them. They belonged at home.

After *Guess Who?* had mysteriously gone missing, I demanded the *Monopoly* set in recompense. Suzi refused to give it up, and in the end, because it was late, and Dad had had enough, he ripped the board in two and gave us half each. Even then we insisted on divvying up the hotels, houses, money and the cards. We almost came to blows over which counter pieces to have. We both wanted the dog and neither of us wanted the iron. I mean, who would ever want to be an *iron*?

I've no idea what happened to my half of the set, but as I rootle through Suzi's boxes I find her half of the Monopoly board, along with all her pieces, including that poor iron. I can't believe she kept it all these years.

I know I shouldn't be going through her things, but it's a real nostalgia-fest, stirring up long-forgotten memories and emotions. Here are the ornaments that used to sit on the shelf above her bed when we shared a bedroom. Here's a wad of birthday cards from when she was five, six, and seven. Here are her old exercise books from infant school. I open one at random.

We went to the Grabledon of tyme. I wor my prety dress with the flowers. My sister Phoebe has trousers. I had a swim in the sea. Phoebe staid on the sand. The sea wos cold. It wos fun.

Four figures with spiky cactus fingers, are lined up on a sunny beach, holding hands. We've all got big blue eyes and bright red splodgy smiling mouths. Below the picture, rather than asking *What on earth is a Grabledon of tyme?* the teacher has instead written *What a lovely time you had at the beach Susie.*

She was still Susie in those days. It was only after she moved out with Mum that she decided she was going to be Suzi. Or rather *Suzi!* Pronounced with an exclamation mark.

Her next act of rebellion was to get her belly button pierced and not tell anyone about it. I only found out by accident and had to promise not to tell Mum or Dad on pain of death. Here's the £10.00 receipt for it from *Pretty Little*

Things, the shop in the Arcade that sold cheap bracelets and hair scrunchies.

I never imagined that Mum and Suzi's move was going to be permanent. I don't think Dad did either. But as the days stretched to weeks, and the weeks to months, we had to accept that they weren't coming back.

When Mum did visit the house, to fetch me for brownies or swimming or whatever, there was always a big row. She'd berate Dad over the fact that I wasn't eating proper meals, or that I needed new school clothes, or that he hadn't brought me round when he said he would.

I couldn't understand why she was having a go at him. She was the one who'd walked out, without any reason. I began to think that maybe it was because of something I'd done.

One of the boxes is labelled *Mum's Things*. At the top is a pile of mildewy-smelling papers. Council tax bills, water bills, home insurance documents dating from 2012, the year she died. Nothing very interesting. But underneath are her old books: *Winnie The Pooh, The House At Pooh Corner, Now We Are Six*.

With their torn covers, foxed pages and broken spines they're like ancient relics from a bygone age. Mum had them when she was a little girl — they'd been passed down from *her* mother — and she read them to us at bedtime too.

I'd forgotten all about them. Flicking through the pages and seeing all these old poems and stories from my childhood brings an emotional rush of recognition: *Christopher Robin; King John's Christmas; Trespassers William; Piglet meets a Heffalump*. They're so strongly associated in my mind with Mum that it feels as if the memories are being beamed to me from beyond the grave. It's too much to handle all at once so I put them aside to look at later, and turn my attention to the bulky plastic Tesco bag lying at the bottom of the box. Its handles are tied together, and it takes me ages to unpick the knot with my fingernails so I can take a look inside.

My heart tightens: bottles of talc. It's the presents I gave Mum every year for Christmas and for her birthday, and they still have their gift tags attached.

To Mummy, with lots of love from Phoebe xxx

On the reverse of each one Mum's written the year, forming a sequence which runs from 2004 up to Christmas 2007, when presumably I was finally old enough to realise that there's only so much talcum powder a woman in her forties really needs.

I can't believe she kept them all. I take a bottle of Yardley's English Lavender talc (lavender was her favourite flower), twist the lid and give it a squeeze. A puff of fine white dust jets up into the air. Although the fragrance has mostly faded, the faint lavender smell is still enough to trigger such a heady rush of memories and emotions from my childhood that I have to fight back the tears. Perhaps this secret little stash of talc proves she cared about me more than I thought?

I give the bottle another, firmer, squeeze, and a cloud of white powder wafts up into my face. I close my eyes and let it settle on my cheeks, on my forehead and on my eyelashes, dusting me like a thin layer of snow. A calmness comes over me. I can't explain it really: it's like I can sense Mum's presence here in this room.

I let out a long, silent breath. For so many years it felt like a part of me was missing because I couldn't let myself believe that Mum loved me. But now, enveloped in this talcy, perfumed cloud, I can finally accept that she did. Tears begin to run down my cheeks and for the first time in many, many years, I feel whole again.

PART THREE

Chapter 24

I'M SQUASHED UP beside Mum on the sofa. We're sitting in the front room of our Aldershot house. It's a warm summer's day, the windows are open, and a gentle breeze is ruffling the pages of the newspaper on the coffee table. I've been telling her about all the worrying things that have been happening to me, and when I've finished unburdening myself, she takes my hands, gives them a warm squeeze, and plants a tender little kiss on my forehead.

'There's nothing to worry about,' she tells me. 'It's all in your head. Everything's going to be all right.'

I close my eyes and surrender to her ministrations with a contented, purring sigh.

But something isn't right. At first I can't figure out what it is, but then it dawns on me: the coffee table. It's the ugly Moroccan coffee table which Suzi carried up to the flat. What on earth is that doing here? And it's not just the coffee table that's wrong. I realise now that we moved out of the Aldershot house years ago. And I remember taking this sofa to the dump with Dad before he left for Spain. And —

I spin round to look at Mum, but her features seem to blur before my eyes and I'm unable to focus on her face. Her hands are slipping from my grasp and the room fills with light as I drift into wakefulness. But I don't want to wake! I want to stay cuddled up beside her on the sofa. Just for a moment longer. I try to fight it, I try not to wake up, but it's no good. The images glimmer for a few moments at the back of my mind, and then, before I can grasp hold of them, they wink out of existence.

But even though the details of the dream have faded away, the sense of Mum's warm presence on the sofa stays, permeating my body with a wonderful sense of serenity.

It's all in your head.

Yes, it's time for me to stop running scared from every stupid little thing. It's time for me to take control of my life, to become the hero of my own story. To embrace my inner Disney princess. I filled out one of those online, click-bait surveys last week, titled *Who is your Inner Disney Princess? Take our quick quiz to find out* — and it turns out that I'm Mulan, which is great because *Mulan* was always my favourite Disney film.

I've never felt very Mulan-ish before though, but now that I've accepted that my fears are all in my head, I feel strong(ish), I feel brave (sort of), I feel capable of (almost) anything!

My blossoming Disney Princess confidence gets a further boost over breakfast when I find two unread messages on my phone. Tom says *am I around on Wednesday next week* because he's got hold of tickets for the opera and thought I might like to go with him. Robbie asks *do I like Scandinavian food*, because there's this Scandinavian restaurant in Wimbledon he's heard really good things about.

My initial thought is to invent some excuse and let them know I'm busy. But then I tell myself: *No! Be brave! Be strong!* I need to stop over-thinking things and I need to start getting out of the flat more. I've never been to the opera before, so that would be a new experience for me. And, unless you count the food hall at Ikea, I've never eaten Scandinavian food either. So I say yes to both of them. Yay! Go team Mulan!

The next test of my new-found braveness comes a few minutes later as I'm returning Boris Johnson to his grassy knoll. I hear a blood-curdling shriek from Denise's flat.

Yesterday I would have suffered a complete meltdown freak-out, but today I march up to her door with a cool head and call to her through the letterbox: 'Denise! Are you okay? What's going on?'

Urgent footsteps pound along the hallway. Then the door's opened and Denise appears wearing a black kimono with embroidered flowers. Her hair's all wet, her face seems drained, and she's panting heavily.

'Phoebe! Thank God. I need your help.'

'What is it?'

She grabs my arm and steers me along the hall to the bathroom. 'In there.'

I peer into the room. I bet it's a spider. 'A spider?' I ask.

'Spider,' she confirms with a breathless nod.

Now, I'm not really the world's greatest fan of spiders either. I hate all those legs and the skittery way they move. Surely no creature on God's earth really needs eight legs, does it? Nothing with good intentions anyway.

Denise gently shoves me into the room. 'It's in the bath. It's bloody enormous.'

'That's not really helping,' I tell her, as I pull back the wet shower curtain. There's a spider trying to climb up the side of the tub. It's one of those small-bodied, spindly-legged beasts, which would normally be throwing me into a tizzy spin, but instead I pull on my inner reserves of strength and tell myself it's not really *so* big. 'The poor little guy can't get out.'

'Just kill it!'

'I'm not going to kill it.'

'Here, you can use this.'

Denise takes off a slipper and tries to force it into my hands, but I refuse to take it. 'I'm surprised at you! That's not very vegan, is it.'

'I'm not planning on *eating* it. I just want it dead. Please Phoebe, it's giving me the fears.'

'Okay, okay. Can you get me a cup and a piece of paper.'

While Denise goes off to fetch the spider-removal equipment I metaphorically roll up my sleeves, and, unable to think of any suitable *Mulan* songs, start humming the stirring "*I can go the distance*" song from *Hercules* instead.

Capturing the spider under the glass is relatively straightforward. The scary part is slipping the paper underneath. The spider is magnified by the glass and looks ten times larger and ten times more spidery. Denise isn't helping much either. She's making a big squealy fuss from the doorway, bobbing up and down like a child that badly needs to pee, but eventually I manage to trap it.

'Quick! Open the front door!' I shout, running along the hallway with my hand under the glass and only the thinnest piece of paper protecting me from the arachnid. I throw the paper and the glass out onto the lawn, telling Denise we'll fetch it later when we're certain the spider has gone.

'Thank you, thank you! You're so brave!' she gushes.

'Brave? Me? Hardly!' I say with a modest chuckle, feeling really pleased with myself. I think of what a scaredy cat I've been over the last few weeks, conjuring up every kind of phantom and bogey man out of the shadows. Channelling my inner Disney Princess felt rather good. Even if it *was* just a spider.

'They can't actually do anything harmful to you, you know,' I tell her.

'That's what they want you to think. They lull you into a false sense of security and then crawl into your bed at night and get tangled up in your hair. Then they'll creep into your ear while you're sleeping to lay their eggs. And when they hatch out, you'll have tiny little baby spiders crawling all over your face. Don't laugh, it's no joke!'

Denise offers me a cup of tea and I follow her through to the kitchen. While she's filling the kettle, she asks: 'Have you read this week's local paper yet?'

The local paper? Who reads the local paper? I wonder again how old she is, adding on another five years to my previous estimate.

'No, not yet,' I answer.

'They've convicted a man for vandalism,' Denise says, handing me the article. 'I bet he was the one responsible for vandalising my gnomes.'

Jonathan Short, 48, of no fixed abode, pleaded guilty to seventeen counts of vandalising gardens in the Clapham area. He was tried at the Lavender Hill Magistrates Court and will be sentenced next week.

A sense of relief percolates through me. 'Thank God for that. I've been worrying that my ex might have done it.'

Denise's face clouds over. 'Alfie? Why? Was he violent?'

'He could be cruel,' I say, avoiding directly answering her question. 'He liked playing mind games.'

'What sort of games?'

I tell her about Luca the Romanian, and she makes a gesture of disgust. 'He sounds like an utter shit. That's exactly why I keep telling you that you're better off avoiding men for a while.'

'Umm, well.' I shift awkwardly in my chair.

'Don't tell me you're planning on dating already?'

I hesitate for a moment and then against my better judgement, I say *not exactly*, and come clean about the fact that I didn't cancel my meals with Tom and Robbie.

Denise ponders what I've told her for a moment, before saying: 'How do you know you haven't fallen for another of his impersonations? I imagine a Geordie or a Yorkshire accent is just as easy to pull off as a Romanian.'

A clammy sense of dread seeps into my bones and I go cold. What if Alfie's been playing a game with me? It's perfectly possible and I'd be completely defenceless against that type of subterfuge. I think about cancelling, but then I notice that Denise is laughing.

'Phoebe? You're not taking me seriously, are you?'

'God no,' I say, 'of course not. I knew you were teasing. Ha ha ha.'

Chapter 25

WHAT DO DISNEY princesses do after the closing credits have rolled and they've entered their *Whole New World*, or brought *Honour To Us All*, or managed to *Let It Go*? I don't know about Jasmine or Mulan or Elsa, but my new-found optimism is fading faster than the scent of cheap lavender talc.

I don't like pointing the finger of blame, but why did Denise have to go and plant those seeds of doubt in my mind just when I'd managed to convince myself it was all in my head? Would Alfie really go to all that effort of befriending me just to get close to me again?

And just to make me feel even more ill at ease, I receive another strange delivery through the letterbox. This one's a small rectangular parcel, stuck up with thick tape; it weighs practically nothing, makes no sound when I shake it, and I suspect it's just an empty cardboard box. I should probably throw it away, but instead I take it up to the kitchen and slit the flap open with a pair of scissors.

I peer inside. At first I see nothing, but then I spot something moving, and with a shriek I drop the box onto the floor. Hundreds of tiny red ants spill out and begin swarming all over the kitchen. They're getting on my shoes, climbing up my legs, and, when I try to brush them off, they're on my hands, on my wrists, and running up the back of my arms.

Eventually I gather my wits together long enough to grab a tea-towel and start flicking them off. When I'm finally ant-free, I fetch the Henry and hoover up as many as I can. But all through the rest of the day I keep finding them marching across the floor, trooping along the windowsills and hiding in the cupboards. The little buggers have been biting me too. When I'm getting changed for my night at the opera with Tom, I find that my legs have come up in an ugly red splotchy rash. I'm tempted to wear jeans to hide the bites, but I'm not sure how dressy it will be, so instead I dig out the thickest, most opaque pair of tights I can find.

Waiting for Tom by the door of the grand red-and-white marble theatre foyer so he'll be able to spot me easily, I find that there's a real mix of styles: some women are in elegant floor-length evening dresses, while others are wearing jeans. Yet even the jeans-wearing women, greeting their friends in bright honeyed voices, seem intimidatingly posh, and I feel completely out of place.

The foyer fills with the pulsating hum of chatter as people stream in off the street. I seem to be in everyone's way, getting bustled and jostled and *'scuse me'd* and *sorry'd* from every direction. The chandeliers glitter and sparkle above my head, there's a palpable sense of anticipation in the air, and I have the overwhelming feeling of being trapped inside a giant, multi-coloured kaleidoscope. I'm regretting ever saying yes to the opera.

We're seeing *The Barber of Seville*, and in order not to look like a complete philistine I've done some homework on Wikipedia. The opera was composed by Gioachino Rossini in 1816, and is about a girl who's locked away by her evil guardian, and is then seduced by a visiting Count who comes to the house in a series of disguises. It's supposed to be a comedy, but it doesn't sound very funny to me.

I gave it a listen on Spotify to try and familiarise myself with the songs, but it just seemed like a lot of high-pitched warbling and wailing, and I had to give up. I shouldn't be so negative though; there must be something good about it if it's still being performed two hundred years after it was written. Who knows, maybe I'll even enjoy it? At the very least it's a step up from going to Nando's to watch Alfie fill his face with peri-peri chicken.

'Phoebe!'

A man's forcing a path through the crowd towards me.

'Gosh, it's busy. How are you?' He kisses me on both cheeks. He's come in smart-casual work clothes — a button-down open-necked shirt, a green jumper and pale grey chinos. 'Shall we go through?'

Our plush red velvet seats are situated right in the centre of the stalls. 'These tickets must have cost a fortune!' I gush.

Tom grins: 'Don't worry, they're freebies. Corporate hospitality for a client who cancelled.'

'Phew!' I give a relieved sigh. 'I was feeling guilty that you'd spent a ton of money on something I might not properly appreciate.'

Tom looks disappointed. 'You don't like opera?'

'No, it's not that,' I reassure him hurriedly. 'I've never been before, but I've always wanted to give it a try.'

'Excellent!' he exclaims, 'You're in for a treat!'

He gives me a rundown of the plot, but I don't learn anything I hadn't already read on Wikipedia, and I wonder if he's such an opera buff after all. He catches me frowning. 'Don't worry. I'm sure you'll enjoy it. Trust me.'

Trust me. Something about the way he says it makes my heart miss a beat. He sounded *just* like Alfie. I sit bolt upright in my seat and stare straight into his face and wonder: *Alfie, is that you?*

His eyebrows knit together in a puzzled frown: 'Everything okay?'

But before I can answer, the lights in the auditorium go down and an expectant hush settles blanket-like over the audience. The orchestra strikes up the overture and, as the strings begin scraping away, I steal another glance at Tom.

Is it Tom, or is Alfie sitting right next to me in the Coliseum, listening intently to an opera? It seems unlikely — Alfie's even less cultured than I am — but I can't be sure. I dismiss the notion from my mind and try to focus on the music. But after listening to the fancy twiddles and irritating thumps and blasts for a minute or two, my thoughts turn back to the question of Tom's identity.

I met him in the coffee shop *the day Suzi told Alfie my address*. Once he knew where I lived, he could easily have followed me around and struck up a conversation, knowing I'd never recognise him.

Tom catches my eye and gives me an I-hope-you-are-enjoying-it smile. I smile back, and return my attention to the stage, telling myself I'm being ridiculous. It's just a coincidence. *Just watch the opera and stop letting your mind run away with itself.*

One thing's for sure: opera's definitely not my thing. The singers sound like they're wailing in pain, the acting's hammy, the plot's convoluted, and because the hero keeps changing disguises to seduce the heroine, I've no idea who's who.

A shudder of fear rattles my system as the realisation hits me: Alfie's chosen this opera because it's all about deception. The action on the stage is reflecting what's going on here in the stalls. He's toying with me. It's exactly the kind of tricky game he loves to play.

I spring to my feet. 'Sorry, I have to go. Something's come up,' I say nervously, avoiding his eye. I hurry away along the row of seats, mumbling apologies to the people who're forced to pull in their legs or hover bent-kneed over their tip-up seats to let me pass.

I don't look round until I reach the central aisle. Tom's following, forcing everyone in the row to get up again, but his progress is impeded by a man with a furious scowl who's making a big fuss.

It allows me time to get away and I sprint up the carpeted steps to a set of double doors, along a darkened passageway to the foyer, and out onto the pavement.

A cold, sharp wind whistles down the street, stinging my cheeks. I turn my face away and, without stopping to think, head downhill, darting through the crowds on the busy pavement, my coat flapping crazily around my legs.

I nip between the queuing taxis and buses at the lights, and find myself facing the illuminated fountains, bronze lions and towering column of Trafalgar Square. Right in front of me a young, good-looking, touristy couple are standing arm-in-arm with their backs to a fountain. They give a joyful shout and throw up their hands. A coin arcs up above their heads and falls into the water with a tiny plop.

I feel a pang of jealousy at the young lovers. My Prince Charming turned out to be a Gaston. I can't believe the evening's gone so horribly pear-shaped. I was really starting to like Tom too.

I perch on the smooth, curved edge of the fountain's basin, wondering if maybe I've made a mistake. Perhaps it wasn't Alfie after all. The only evidence I've got is that he said "*trust me*", and that he took me to an opera with a plot about a man who adopts a disguise to seduce a woman. I don't think it would hold up in a court of law.

I stare dejectedly at the pavement. I'm never going to find my Prince Charming if I flee every time something unexpected happens. If only Denise hadn't planted such alarming notions in my head.

A pair of men's shoes — black leather with a pointed toe — walk into my field of vision and I look up.

'Was the Rossini really *that* bad?'

It's Tom, not Alfie, I'm 99.9% certain. Alfie wouldn't be seen dead in pointy shoes like these. *Wanker-winkles* he called them once when we were out shopping and I suggested he try on a pair. *Are you trying to make me look like a fucking clown?*

'I'm sorry. I was feeling claustrophobic. I needed some air.'

'D'you feel any better now?' He seems genuinely concerned.

I nod. 'Yes thanks. I'm really sorry. It was all the people and all the noise and —'

'And all the *singing*?'

'Well, maybe. But I'm fine now. We can go back if you like?'

'Not unless you want to. To be honest I don't like opera much either. I just wanted to impress you.'

We decide to go for a drink instead and spend the rest of the evening in the cosy upstairs room of the pub on the corner. Tom opens up to me about his family, his job, his life's goals and aspirations. He asks me a lot about my life too and seems genuinely interested in what it's like working at St George's. He's also very sympathetic when I tell him about Mum — it turns out he lost his father when he was about the same age. He's a really good listener, he's got a good sense of humour and we get on really well. It's all very easy. Too easy perhaps?

I stare at his ugly footwear to remind myself that it can't be Alfie. And just to be sure, I steer the conversation to the subject of trainers, dropping the names *Huarache* and *Roshe* into the conversation, but Tom's face is a total blank. Not even the tiniest ripple of suppressed understanding troubles his features. And if that weren't enough proof, he's drinking bitter, and I've only ever known Alfie order lager.

It's late when we leave the pub. We're standing on the pavement outside, our warm breath blossoming cloudily above our heads. I'm studying his face, unsuccessfully trying to tease some form of recognition from his features, when he mistakenly thinks I'm puckering up for a kiss and moves his head towards mine.

For a brief second I allow myself to be carried along by the moment, not even caring about the sour, hoppy smell of beer on his breath. But just as our lips are about to meet, I snatch my head back, suddenly appalled at the prospect. It all comes tumbling back to me — trapped under Alfie's sweaty body, unable to move, wanting to cry, wanting to shout out, the shame of sex, the mortification that my body betrayed me.

I thought I was making progress, but I'm clearly not ready for any level of intimacy with a man.

Tom looks dejected and a little hurt, but even though I make light of our little misunderstanding, I know that even one small kiss would be too much. And I promise myself to be more on guard when I see Robbie tomorrow and make sure that the evening doesn't end on such an awkward note.

Chapter 26

WALKING TO THE restaurant from the hospital the next evening, rather than getting the tube, seemed like a good idea because I thought it would give me time to decompress after work. But I didn't manage to get away on time because we were so busy, and then, just as I was leaving, a junior doctor grabbed my arm and told me he's discharged his patient so could I take out the cannula, which was really irritating when it would have taken him all of three seconds to do it himself.

So, I didn't have time to shower, and now I'm feeling really grimy. Plus, this walk is taking much longer than I thought. Unless he arrives late, I'm not going to make it before Robbie, and I'll have to run through that whole embarrassing guppy-in-a-fish-bowl routine while I scan the room for him.

A bleep from my phone interrupts the music playing through my headphones. I've got a text, from an unknown number. I open it with trepidation:

When you walk down a London street,
Be careful to watch both your feet.

What? Before I can work out what's going on, I get another text:

Keep in the squares,
Cos the dangerous bears
Are waiting for someone to eat.

A cold fear rises in my throat, and I spin around, convinced someone must be following me. There's no-one there, but someone, somewhere, knows I'm walking along a pavement in London. And that same person must also know that Mum used to read us the poem about bears and cracks in the pavement when we were little. On the way to school Suzi would tease me and give me a little shove, to try and get me to step on the lines between the paving slabs. She'd tell me *the bears are going to get you*, and when I ran crying to Mum, she'd deny she'd done anything.

But who would send this? It surely can't be a coincidence that Mum's old Winnie The Pooh books are lying on the coffee table in the flat, can it? Has Alfie broken in and been through my things?

Another text pings through. It contains just one word:

Grrr!!!

I look round again, but there's no-one behind me. I quicken my pace, unable to shake the feeling that I'm being watched, and arrive five minutes late, panting from exertion, my armpits unpleasantly damp, and feeling grubby from work. As I stand in the doorway scanning the room for Robbie, I try to dismiss the texts from my mind. After all, it's just a poem, and the bears waiting to pounce on people are no more real now than they were when I was six, are they.

'Phoebe!'

Robbie's on his feet, waving. 'You looked right at me but didn't see me!'

'I didn't have my glasses on,' I say with a self-deprecating little chuckle. I don't wear glasses, but it's one of my go-to excuses when I don't recognise someone.

'You look nice!' he tells me as I take my seat.

'Thanks.' I can't help blushing because I know it isn't

true. After walk-running all the way here from work, I know I must look like I've been dragged through a hedge backwards.

'I ordered you an aperitif: vodka lime soda.'

'How did you know?' I ask, suddenly mistrustful.

'You told me,' he replies with amused surprise.

'Did I?' I can't remember. I'm becoming paranoid. First I think Tom is Alfie, and now it's Robbie's turn to fall under the spotlight of suspicion. I study his face and try to unlock the secret code everyone else possesses which would allow me to recognise him, but it's as futile as trying to win a blinking competition against a fish.

He catches me staring: 'You okay?'

'I'm a bit squinty without my glasses,' I say, screwing up my eyes and wondering if I should actually get myself a pair of clear-lensed spectacles to make my lies more believable.

Robbie holds up his glass. It contains something amber-coloured and has an orange peel twist hooked onto the rim. 'Cheers!'

I raise my glass and, as we chink, I wonder if I'm clinking glasses with a trainee accountant from Yorkshire, or with the guy who posted me a box of red ants and sent me scary bear texts.

I survey the restaurant. With its white walls, the pale wood furniture and pastel fabrics, it's not the type of place Alfie would ever have taken me to. Although there's a busy bar on one side, the acoustics aren't too bad and you can actually hear the conversation without raising your voice. It's about a thousand times more upmarket than the Ikea food hall in Croydon, that's for sure. Alfie took me there on our third or fourth date. We didn't go to look at furniture, we actually went just to eat. My warning bells should have been ringing like crazy, but I was too besotted to pay any attention. *No, my treat* he insisted at the till, and I let him stump up the £3.80 or whatever it was for a plate of vegetarian meatballs. I should have treasured that moment because it's the only occasion I can remember that I didn't end up footing the bill.

'It's nice here,' I say, 'very hygge.'

'Hue-guh,' Robbie says, correcting my pronunciation. 'I thought it would be a good choice as there're lots of veggie options.'

There aren't actually that many vegetarian options, but it's better than the last restaurant, and vegetarian beggars can't be choosers.

A blond, Scandinavian-looking waiter arrives and — with a disappointingly non-Scandinavian accent — takes our order. I have the Swedish potato dumplings filled with peas, mint and goat's cheese (hello again goat's cheese!), while Robbie gets something called *frikadeller*, which comes with a creamy mash, pickled cucumber, lingonberries and gravy.

When Robbie's frikadeller arrives, it turns out just to be meatballs, and I immediately think about Alfie and Ikea. Then I tell myself to stop fixating on the notion that just because Alfie and Robbie like eating the same food, it follows that they must be the same person. I mean, there are more than thirty million men in the country and a good proportion of them must like meatballs.

'I'm just popping to the *toaletten,*' Robbie says after dessert.

I fiddle with my napkin while I wait. My phone buzzes. It's a text:

Hope you enjoyed your dumplings Phoebe ;)

I jerk round to look over my shoulder, half-expecting someone to be standing beside me. There's no-one there. But *someone* is spying on me. I feel a nervous chill and my pulse races as I survey the room, scanning every face to see if I'm being watched.

The restaurant's pretty full. It's mostly couples or small parties of three or four, but over at the bar a group of a dozen or so guys are laughing together, their bright, shining faces aglow with excitement. Is Alfie standing among them?

I spot Robbie's blue shirt weaving a path back through the tables from the toilets. When he sees me, he gives a little wave of acknowledgement, and I'm about to wave back when I notice him tucking his phone away in his pocket. A chill of fear ripples through my system. Oh God! Did he just send that text?

'You okay?' he asks as he approaches the table.

'Yes. But d'you think we could go?' I say casually, trying to maintain my cool.

'Oh! I was thinking we might go on for a drink. I know this great place just round the corner from here. It's usually pretty quiet on a weekday —' He breaks off. He can sense from my expression that I'm not up for it.

I tell him: 'I'm sorry.'

'What about coffee?'

'D'you mind? I've suddenly been overcome with exhaustion.'

'Long day?' he asks with a smile that could be understanding but might be duplicitous.

I nod. 'Twelve hours on your feet is always a long time. I shouldn't really have come out on a school night.'

In my desperation to get out of here I forgo my feminist principles and let Robbie pay, but when he says *shall we get a cab?* I come to my senses. There's no way I can risk sharing a cab with him, giving him the side-eye and dreading what will happen when we get back to Laithwaite Road. But because we're neighbours and because I can't come up with any logical reason why we shouldn't travel together, I have no choice.

In the taxi I catch Robbie checking his phone and he sheepishly admits that his flatmate has been messaging him all evening to find out how things have been going.

I slump back in the seat with a big sigh of relief. So Robbie most likely wasn't responsible for sending me that text after all. But on the other hand, does this mean he told his friend that we were on a date?

'What should I tell him?' Robbie asks.

I shrug uncertainly.

'Can I say that you had a good evening?'

'Yes, if you like.'

'Can I tell him that we'll be doing it again some time?'

He's giving me such a hopeful, optimistic grin that I can't help smiling back at him. 'You can tell him we might.'

Chapter 27

I HAVE A shower and go straight to bed, but I'm wrenched out of sleep by a noisy banging. I examine the clock in sleepy confusion: 11.39 p.m. I peep nervously through the chink in the curtains and see a man in the front garden, banging on my door. When he looks up, I quickly pull away from the window, but it's too late; I've been spotted.

'Phoebe!' the man shouts.

I'm overwhelmed with panic. What do I do?

'Phoebe!'

When he calls my name again, I realise that the time has finally come to get the police involved. I drop to the floor, crawl across the bedroom with my head down, and take my phone from the bedside-table.

The fingerprint sensor never works reliably, and I have to use the pattern-unlock, but my hands are shaking so much I keep messing it up. 'C'mon, c'mon' I mutter in frustration.

The thumping outside starts up again. After my fourth attempt, I realise there's an emergency call button. I press it and dial 999. It's answered straight away.

'Emergency. Which service?'

Before I can reply, there's another shout from outside:

'Phoebe! Open up. It's Alistair?'

Alistair?

The voice in my ear is speaking to me: *'Hello are you there? Which service do you require?'*

'I'm sorry. I've made a mistake. I thought someone was trying to break in, but they aren't. Everything's okay now. I'm sorry. Sorry.' I hang up.

My fingers are still trembling and my heart's still pounding in my chest, but the danger's passed. It's only Alistair. Though I can't think why on earth he's banging on my door in the middle of the night. I go down to let him in, but just as I'm opening the door, it occurs to me that this could be a trick. I quickly shut it again, then slide the door chain and open it just enough to peep out.

The man standing in the doorway has a receding hairline and glasses. I let out a relieved sigh: it's Alistair. Or at least it's what I imagine Alistair would look like after a rough evening. There's grey stubble on his chin, his hair's dishevelled and I can smell alcohol on his breath. I've never seen him like this before.

'I need to speak to Suzi,' he demands impatiently when I've opened the door.

I frown at his face in confusion. 'Suzi? But she isn't here.'

'You don't have to cover for her. I know she's up there,' he snaps angrily, pushing past.

I follow him up the stairs. 'Honestly, it's been three weeks since she was last here,' I protest, but it's no use. He has to go through every room calling her name, and even checks in the wardrobe, behind the shower curtain and under the bed. He's so thorough that I half-expect him to look in the little cupboard under the sink next.

'Satisfied?' I ask, with a sleepy yawn.

'Wait —' He hurries through the kitchen with a triumphant smile on his face, and with the showmanship of a magician revealing his assistant, flings open the back door to the fire escape. He almost had me convinced Suzi was out there, but of course the fire escape's empty.

'She's not here then,' he concludes in a glum tone.

'No.'

He regards me with a look of guilty embarrassment and only now seems to notice that I'm in my pyjamas. In a sheepish voice he asks: 'We're you asleep?'

I nod.

'I'm so sorry Phoebe. I've been such a fool, barging into your home in the middle of the night. God, you must think I'm such a twat.'

'It's okay. It's your flat after all. Don't worry about it. I'm guessing that you and Suzi have had an argument.'

He gives an emphatic nod. 'The mother of all arguments. I mean, we have our little rows from time to time — you know what she's like! — but this evening —' He shakes his head in dismay, his gaze slipping from my face to the kitchen floor and I can see him running through the evening's events in his mind.

'She wouldn't listen to me. She flew off the handle and ranted and raged and wouldn't let me speak. Then stormed off. And it's all over nothing.'

I wait for him to expand on *nothing*, but he's clammed up and just stares vacantly into space. Eventually I ask: 'So, where might she be?'

'Fuck knows. The last thing she said was that she couldn't stand the sight of me. She grabbed her keys, carried an overnight bag out to the car, and drove off. I was convinced she'd be here.'

'Perhaps she just drove around for a bit. She might be back at your house?'

'Maybe,' he says vaguely, thinking about it for a moment before he gets the hint. He checks his watch. 'Christ it's late. I'd better leave you alone. I really am sorry about all this. I'll make it up to you somehow.'

'Don't worry. Stuff happens. Are you okay to be driving?'

'I'm fine.'

I don't really believe him, and I probably should try to stop him from getting into his car, but I'm just so exhausted after everything that I haven't got the energy. As soon as he's gone, I clean my teeth again and go back to bed.

Chapter 28

THE DOORBELL RINGS as soon as my head hits the pillow. Alistair must have forgotten something. Or maybe he's thought of some other little secret nook in the flat where Suzi might be hiding? I wish he'd just let me get some sleep.

I go down to let him in, and find my sister on the doorstep, giving me the special nod.

'Suzi!' I exclaim. 'Alistair's looking for you.'

'I know. I've been sitting in the car round the corner, waiting for him to go. Give me a hand with this will you?'

She passes over a heavy overnight bag. On the ground behind her are three cardboard boxes and a heap of plastic bags.

'God! How long're you planning on staying?'

'I don't know. A night or two.'

'So, what's with all the boxes and bags?'

'Just stuff.'

'Do we have to carry them up now? You do know it's almost midnight?'

'I couldn't leave them in the car all night.'

'Because it's such a dodgy neighbourhood?'

'You can't be too careful.'

'But you're okay with your little sister living here all on her own.'

'Don't be silly. You're a big girl now. Come on, give me a hand and stop complaining.'

We hump the boxes and bags up the stairs and pile them up in the living room. 'Is that it, or have you brought another coffee table with you?' I ask.

Suzi makes a face at me. 'Not funny. You sound just like Alistair.'

'And talking of Alistair —' I leave his name hanging in the air.

She refuses to take the bait, so I'm forced to ask more directly: 'What's going on between you two?'

She sinks into the sofa with a dramatic sigh, then shuts her eyes and places her hand to her forehead. I can't tell if she's crying or thinking or what, until I spot the little tears trickling down her cheeks and pooling in the little indentation above her protruding top lip.

'You okay?' I ask.

Her eyes snap open and in a bitter tone she tells me: 'He's having an affair.'

'No-oo!'

'Yes!' Her tone is emphatic.

'Alistair?'

'Yes, *Alistair*.' She finds a tissue in her bag and blows her nose.

'Are you sure? He doesn't seem the type.'

She scowls at me over her tissue. 'He's a man, isn't he. He's got a penis and a pair of balls. That's enough, isn't it?'

'I suppose so. But — Alistair? He's always struck me as too —' I try to come up with a suitable word.

'Too boring?'

'No, not boring. Steady. Or staid.'

'Staid?' Suzi gives a sour laugh. 'He should have *staid* at home with his penis in his trousers instead of sneaking off behind my back to see this woman. Rachel — she's called *Rachel*. I've suspected something's been going on for a while now. He says he's working late, but when I ring him he doesn't answer, so I try his work number and there's no reply, and when he gets home he tries to cover it up with an obvious lie. He denies there's anything going on, but I went through his phone, and it's obviously been going on for months—'

'You've been looking through his messages?'

'I had to know. Anyway, he caught me red-handed and we had a massive row and he kept trying to make out that *I* was the untrustworthy one, when he's the one who's been cheating. I found all these entries in his calendar. Whenever he said he was working late he was with this Rachel Green woman.'

'Rachel *Green*?'

'Yes. *Green*. So?'

'Like in *Friends*. Jennifer Aniston's character.'

Suzi and I grew up on reruns of *Friends*. We must have seen each episode at least twenty times. I'm surprised it wasn't the first thing she thought of.

'Oh God! Now I've a picture in my head of a gorgeous young woman with perky breasts and *amazing* hair. How can I compete with that? Look at me! I already know he doesn't find me attractive. Do you know how long it is since we had sex? Actually, it's been so long that I can't remember. And when we do have sex, I know he's just going through the motions. I have to lie there, moaning occasionally, and pretend to be enjoy myself, but in reality I'm just waiting patiently for him to finish so that the whole thing'll be over. Don't laugh! God, I need a drink. What have you got?'

'It's a bit late, isn't it?'

Suzi glowers at me: 'Seriously?'

'I don't actually think I've got anything alcoholic in the flat.'

'Come on, you must have *something*?'

I shrug my shoulders emptily. 'Nothing.'

She gives me a withering stare and shakes her head

sorrowfully. 'You poor, sad thing.'

Then she gets to her feet.

'Where are you going?'

'To get some alcohol. *Duh!*'

'At this time of night?'

'The Tesco Metro will be open. You want anything?'

Just my bed, I think ruefully. I can tell it's going to be a long night.

Chapter 29

WHILE I WAIT for Suzi to return, I make a cup of tea, and then have a rummage through her boxes to see if she's brought anything more of interest with her.

Although the first box contains boring paperwork — credit card statements and papers from Alistair's office — I strike gold in the second one. Suzi's teenage diary; a pale-blue book with a drawing of a peacock feather on the front, across which is written in heavy capital letters: PRIVATE KEEP OUT!

I experience a guilty thrill of excitement. Watching Suzi writing in her diary each night, and knowing she'd never let me read it no matter how much I begged and pleaded, would drive me mad with frustration. She bought a lock for it after she caught me searching through her bedside drawer, and then would leave the locked diary out on her shelf just to taunt me. I'd try unpicking the lock with a pin, like they did on TV, but I could never get it open.

Luckily time is on my side; although the lock itself is still intact, the faux-leather strap it's attached to has become unglued from the cover and it's easy enough to slip the whole thing off.

The diary falls open on a page dated 19th April 2004. Five months before Mum and Suzi moved out. I would have been eleven and she would have been fifteen.

Monday

Back to school today. It was okay, but we had PE. How unfair is that? PE on the first day back!! I don't know why we still have to do PE as well as games because everyone hates it. Everyone except Anne Cooper of course, because it gives her a chance to watch everyone getting undressed in the changing room.

Tuesday 20 April

Boring Old School. Double physics and triple chemistry. Why did I choose to do three science subjects for GCSE? Big regrets.

According to Caitlin, Becky is pissed off with me because I lectured her about going on a date with Thomas Devonish. She thinks it's because I fancy him! That could not be further from the truth. If she wants to go out with him, that's completely OK with me. But I'm not going to be her shoulder to cry on when she finds out he's two-timing her. Which he will. For certain. Because that's what he's done before.

BTW It's Hitler's birthday today, which seems very appropriate for such a long boring day.

Wednesday 21 April.

Boring Old School. I got 76% for yesterday's chemistry test, which I'm pretty stoked about. It makes up for the fact that Becky is still pissed off with me and now Amy's not talking to me either because of what I said on Monday. Honestly, you try and help people and this is how they act!!! I'm never helping anyone again, eva! At least Caitlin is on my side. But that's not the worst thing that happened today. In chemistry I had my phone confiscated by Mrs Thornley for texting in class and I won't get it back until Friday. Heeelp!!! What am I gonna do until then? My phone is my LIFE!

It's weird. I can barely recall the names of anyone I went to school with, and yet I can remember all of Suzi's friends. I'm more interested in what she has to say about me though, so I rifle through the pages until I spot my name:

Saturday 1st May

I planned to wear my favourite green halter neck top to Mark's party tonight BUT IT HAS DISAPPEARED. So I had to wear my sparkly vest top instead. I bet Phoebe's been through the laundry basket again and pinched it. It's SERIOUSLY ANNOYING. Why does she keep taking my things? Mum says it's because PB looks up to me. I say it's because she's an irritating little brat who's hoping to get me into trouble when I get caught telling her off.

Ha, she's right! I did borrow her top and she did get in trouble with Mum for shrieking at me when I returned it. I was only trying it on. I thought it made me look really sexy and sophisticated even though it was at least two sizes too large. I couldn't get away with a halter-neck top like that these days though, because of my boobs. It'd look like I was carrying a sack of potatoes round my neck.

I have to flip forward several weeks before I find another reference to me. I obviously wasn't as much a part of her life as she was of mine.

Wednesday 2nd June

After tea Phoebe forced me to play a game of Scrabble with her and for the first time, she beat me!! To save face I pretended I let her win, so she got cross and demanded I play another game, and I refused.

This means that she's beaten me at Cluedo, Monopoly, Guess Who? and now Scrabble. The only game I can still beat her at is Hungry Hippos! And she's four years younger than me! How fair is that?

I overheard Dad asking Mum whether she thought Phoebe or I was the cleverest. Mum refused to answer at first. She said we were both clever. But Dad pushed her for a response and eventually she said, 'Suzi I suppose'. But Dad disagreed, and said that although I get better exam grades, it's only because I work harder, and that

Phoebe's smarter because she has a more logical brain.

*I was p**ed off with Dad, but annoyingly, I think he's right.*

More logical? Then how come I panic so much whenever I'm faced with a maths equation? I've always thought Suzi was far cleverer than me. She always did better at school. But, thinking about it, perhaps she isn't always that logical. If she was, I don't think she'd be on her third marriage, and heading for her third divorce.

I don't dwell on it too long though because my attention's caught by an entry on the opposite page:

Friday 4th June

I went to see Harry Potter and The Prisoner of Azkaban with Paul. It was supposed to be just the two of us, but Mum made us take Phoebe. Again. On a date? Why does she use me like a babysitting service. It's so annoying. Can't I have my own life?? Surely I'm old enough to be treated like an adult now?

PB wanted to sit in the front row, but Paul insisted we sit at the back, for obvious reasons. We kissed a bit, and it was nice, but I didn't want to miss the film so I kept having to push him off me.

The film was great, exactly how I'd imagined it would be, and you can see that Daniel Radcliffe is becoming a really good actor.

My favourite Harry Potter films in order now are:

1. Harry Potter and the Philosopher's Stone — always going to be the best because little Daniel is sooo cute in it.

2. Harry Potter and the Prisoner of Azkaban — it's got time travel, lots of Hermoine, and a really good ending. What's not to like?

3. Harry Potter and the Chamber of Secrets — Bottom of the charts because of SNAKES. Yuck!

Paul is a good kisser, but I think I'm going off him. Mainly because — BIG NEWS — Kyle likes me!!! That's what Amy told me anyway. Apparently, ever since I started going out with Paul, he's been showing an interest.

Kyle is SO much better looking than Paul and I've fancied him for ages. Also, Paul has very sweaty hands.

Hang on? *Prisoner of Azkaban*? I thought we went to see *Harry Potter and The Order of The Phoenix* with sweaty-palmed Paul? We must have, because Dolores Umbridge isn't in *The Prisoner of Azkaban* and I've got that clear memory of Mum acting all nice-but-evil, like Dolores Umbridge, when she announced she was moving out.

I'm so convinced I'm right that I get out my phone to check.

I'm wrong.

Azkaban was released in 2004. *Phoenix* wasn't released until 2007, so I must have added that little detail about Mum afterwards. I wonder what other memories from that evening are unreliable. Perhaps I've misremembered the whole thing?

As it was such a significant event in our lives, I'm sure Suzi will have written about it in her diary. I flick forward to the end of August, but before I can find the entry, I hear the creaking of the front door, and then Suzi's voice from the stairs:

'Hellooo. I'm baa-ack.'

I spring to my feet and hide the diary guiltily behind my back. She enters with a heavily-loaded plastic bag in her hand.

'You planning a party?' I joke.

'I couldn't decide between red, white or rosé. So I bought one of each. What've you got there?' She tries to look behind me.

'Nothing,' I tell her, turning so she can't see.

'What're you hiding there? Show me!' Suzi demands, becoming irritated.

I smile sheepishly and let her see. 'I was just having a little look through those boxes.'

'My diary!'

'I didn't think you'd mind after all this time.'

She snatches it from my hands and draws my attention to the words on the cover: 'It's *PRIVATE*. Can't you read? You always were a snoopy little cow,' she adds, teasingly.

'Hey!'

She grins. 'Well, you were. You can't imagine what a nightmare it was having to share a bedroom with you. Going through my things. "Borrowing" my stuff.'

'Was that why you jumped at the chance to move out?'

The smile dries on her lips, and she looks at me strangely for a moment, before snapping out of it and asking: 'Where's the corkscrew? I *really* need a drink. And two glasses,' she adds as I walk over to the kitchenette.

'Two glasses?'

'You're having a drink too.'

'It's midnight!'

'It's your punishment for reading my diary. You're not working tomorrow are you?'

I shake my head.

'Well then.'

'Fine!' I exclaim with a long-suffering sigh and reach up to fetch two glasses down from the cupboard.

When I turn round, I catch her stuffing a wad of pages into her handbag. She shuts the bag with a click and shoves it down beside her on the couch. Then she crosses her legs and looks up at me with a defiant smile.

Has she just ripped some pages out of her precious diary? What on earth could inspire her to butcher it after all these years? What teenage secrets doesn't she want me to know?

She lines the wine bottles up on the coffee table, takes the corkscrew from me, then flips up its arms and waves the pointed tip at me as if it were a dagger. 'Let's start with the white and work our way up to the red.'

She fills the glasses to the brim, slides one across the coffee table towards me and raises her drink.

'Fuck men. They're all worthless bastards!'

'Worthless bastards,' I repeat, bringing my drink to my lips. The alcoholicy fumes turn my stomach, and remind me how late it is and how tired I am. But Suzi's got such a look of grim determination on her face as she gulps down her wine that I daren't refuse. I take a tiny sip and put my glass onto the coffee table with a grimace.

'Do you think I should have some work done?' Suzi asks, pressing her fingers to her temples and pulling back the skin, to give herself the smooth, surprised look of someone who's walked into a sheet of cling film. 'What d'you think? A little Botox?'

'You're thirty-three! You're way too young for Botox.'

'Thirty-three's old for a Botox virgin. These days people start having it done in their early twenties. I bet Rachel Green's had Botox. Maybe I should get my lips done too?'

She purses her lips like a fish and makes kissy noises at me.

'Don't!' I exclaim. I find her suggestion alarming.

'I'm only *joking*,' she replies, in an over-exaggerated way that doesn't entirely convince me that she is.

'Not funny. You know that lip-fillers freak me out.' I don't know if it's connected to my face blindness, but there's something about the way that lip-fillers alter the look of a face that I find disturbing.

'Why would you want to have work done anyway if

all men are worthless bastards?' I say.

'It wouldn't be for the worthless bastards; it would be for me.'

'Really? You want to join the ranks of those women who have surgical procedures done in the name of self-empowerment, without realising that they're sexualising, infantallising and mutilating themselves in the pursuit of unhealthy, unattainable societal norms derived from masculine notions of beauty.'

'Oh!' Suzi blinks at me in surprise. 'I didn't know you felt so strongly about it.'

I give an embarrassed laugh. 'Neither did I! I'm sorry, I think it's Denise's influence. You should do what you want, it's your body.'

I decide to change the subject. 'Suzi?'

'Hmmn?'

'You remember the day Mum and Dad announced they were splitting up?'

She shoots me a suspicious glance and pauses for a moment before answering. 'Of course I remember.'

'Do you remember how Mum was about it?'

'What do you mean?'

'I'm just wondering how well I actually remember that day.'

'*I* remember it all too well. It was the shittiest time of my life. Thanks a lot for bringing it up. Do we have to talk about it now?'

'It's just that I've been thinking about it a lot recently. Seeing your diary made me wonder if I've been wrong about how things happened.'

Suzi gives her nose an irritated rub. 'Maybe you don't remember because you were so little. It was much harder for me because I was that bit older. And of course, unlike you, I had to leave the home I'd grown up in and move to that miserable little flat.'

Her words have the same effect on me as pouring sugar into a glass of coke: years of repressed resentment bubble up and spill over the edge. 'Have you ever thought about what it was like for me being left behind? Do you have any idea what it felt like to be deserted by your mother and your big sister?'

She squares up to me and snaps: 'It was your choice!'

'How was I supposed to choose? I was only little, remember?'

She purses her lips, gives the tip of her nose another rub of annoyance, and picks up her glass. 'Can we *please* not talk about it. I want to try to forget about all the horrible things that have happened in my horrible life.'

She makes a good job of forgetting. While I'm nursing the same drink, she manages to polish off the rest of the white wine, and most of the rosé, before breaking off mid-sentence and smacking her glass down onto the table. Her face has acquired a green, sickly tint, and her skin shimmers with an oily sheen of sweat. She lolls back into the sofa and closes her eyes.

'Are you okay?' I ask.

With a great effort she lifts her head, opens her eyes, and in a crystal-clear voice announces: 'I think I may be a teeny bit drunk.' Then she belches twice and is sick all down the front of her blouse.

After I've cleaned her as best I can with kitchen roll and a damp tea towel, I pull her to her feet and escort her to the bedroom.

'What're you doing?' she asks confusedly, her sour vommitty alcohol breath in my face as I undo her buttons, remove her blouse and put her into one of my baggy bed-time t-shirts. She can have the bed tonight and I'll sleep on the couch.

I rinse out her blouse and fetch the washing-up bowl from the kitchen, just in case she needs it in the night. When she's all tucked up in bed I wish her goodnight, but she pleads forlornly with me to stay: 'Don't leave me. I'll be lonely on my own. Please!'

'Okay,' I reply without enthusiasm. 'I'll stay on one condition.'

'What?'

'If you let me read your diary.'

'Diar-ee. My diar-ee?' she slurs.

I give her a nod of encouragement. 'Yes, your diary.' I know it's not really fair to ask while she's in this state, but she's brought it upon herself.

She tells me *yes*, with a happy, intoxicated smile, then rolls over with a convulsive groan and pukes her guts up over the side of the bed. Luckily most of it goes in the washing up bowl. And lucky too that I'm a nurse and not easily grossed out. If it had been the other way round, I don't think Suzi would be coping so well.

When I've cleaned everything up, I take a quick shower, then change into my pyjamas, fetch the diary from the coffee table, and settle down in the bed beside her.

She's already asleep, curled up in the foetal position. Every so often she emits a low moan or a soft groan, but her noises sound less urgent than earlier and hopefully, having emptied the contents of her stomach, she'll be feeling a bit better.

The diary opens at the jagged stumps of the pages she tore out. I wonder again what was so bad she couldn't risk me seeing it? She'd never know if I sneaked them out of her handbag, but that would be a breach of trust too far even for me.

Fortunately, the terrible thing I'm not allowed to read happened in July, and the entries resume in August, so I'm able to flip through the pages until I find what I'm seeking.

Tuesday 31st August

OMG. Yesterday was a fucking trainwreck. I'm so pissed off right now that I can't write. Seriously. WTF.

Wednesday

I still don't want to talk about it. So instead this is a list of the top five things I can't stand.

1. I hate people who stare at you and think they're better than you.

2. I hate people who go on and on about how great Mean Girls is, and how special it makes them for liking it.

3. I hate people who use Americanisms all the time because they think it makes them sound smart.

4. I hate smoking cos it's gross and smells so bad.

5. I hate people who say they're happy when they're not

6. I hate my dad.

7. I hate my sister.

8. I hate the situation I'm in.

Okay, that's eight things. So bite me! (see No. 3)

Thursday

I have to accept what happened because WHAT THE HELL ELSE CAN I DO? But I don't think things are ever going to be the same.

WARNING — this may be a long and jumbled entry, if I even bother to finish it.

So — on Monday night Mum, Dad and I were waiting in the sitting room for PB to come downstairs so Mum and Dad could tell her they're separating.

Mum's eyes were already all red from crying, and she made me sit next to her for "moral support". Mum had wanted to tell Phoebe a week ago, but Dad told her to wait.

Of course, Mum and Dad couldn't help having ***another*** *argument while we were waiting for PB.*

Mum said — we ***mustn't*** *break the girls up*

Dad said — then let them both stay here.

Mum said — Suzi doesn't want to, do you?

I said no.

So Dad says — okay, but it's only fair to let Phoebe choose where she wants to live.

I said — but I want Phoebe to live with me and Mummy.

Dad didn't say anything to that. He was really angry and his stony face was screwed up tight and he looked like he wanted to hit something.

PB took ***ages*** *to come down. Obviously she knew what was coming. But then, when she walked into the room, she acted all stupid, pretending like she didn't know a thing. How dumb does she think we are? Even if you're only eleven, you can't be blind to what's been going on, can you?*

Dad was supposed to be the one to tell Phoebe, but he wouldn't speak, so Mum ended up having to do all the talking. And before she had even finished Phoebe started crying and said — I want to stay with Daddy.

Nothing we could do would persuade her to change her mind. She's so stupid and so stubborn.

Mum started crying then, but Dad had a big smile on his face, like he'd won. I hate him. It's all his fault we have to move out. He should be the one moving out and let us all live here with Mum, but he won't.

And now Phoebe is refusing to speak to me. She kept it up all Tuesday, all Wednesday and today as well, acting like it is all ***my*** *fault!! WTF! I tried to convince her to come with us to the new flat, but she just ignored me and in the end I had to give up.*

Tomorrow is moving day and I can't get to sleep. Mum and Dad are arguing. I can hear their voices coming up through the floor from the kitchen below, but not their words.

First Mum's voice — a high-pitched whiny wah wah wah wah.

Then a deeper, angry reply — wah wah wah wah

And on and on like that. Like they've done for years. Thank God I won't have to put up with this ever again after tonight. That's probably the only good thing about moving.

Friday

So, we moved in to the new flat today. Mum had promised me that it was only ten minutes away. But she meant ten minutes IN THE CAR. None of my friends live anywhere near here and we're two bus rides away from Phoebe. Also, this flat is a shit-hole and I hate it and I miss home.

Look on the bright side. At least you've got your own bedroom now Mum said. And I wanted to tell her that I don't want this shitty little bedroom, but I didn't say anything because I know it's not her fault and she's miserable too. We're both going to be miserable as hell here in our miserable flat all on our miserable own. Welcome to your new life Suzi.

Friday - later

I can't sleep. I never thought I'd be writing this, but I miss having Phoebe in the room. I'd even put up with her snoring. I always wanted my own room and I used to get sick of Phoebe never leaving me and my friends alone. But now I'd give anything to be sharing with her again.

I break off to wipe away the tears that trickle down my cheeks. For years I told myself Suzi didn't care about me. My defensive coping strategy was pretending I didn't care about her either. I was so good at it I almost managed to convince myself. And now I find that she cared about me all along. First Mum and now Suzi: I've been wrong about everything.

I give her a little prod in the back. 'Suzi?'

I prod her again until she turns and looks up, squinty-eyed, and says: 'Uh?'

'Suzi, I want you to know that I'm really, really sorry —' But even before I've finished speaking, she's rolled back over and fallen asleep.

I reach over the duvet and squeeze her tightly. She gives a sicky little belch, and I tell her: 'Love you too.'

Chapter 30

THE NEXT MORNING Suzi staggers into the sitting room with the duvet wrapped all cocoon-like around her, then slumps onto the sofa with a sigh, like a soufflé that's been taken out of the oven too soon.

'My head hurts!'

'I'm not surprised.'

'Ouch!' she moans, splaying her fingers against her forehead, 'd'you have to talk so loud?'

I bend down to ear-level and whisper-ask: 'Coffee?'

She nods, winces from the nod, and in a quiet, unsteady voice replies: 'Please. Black. *Very* black.'

I've been up for hours, pottering around the flat with a broad grin of contentment on my face while I waited for Suzi to wake. Learning how much she missed me after she moved out has changed everything. She's not the stony-hearted, unfeeling, mean big sister I thought she was.

What I can't figure out is this though: if she cared about me so much, why did she leave with Mum? Couldn't she have at least tried living with Dad and me for a while? Whatever the reason, I'm pretty sure it must be connected with the pages she ripped out. What was so terrible that she still has to hide it from me?

I make the drinks and as I hand over her coffee I casually say, 'Suze, you know you let me read your diary last night?'

She sips her drink, mutters 'fuck' because she's scalded her tongue, then gapes at me like I'm speaking a foreign language. 'What?'

'Your diary,' I say slowly, but she isn't listening. Instead, she heaves a despondent sigh, and in an over-dramatic voice that drips with anguish announces:

'I'll never forgive him for this.'

'Alistair?'

'It's all over between us. I'm leaving him.'

I sit beside her and put a consoling arm around her shoulder. 'Maybe you're wrong about it? Has he actually admitted to anything?'

She eyes me sharply: 'Who's side are you on?'

'Yours of course,' I say quickly, giving her shoulder a little squeeze.

'It's confirmed all my fears about men. Why did I ever think Alistair was any different? Relationships always turn sour sooner or later.'

'Not all,' I say optimistically.

'Really? So your relationship with Alfie is going to have a happy-ever-after ending?'

'Well, no.' A ghastly image of Alfie's contorted face flashes into my mind and I quickly have to bat it away. 'But I still have faith that one day I'll find the right man for me.'

'Don't count on it. D'you know what I've learnt that all men have in common?'

'They're all worthless bastards?'

'Yes!' she exclaims in surprise. 'How did you know I was going to say that?'

'Lucky guess. I don't think you're right though.'

'About men in general?'

'About Alistair. I always felt he was one of the good guys.'

'So did I!' she declares despairingly.

The matchmaker in me hates seeing Suzi sacrificing her relationship on such a flimsy set of suspicions, and I don't believe she really wants to end it. She's got some inner compulsion driving her to find fault in her men. 'Maybe you should wait before doing anything you might regret later. You haven't actually got any solid proof that he's been unfaithful.'

Suzi rolls her eyes in vexation. 'Which is exactly why I grabbed those papers from his desk. I'm going to check his credit card receipts, his bank statements and his desk diary. I'm sure I'll be able to unearth some more dirt.'

The bemusement I feel must be showing on my face because Suzi shoots me a look of annoyance and says: 'What?'

I hesitate from saying anything to piss her off, but if I don't speak now, it might be too late: 'It seems to me that your mind's already made up. I just wonder whether running from your problems is the answer.'

'What d'you mean?'

'You do have a track record of running away when things aren't going well.'

She looks askance at me. 'You mean because I moved out with Mum and left you with Dad? I was hoping we'd progressed beyond this conversation.'

'No, I meant your last two marriages, plus all the men you've ever dated. There seems to be a definite pattern to your behaviour. But now that you mention it, maybe it did all start when Mum left Dad?'

Suzi studies me coldly. 'Are you trying to psychoanalyse me?'

'I'm just thinking out loud.'

'I suppose you were unaffected by their divorce?'

'No. We were all affected. You lost your faith in relationships. I developed a fear of abandonment. And Dad began using alcohol to numb the pain of her leaving.'

Suzi shakes her head. 'He was already drinking.'

'He was?' I don't remember him drinking before Mum

left. Afterwards he was drunk all the time though. He'd stumble around the house with a desolate, sorrowful look in his eyes, and in a heart-wrenching, slurred voice, tell me *I didn't want any of this to happen.*

I set my mug down on the coffee table and steel myself to ask something I've never asked before because I've known I wouldn't get a straight answer. Perhaps this time I will.

'Suzi, why did Mum leave Dad? Was she having an affair?'

Suzi doesn't look me in the face. Her eyes dart around the room and she taps her fingernails against her teeth. I knew it! She knows. She just can't decide whether to tell me.

Eventually she stops the teeth rattling, her mouth snaps shut, and just when I think she's finally going to spill the beans her phone rings. She glares at the screen and in a venomous voice hisses: 'It's Alistair!'

'Maybe you shouldn't answer. You can ring him back when you've calmed down a bit. You don't want to say something you'll regret.'

'I already regret wasting five years of my life on that worthless bastard,' she snaps, giving the phone-screen an aggressive swipe.

'What?' she barks.

Then: 'Oh!'

I can tell from the change in her tone and body language that something's up.

'Is he all right? — uh-huh — what happened? — uh-huh, uh-huh. Well, I really don't have much choice, do I? — Okay, okay. I'm *sorry*. I said I'll come — *yes*, I'll leave straight away.'

When she's hung up, I ask: 'What's happened?'

She blows out her cheeks with a stagey sigh: 'Alistair's

father's had a fall. Maybe broken his hip. He's been taken to casualty and Alistair has to schlep it up to Bishop's Stortford to be with him, because apparently none of his brothers can go, even though every one of them lives closer.'

'Are you going with him?'

'No. *I've* got to get back because Alistair had agreed to have the neighbour's dog for the week, and the dog can't be left on its own because it'll chew up the furniture. That bloody dog! I don't know why he agreed to have it.'

'Maybe because he's basically a nice guy?'

She snorts dismissively. 'Nice to other people perhaps. Anyway, I'm not going to get into another argument with you. Have you seen my car keys?'

I try to persuade Suzi that she's in no fit state to drive considering how much alcohol must still be in her system, but just like her husband the night before, she refuses to listen.

Chapter 31

WHEN SUZI'S GONE, I wash up the mugs and finish cleaning the flat. I'd left the hoovering until last because I didn't want to disturb her beauty sleep, but when I go to the cupboard, the Henry Hoover isn't there. Which doesn't make any sort of sense because there's nowhere else in this tiny flat it could be.

I wander through the rooms with a puzzled expression on my face and am even more confused when I find it grinning at me from the back of the wardrobe.

How on earth did it get in here? Was Suzi playing some kind of drunken game of hide 'n seek with me last night? It seems unlikely, but it didn't wheel itself from the cupboard to the wardrobe all on its own. I just can't account for it.

Over the next few days, I begin to notice that other items are turning up in the wrong place. When I get home from work on Monday, I find my raincoat lying on the bed, when I'm almost certain I left it on the peg in the hallway. Later in the week I discover a mug beside the sink in the bathroom. Nothing odd about that maybe, except it's one of the chipped mugs that were left behind by the Henry-phobic, which I've never even taken out of the cupboard. And then on Thursday I find an empty shampoo bottle sitting at the top of the stairs. Although I can't be one hundred per cent sure I didn't leave it there in some scatter-brained moment of madness, I'm becoming increasingly suspicious. Is someone messing with my things when I'm out? It seems so benign — it's just a coat, a mug and a shampoo bottle after all — but it's got me so unsettled that I decide to do something about it.

I google *how to find out if someone is coming into your flat while you're out.* The simplest method is to use a tennis ball. You pop it behind the front door when you leave and if someone opens the door while you're out, the ball will get knocked across the hallway. Of course, you have to open the door carefully when you get home, or you'll spring the trap yourself.

It's not going to help me identify who's breaking in — for that I'll need to invest in one of those video doorbells they keep advertising — but it'll be a start. At the very least I'll be able to prove to myself that I'm not imagining it all.

In one of Suzi's boxes of toys I find an old balding tennis ball with a smiley face on it, which Suzi or I must have drawn on with a Sharpie. The ball may not be up to Wimbledon standard, but it'll do the job.

I set the trap on my way out to work the next morning and head off down the road for the tube with a bounce in my step, more excited than apprehensive, because I feel like I'm finally doing something to take control of the situation, instead of just sitting back and letting things happen.

I never thought I'd complain about it not being busy at work, but today's the quietest I've known it for ages. When the clock finally says it's half past seven, I'm the first one upstairs, the first one throwing their uniform into the ScrubX machine, and the first one changed and on their way home.

I gingerly open the front door and squeeze my way into the hallway, my heart in my mouth.

The stupid ball hasn't moved. It's sat there on the floor, nuzzling up against the door, its Sharpie-d face staring up at me reprovingly as if to say: *what did you expect?*

I'm so disappointed, which is ridiculous because I

should be glad that no-one's broken in. I should savour the fact that for once I can be certain no-one's been messing with my things while I was out. Perhaps it *is* all just a figment of my imagination?

Tonight, I'm going to have some me-time. I'll take a long hot shower, then slob around on the sofa gorging myself silly on toast and peanut butter, while watching one of the box sets on Netflix I've been saving up. And if Denise invites me down, I'll just tell her I'm busy.

As I wait for the kettle to boil, I notice that the paddle-shaped leaves of the umbrella plant on the kitchen windowsill have turned yellow. I could have sworn it was looking perfectly healthy this morning. I know I've not got the greenest fingers in the world, but even I don't usually finish off a house plant so quickly. I bought this palm after reading an article that listed the *30 Indoor Plants That Are Almost Impossible to Kill*, and it's been surviving perfectly happily until now.

Perhaps it needs watering? I probe a finger into the soil, but it seems quite damp. Have I been over-watering it then? There's a label buried in the soil, presumably with the plant care instructions on it. I pull it out.

I give a tiny *oh!* in surprise. It's not a plant label; it's one of the little plastic cards from the *Guess Who?* game: Robert, a floppy-haired, canoe-faced man with a big nose and sad blue eyes. I stare at him in puzzlement. How on earth did he get buried in the soil? Maybe Suzi did it when she was here, as some sort of not very funny joke?

More disconcerting though, is the chloriney smell coming off it. If I didn't know better, I'd say that someone has been watering my plant with bleach. The notion makes me shiver, and as I rinse the card under the tap, and leave it to dry on the draining board, I can't shake the uncomfortable feeling that I've got the clammy imprint of someone's sweaty hand on my back.

I make a second discovery while buttering my toast. Probably because I'm feeling so jittery, I drop the knife onto the floor, and when I bend down to pick it up I find another *Guess Who?* card shoved under the fridge. I use the knife to slide it out, and wipe the card clean on a piece of kitchen roll.

This one's Tom: bald, with round glasses and a pinched look of surprise on his face. I place him beside Robert on the draining board. Tom and Robert. Robbie and Tom! I go cold with fear. Surely it can't be a coincidence. Did Alfie enter the flat while I was out, and set this up as a way of warning me off them? Perhaps they're in danger? Should I warn them? Or should I go straight to the police? But what would I say? They're hardly going to take me seriously when I tell them I found two pieces from a children's game in the kitchen. I need to be able to show them concrete proof that someone's broken in.

I google it again, and on an American website offering handy household tips, I find a fool-proof method for collecting evidence that someone's been entering your house while you're not there. It's all laid out like a recipe.

1. You'll need cooking oil (any cheap oil will do, like soybean or canola) and talcum powder.

2. Next spread a very thin layer of oil around the entrance to your building.

3. Sprinkle the powder over the top of the oily layer. Make sure to cover as wide an area as possible.

4. You can also apply it to your door handles.

5. Now, if someone steps on this or touches the door handle while you're out, they'll leave a print. Even if they've figured out what you've done, they won't be able to remove their marks without using soap and water.

6. You're bound to make footprints of your own when you

leave, so take a photo before you go so you'll know which footprints were yours.

7. Warning — this can get messy, and you might have a lot of cleaning up to do afterward!

I set the trap the following morning before I leave for work. I don't know what canola oil is and I've never seen soybean oil for sale in the supermarket, but there's an expensive bottle of extra virgin olive oil in the cupboard and even though it feels a bit wasteful, I pour it liberally around the front step. Then I sprinkle a fine layer of powder on top, using one of Mum's bottles of talc. It's for a good cause so hopefully she would approve. I rub a little oil and a dusting of powder onto the door handle as well, for good measure, then get out my phone and take a photo before I go.

Chapter 32

I'M IN 'MAJORS' again today, and it could hardly be more different from the relative peace and quiet of yesterday's shift. By ten o'clock the waiting room's already packed, there's no cubicle space, and the resuscitation bays are full. There's a never-ending succession of chest pains, abdominal pains, chronic infections and broken bones. On top of everything, because they've run out of small, medium and large-sized scrubs, we've all been forced to flap around like clowns in ridiculously ill-fitting extra-large uniforms until the ScrubEx man finally comes to refill the machine at midday.

One of my patients starts acting really obnoxiously for no reason, and then all the people with him join in and accuse me of misconduct. One of them is filming it all on their phone, and they're obviously planning on filing a complaint against me, hoping for a big compensation payout. This scam is not uncommon, but when it happens there's nothing you can do about it except act professionally and try not to let it get to you.

I've got too many patients to look after and spend the day running back and forth between cubicles. It's like spinning plates. I once borrowed Claire's FitBit to find out how much walking I was doing on a typical day at work: 26,000 steps, which is over eleven miles! It's no wonder we're all so exhausted and our feet aching so much when the shift is finally over.

I wearily make my way up to the changing room on the first floor and grab my bag from under the bench in the corner where I'd had to leave it because, as usual, there weren't any free lockers.

I unzip my bag. What I find inside makes me blench: lying on top of my clothes is another *Guess Who?* card. This time it's Anita, a young blonde girl with big blue eyes, rosy cheeks, and her hair in bunches. *Just like I've got my hair today.*

My hand shakes as I turn the card over in my fingers. Alfie must have slipped it into my bag while I was down in A&E. But the room's card-accessed, so how did he get in? Am I not even safe from him at work? I slip the card into my coat pocket and hurry out by the Coverton Road exit, speed walking through the darkness with the jittery, self-conscious feeling of being watched.

My ears prick and I think I hear footsteps approaching, but when I turn to look behind, there's no-one there. My pulse is racing and a growing sense of panic is taxiing along the runway of my mind. I'm so spooked now that I daren't go down into the tube, so I hurry on past and duck into the coffee shop next to Greggs.

The cosy atmosphere inside the café, with its wooden tables and chairs, the chalk board on the wall, the cakes, pastries and the rich aroma of coffee, makes me feel safe. I decide to get myself a hot chocolate, and wait here until I've calmed down.

'Hello!'

I spin round and find a man in a striped jacket grinning at me. Alfie?

'We've got to stop meeting like this!' the man jokes.

'Yes,' I reply uncertainly, my eyes frantically scanning his features for clues, in the same way that the needle of a record player might skitter impotently across an old piece of vinyl, unable to lock into the dusty grooves.

'Have you finished for the day, or are you on your way in?'

'I've just got off. What about you?' I ask, hoping to

pin him down.

'Just working late,' he replies vaguely.

'Anything interesting?'

'Well, *I* think it's interesting. We're working on a product launch for a new range of cat food. They're sponsoring an exhibition of cat-related artworks at the Tate and we're organising the press launch. It's been an absolute nightmare getting it all together in time.'

It's Tom! I get the usual rush of memories from the various times and places we've met before, and am surprised by how warm it makes me feel. Of course, it may just be relief that Alfie hasn't followed me from work, but I think it's more than that.

He apologises because he can't stay. He's meeting an old school friend for a drink and has to be in Clerkenwell at eight. We take our drinks outside, but then he doesn't seem in a particular hurry to get away.

He takes the lid off his coffee to let it cool down and as we watch the steam rising up into the cold air, he's struck by a sudden thought. 'I'm glad I bumped into you. I've got something — sorry, could you hold this for me? Thanks.'

I take his coffee and he unbuckles the flap of his messenger bag, then takes out a CD. I cock my head sideways to read the writing on the box.

'*The Barber of Seville*. Thanks,' I say, cringing inwardly because my *thanks* didn't sound too genuine.

Tom looks crestfallen. 'It was only £1.50 so I won't be offended if you bin it. I just thought that, seeing as you missed out on watching it live, you could listen at home. You never know — maybe you'll like it?'

'That's really nice of you. I'll give it a go!' I say, injecting a bit more enthusiasm into my voice. I don't tell him that I've already heard more than I can bear and also, I don't actually own a CD player. Who even does these days?

Tom blows on his coffee and takes a hesitant little sip. Just as he's lowering the cup from his lips, a man hurrying past knocks smack-bang into him, and rushes on without stopping.

'What the f— !' Tom exclaims, glowering into the distance. 'Did you see that? Not even an apology. What —'

He breaks off when he notices me staring at his crotch. Coffee's slopped all down the front of his pale grey trousers.

'Shit! That bastard! Now it looks like I've pissed myself! Don't laugh. I've got to go to the pub like this!'

I try not to smile. 'I'm sure no-one will notice,' I lie.

I take his coffee from him again so he can root around in his pockets for something to clean himself up with. As he pulls out a hanky, I see a small object fly out. It hits the pavement at my feet with a plasticky rattle. I bend down and pick it up.

It's another *Guess Who?* card — a middle-aged woman with dark skin, short curly hair and gold hooped earrings, called Anne, who despite not having pink hair, reminds me an awful lot of Denise.

My blood runs cold. 'Where did you get this?' I struggle to keep my voice from quavering.

'What's that?' he asks, calmly taking it from my fingers. He studies it for a moment and then hands it back with a shrug. 'It's not mine.'

I stare at him in disbelief. Fronting it out so brazenly. 'I saw it fall out of your pocket,' I reply in a flat tone, trying to control my urge to flee.

'I've never laid eyes on it before in my life, I swear!'

He's a convincing liar. I could almost believe him, but Alfie always had a talent for acting.

'Honest Phoebe,' he continues, examining me with a curious frown, 'it has nothing to do with me. Maybe that bastard who made me spill my drink dropped it? Why are you so interested in it?'

He seems genuinely puzzled. Perhaps he is telling the truth? I don't know what to think, but either way, I don't want to take any more risks. I just want to get home, so I slip the card into my pocket and tell him: 'I have to go.'

He looks disappointed but tries to make a joke of it. 'Is it the stains on my trousers? I didn't piss myself, honest!'

'Sorry, Denise is expecting me,' I mumble, and hurry off to the tube.

I keep turning to check over my shoulder as I travel down the escalator to make sure I'm not being followed, and when I get down to the platform, I'm a jittery bag of nerves.

Next Train: High Barnet via Charing Cross 10 minutes

Ten minutes! How come there are never any trains when you're in a hurry?

I can't stop fiddling with the *Guess Who?* card in my pocket as I wait. I keep turning it over and over with a growing sense of foreboding, until finally a warm whoosh of air whips my hair across my face. There's an angry glare of lights, and the train comes rattling out of the darkness and screeches to a halt by the platform. The doors slide open, and I go and sit down in the centre of the long bench of seats.

The jittery feeling hasn't subsided and I'm starting to feel travel sick from the jerky side to side motion of the train. I fix my eyes on the ghostly reflection of my face in the window opposite. I look panicky and tell myself to do my breathing exercises to calm down.

Breathe in slowly. One, two, three, four, five.

The scraping of the wheels on the tracks sends up bright sparks that illuminate the tunnel with an eerie blue light, fleetingly revealing the dirty cables and dusty pipework that lines the tunnel's walls. And then I'm staring at the reflection of my anxious face again.

Hold for five. One, two, three, four, five.

The exercises don't seem to be helping much, maybe because I'm still fiddling with the *Guess Who?* card in my pocket. I take it out and examine it again. I hadn't spotted earlier that the eyes have been carefully gouged out with a sharp implement, in exactly the same way that the faces in the magazines were defaced. Is it a warning that some gruesome fate awaits Denise?

As the train rattles on through the darkness my thoughts oscillate wildly between the conviction that Alfie's just playing mind games with me, and the fear that Denise is in real trouble. And then I worry whether that was really Alfie in the coffee shop just now, or should I trust my gut, which is telling me that Tom was telling the truth and had nothing to do with the card? Even though I swear I saw it shooting out of his pocket.

The building looks quiet. The lights are on in Denise's flat and there's no sign of anything out of the ordinary. I cross the road and head up the path, too busy staring up at my bedroom window to notice anything until I'm halfway to the front door.

A jolt of shock surges through me and a convulsive shriek escapes my lips. Denise's body lies on the ground, her short pink hair matted with blood. I feel myself go cold. *Please, please, please don't let her be dead.*

I squat down by her side to check for a pulse, so panicked that I have to reposition my fingers three times before I find the fluttering throb of an artery on her neck. *She's alive! Thank God!*

The sudden relief opens the floodgates and tears pour down my cheeks. But I tell myself to get it together, and snap into nurse-mode. First, I check her airways, then examine her for injuries, and finally put her in the recovery position before ringing 999.

'Emergency. Which service?'

'Ambulance please.'

I tell them that she's unconscious, but her breathing is steady, and that she has a haematoma to the back of her head with no other signs of injury.

'How long has she been unconscious?'

'I don't know. I just got home a moment ago and found her on the ground. Oh, hold on —'

Denise opens her eyes and tries to lift her head. In a watery, confused voice she asks: 'Where am I?'

'You're outside the flat,' I say. 'I've called an ambulance. You're going to be okay.'

The operator tells me it'll be a forty five minute wait, which I don't really believe because we've had patients this week who've had to wait four hours. A wave of exhaustion passes through me at the realisation that it's going to be a very, very long night.

I fetch a cushion for her head and make her as comfortable as I can. When I ask her what happened she says she thinks she slipped over but can't really remember.

'You weren't attacked?'

'No,' she replies, surprised at my question. 'I slipped.'

Slipped? I glance behind her at the blood-stained step and the oily sheen of talcum powder glinting in the yellow light cast by the streetlamp. I experience a sharp pang of guilt. She must have slipped on the oily mixture I laid down this morning. Which means I'm to blame for her injuries.

'Don't worry. It's going to be all right. I'm here,' I tell her, remorsefully.

The ambulance actually arrives when they said it would. Denise is put onto a stretcher, and I travel with her to the hospital. As we arrive in the loading bay at St Georges, I think how strange it is experiencing things from a patient's point of view. There's a long wait before we're seen, and then

I help out by taking Denise's bloods and wheeling her round for her CT scan. The head injury doesn't seem too bad, but because there's a small bleed on her brain, they decide to keep her in for observation.

I push her wheelchair into the lift, take her up to Gunning ward, help her into the bed, and once she's settled in, I tell her I'll come back later, after I've caught up on a bit of sleep.

'You don't have to do that. You've been such a saint,' she tells me with a groggy smile of gratitude.

I wince guiltily. 'Don't worry, it's the least I can do.'

I say goodbye and make my way towards the exit. It's gone half past three in the morning and I'm so tired I can barely walk. I can't believe I'm still at the hospital eight hours after my shift finished. That's dedication for you.

A woman with a bandaged head is watching me intently as I pass by her bed. She's got bruising under her eyes, her lips have been bleeding, and then there's the trauma to her head — all unmistakable signs that someone's beaten her up, poor girl.

I can tell by the reaction when I catch her eye that she recognises me. In all likelihood she's someone I treated in A&E earlier today — or rather, I mean yesterday. I give her a warm, professional smile, and am taken aback by the hostile scowl she returns.

'What're you staring at?' she demands.

'Sorry. I didn't mean to stare. Are you okay?'

'Do I look it?' she replies, a sarcastic sneer on her swollen lips.

I quickly check the name written on the white board above the bed: Nisha Harlan. Oh God! I experience a sudden upwelling of empathy, and, forgetting all about what we're trained to do when dealing with suspected victims of abuse, I can't stop myself from blurting out: 'Did Alfie do this to you?'

I see a flicker of hesitation in her eyes, but then, with the suddenness of a door slamming shut in a draft, it's gone. Her bruised eyes stare at me defiantly. 'I don't know what you're talking about. I fell.'

Clearly she's lying. This was Alfie's handiwork. And if Alfie was capable of doing this to Nisha, then he probably attacked Denise too? Two women lying in the trauma ward. And it's all my fault — if I'd gone to the police after he attacked me, I might have prevented it. I feel so ashamed. Denise and Nisha are suffering on account of my cowardice. I want to redeem myself and blurt out:

'Alfie attacked me too. He raped me.'

I can't believe what I've just told her. *Rape*. Actually saying it out loud for the first time forces me to fully confront what happened. He *raped* me. I recoil from the word as if from an unpleasant odour. I feel embarrassed and ashamed and guilty and dirty. I feel my face reddening and find it hard to look Nisha in the eye.

But she's staring back at me with an expression of pure disgust. 'Why are you lying? Alfie would never do something like that.'

My heart goes out to her. I know what it's like to live in denial. All the time I was with Alfie I knew deep down that something was wrong; I just couldn't admit it to myself. I thought it was my fault when we argued, and that our problems would be fixed if I loved him more. He was like a half-full glass of water which I just needed to fill with love to make him whole. But that isn't how it works; Denise explained it to me. People like him are like a broken vessel, with a crack in their glass, and no amount of love would ever be enough.

Only how do you convey this to someone who's looking at you with murderous intent because they think you're trying to steal their boyfriend? As far as she's concerned, I'm the problem not part of the solution.

'Alfie's like a broken vessel —' I begin, but she stops me.

'What are you on about? What are you even doing here in the middle of the night anyway?'

'I just want to help you.'

'If you don't leave me alone, I'm going to ring for someone.'

She looks more scared than aggressive, but I raise my hands submissively as she glares at me, call button in her hand. 'One, two —'

'Okay, okay, I'm going.'

Chapter 33

I USUALLY MAKE an effort to chat with Uber drivers, but it's four o'clock in the morning and I'm too exhausted to string two coherent words together. I get out of the car and trudge up the path to the front door in a daze. As I'm fumbling in my bag for the key, a dark, formless shape on the grass by the fishpond catches my eye. I squint at it wearily but can't figure out what it is.

Then, as if summoned forth by some kind of magic, the moon emerges from behind the clouds, and the garden is filled with a silvery light. I let out a horrified gasp: the shape on the grassy mound is the headless body of a cat. Denise's cat, Bernard. His ginger fur is smeared with blood, congealing around the stump of his neck and gleaming like jewels in the moonlight. There's blood too on the faces of the gnomes which stand in a gory circle around his body.

A chill of fear wells within me. First Denise, then Nisha, and now Bernard. Denise may have slipped, Nisha may have fallen, but nothing could explain away Bernard's decapitated body. Finally I have gory proof that it isn't all in my head.

With shaking hands, I get out my phone, and for the second time tonight dial 999. I'm put through to the police and explain that I've found the body of my neighbour's headless cat in the front garden.

'Thank you. We'll log a record of the incident.'

They don't seem to be treating the situation with much urgency. 'Aren't you going to send someone round?'

'I'm sorry, we no longer investigate reports of cat

decapitation. A thorough investigation was carried out a few years ago, which found no evidence of human involvement. Your cat was most likely hit by a vehicle and then mutilated by urban foxes.'

Urban foxes? I look at the horror-show in front of me. It must have been a particularly dexterous film-buff of a fox which placed Bernard's body on the grassy knoll, smeared the gnomes' faces with blood, and placed them in another Wicker Man-style circle. But I've exhausted my last reserves of energy and don't have anything left to start arguing with the woman on the phone.

I hang up, and slump to the ground on my knees. My eyes fill with tears of frustration, of self-pity, of despair. I've no energy left and I don't know what to do.

'Phoebe?'

A man is standing over me, holding out his hand. Though I've no idea who it is, I let him pull me to my feet. Even if it's Alfie, I'm too tired to make any attempt to escape. Instead I ask: 'What're you doing here so late?'

'I've been out with the guys from the office,' he says with a drunken grin.

I'm none the wiser, and frown at him as I examine his features.

'What? You think accountants can't have fun?'

'Robbie!'

'At your service,' he replies, with a silly, chivalrous flourish of his hand, followed by a deep bow. 'So, what are you doing camping out in your front garden in the middle of the night?'

Without replying, I move aside to let him see what's behind me.

'Fuc -king-hell!' He goes over and takes a closer look at the bloody scene. 'D'you know who did this? Did you call the police?'

'They weren't interested.'

'Really? Uugh! My God, what a mess!' He screws up his nose and with a slow, sorry shake of his head asks: 'What're you going to do?'

'I don't know,' I say helplessly.

'I could give you a hand cleaning it up if you like. Have you got a bin bag or something I could use?'

'You don't have to do it now. It can wait until the morning.'

'I don't know; it's pretty gross. You don't really want to be waking up to that, do you?'

'I suppose not. Thank you,' I say, my eyes welling up with gratitude.

Robbie follows me up to the flat and bustles around with a clumsy alcohol-fuelled enthusiasm. He insists I wait up here, while he goes down with the bin bag, some cloths, rubber gloves and a washing up bowl filled with soapy water.

I sit on the sofa in a state of numbed anxiety, trying to figure out what's going on. Denise, Bernard, the *Guess Who?* card which fell out of Tom's pocket. Everything's pointing to Tom. Was it really just by chance that I bumped into him? Was he really working so late on a Friday night? But he seemed so convincing when he said he had nothing to do with that card. I'm going round in circles.

I go to the bedroom window and watch Robbie wiping the gnomes clean with a cloth. He glances up, and when he sees me he gives me a wave. Can I really trust him? Or is this knight in shining armour behaviour just an act?

It doesn't take him too long before he's back in the room, peeling off his gloves, and telling me *it's all sorted*.

'Thanks Robbie!' I gush enthusiastically so he won't be able to pick up on my uncertainties. But I needn't have worried; I can tell from the squiffily lopsided grin on his face that he's still pretty drunk.

'I didn't know what you wanted to do with the body, so I left it by the bins,' he says.

The body? For a brief moment I picture Denise lying on the ground covered in blood, but of course he means the cat. We'll need to give him a proper burial when Denise comes out of hospital. She's going to be heartbroken when I tell her what's happened. And then it all hits me at once: gratitude towards Robbie; guilt over Denise and Nisha; and the utter exhaustion of everything. I start to cry.

'It's all right,' Robbie says, reaching out his arms and giving me a hug.

I feel myself melting into the solidity of his embrace and let him pull me to his chest. I'm so tired, so confused and so afraid. I want someone to look after me, to protect me.

He mutters something I don't catch, and when I turn my head to look up into his face I suddenly feel really uncomfortable. The way he's stroking my hair, the smell of alcohol on his breath. This is *such* a bad idea. It's so late, I'm so tired, he's so drunk and I'm already borderline hysterical.

I wriggle out of his arms and as I step back I spot a line of bloody splatters running like a child's straw-blown painting up the back of his shirt sleeve. A gruesome image forms in my head: Robbie is sawing through Bernard's neck with a sharp knife and blood is spurting up from a severed artery.

I carry on backing away from him until I'm up against the fridge.

He looks at me puzzledly. 'What?'

I can't speak. He follows the line of my gaze, twisting his arm round to examine the back of his sleeve. 'Oh yeah, thanks. D'you have a cloth?'

'How did it get there?' I ask in a quavery, staccato voice.

'What d'you mean?'

'How come you have spatters of fresh blood up your arm?'

He rubs his bristly chin and smiles hesitantly, as though uncertain whether I'm making a joke. 'Maybe it has something to do with your neighbour's decapitated cat, which I've just cleared up for you?'

'Oh.' I close my mouth with a plop. Now I feel foolish. Of course he was going to get blood everywhere. I'm so tired I'm not thinking straight. But — hang on — how did he know the cat belonged to my neighbour? I don't remember mentioning it. But I'm so befuddled from lack of sleep that maybe I did. I need my bed.

I pretend to yawn, hoping he'll get the message, and then the yawn turns into a long, unsatisfactory, half-real one.

'Keeping you up?' he asks, fiddling with his clumpy, over-gelled hair.

'What's the time?'

'Half past four.'

'I've been awake for over —' I try to do the maths but it's beyond me.

'Don't worry, I can take a hint!' Robbie says with a laugh, and I go downstairs with him, thanking him again for his help. After I've watched him cross the road to his house, I bolt the door firmly and go back upstairs to bed.

PART FOUR

Chapter 34

STARING OUT OF the window after a fitful sleep, I try to convince myself that last night's drama was just a bad dream. The gnomes are fishing and gardening and wheeling their wheelbarrows as if nothing had happened. But when I come across the pair of blood-splattered rubber gloves in the kitchen bin, I'm forced to confront the appalling reality of my situation.

Bernard's headless corpse is wrapped in a bin bag and Denise is recovering in a hospital bed. What will Alfie's next move be? He's hospitalised two women and maybe I will be the third? I can't bear to think about it. For all I know, he's waiting outside the house this very minute, and there's nothing I can do about it because the police aren't interested.

And then there's the unsettling notion that he's wormed his way back into my life by pretending to be Tom or Robbie. Or both. It's a crazy thought, but it's something he might be capable of pulling off.

If only I could recognise faces. The way that Alfie's able to exploit my weakness so easily makes me feel sick. I really wish I'd not been born this way, but sitting here whining like a baby isn't going to help anyone. I need to start tapping into that reservoir of logic which has, unbeknown to me — but apparently obvious to both Dad and Suzi — lain hidden inside me all these years.

What I need is to get hold of photos of Alfie, Tom and Robbie, to compare. Unfortunately I didn't take any photographs of Alfie while we were dating, I've just got the occasional picture of places we'd visited, and when I search on social media I can't find any trace of him at all. I scroll back through the photos on my phone again, just in case I've missed something, and stop at a snap I took in March of a heron perched on the riverbank in Garret Park.

There's a figure sitting on the bench in the background. Zooming in I can see that he's wearing a pale grey Jack Wills hoodie, exactly like the one I bought Alfie last Christmas. I enlarge the image as far as it will go, but when it's zoomed in so much it's impossible to make out the features. He's got darkish hair and angular cheekbones, but the rest of his face is lost in blocky pixelated shadows.

I have more success finding pictures of Robbie and Tom online, and compare their two profile pics to try and at least establish whether they're the same person or not.

The photos both show handsome, smiling, confident-looking young men. Tom's nose is perhaps a little thinner and longer, and Robbie's eyes are maybe a bit wider-spaced, but there's nothing particularly distinctive about either of their faces. So I adopt a systematic, mathematical approach, measuring the size of their foreheads, the distance between their noses and mouths, the shape of their ears. But because the photos were taken at slightly different angles it's impossible to come to any conclusions and I have to give up. I should have kept my promise and befriended only bug-eyed, beaky-nosed freaks.

My phone's ringing. Another unknown number, probably one of Alfie's burner phones. I keep adding numbers to my blocked caller list, but he seems to have an unlimited supply of them and the calls keep coming.

I'm about to reject the call when I notice that it's an 0208 London number, not one of the usual mobile numbers he uses. I press *Answer* but it's already gone to voicemail. I check my messages and a robotic voice tells me:

You - have - *one* - new - messages.

Message - left - on - Sunday - eleventh - December - at - eleven - twenty - four - a.m.

'Oh, hi Phoebe it's Suzi. Listen, could you do me a big favour? You know last week I brought round a box containing a whole pile of Alistair's papers? Well apparently there's a really important work document in there that he needs really urgently. D'you think you could bring the box to Dulwich for me? Pretty please? Thanks. Love you. Bye.'

I call her back on the 0208 number, which turns out to be Alistair's home-office line. No doubt she's in there rifling through his things to find more incriminating evidence.

'Will you bring it over?' she begs. 'He's *desperate* for this particular document, and I said I'd courier it up to him this afternoon as soon as I find it.'

'Can't you drive over here and collect it?'

'The traffic's *so* bad.'

'On a Sunday?'

There's a pause. 'I can't leave the dog on its own.'

'So bring the dog with you.'

'I can't. It's — it's really disgusting, Phoebe. It slobbers continually. There's all this disgusting drool dripping from its mouth, and it leaves hair everywhere. I don't want it making a mess in the car. There's a reward in it for you if you come.'

'What kind of reward?' I ask suspiciously.

'You'll find out when you get here. *Please* Phoebe!'

I sigh. I'm really not keen on leaving the security of my flat to go traipsing across London just for the sake of Suzi's car upholstery. Plus, I promised I'd visit Denise at the hospital later. But Suzi knows I'll end up giving in, because I always do and there's no point prolonging it any longer, so I say: 'Okay, I'll do it. But it had better be a worthwhile reward.'

I tip the contents of the box out onto the carpet and

start packing it into two bags-for-life so it'll be easier to carry. I can't believe how much of Alistair's stuff she brought round. And now I've got to lug it all the way back to her house.

When the bags are all packed and ready, I notice a little card lying in the bottom of one of the empty boxes. It's a business card, with the name Rachel Green printed on it, along with a website address. I can't help smiling. Time for some more detective work.

Chapter 35

AN HOUR AND a half later I arrive at Suzi's with a bag-for-life in each hand and a big grin on my face. All the way over here I've been bursting to share my discovery with her.

'Come in, come in. You have *literally* saved my life!' she tells me as I hand over the bags and follow her through to the kitchen.

'Suzi —' I begin, but she interrupts me.

'You wouldn't believe how many times he's rung this afternoon to see if I've found his precious document.' She empties both bags onto the kitchen table and starts flicking through the bank statements and credit card bills.

'Suzi,' I say again, 'you know —'

'Ah -ha!' she declares victoriously, holding up some A4 sheets held together by a purple paper clip and waving them in front of my face.

Then she switches her attention to me. 'What?' she asks, 'were you going to say something?'

'Never mind, it can wait.'

'No, you know what?' she announces, putting the papers down and slapping the table with her hand. 'Fuck him. You've come all this way and I haven't even offered you a drink yet. It won't hurt if he has to wait a little bit longer. Would you like a drink? Tea? Coffee?'

'Tea please, but wait a mo', I've got something to show you. You know Rachel Green —'

Suzi shoots me an angry glower. 'Just don't go there, Phoebe. I don't want to have to think about that skinny, flicky-haired floozie that Alistair's been seeing.'

'What if I told you that Rachel Green wasn't a pretty young flicky-haired floozie? What if I told you that Rachel Green looked like this —'

I whip out my phone with a *ta-da* to show her the fruits of my research. It's a photo of an elderly-looking woman with short, nondescript grey hair, and heavy-framed glasses.

'Who's this?'

'Rachel Green. Alistair's Rachel Green.'

'Oh my God, it's worse than I'd imagined. I thought I was married to your common-or-garden adulterer, but apparently I'm married to a granny-lover. What am I going to do!'

'Don't be silly, you've got it all wrong,' I tell her, unable to keep from smiling at her over-the-top reaction. I hand over the business card I found and she reads it out loud:

'*Dr Rachel Green. Sex and Relationship Therapist. 185b Harley Street, London W1G 9QT.* He's been seeing a sex therapist? Why wouldn't he tell me?'

'Maybe he's too embarrassed.'

'He'd rather let me think he was having an affair?'

'Did you give him a chance to explain?'

'Yes.'

'Really? Even bearing in mind how pig-headed you become when you've made up your mind about something?'

She eyes me guiltily, like a schoolgirl caught lying about her homework. 'I might have over-reacted just a teeny bit. Come here —'

She wraps her arms around me and gives me a hug. 'My clever little sister, finding that business card. Dad always said that you were the smart one.'

'Did he?' I say, pretending to be surprised.

'Mmn. He said you had all the natural intelligence.'

'But you're the one who got all the A's and went to

the good university,' I counter.

'Only because I worked harder than you. You were the one with all the common sense.'

I get a tingling buzz of pleasure listening to Suzi stroke my ego, and can't resist asking: 'I wonder where it's all gone then, because nothing I've done recently seems to demonstrate much common sense, does it?'

'What about at work? You deal with the stress of life-or-death situations every day. I could never do that.'

'I suppose.' And it's true that at work I'm able to keep a level-head in an emergency better than most of the nurses. Better than most of the junior doctors and registrars too. It's just the rest of my life that's a mess.

Suzi makes the tea and produces some prettily decorated cupcakes from a tin.

'These look nice,' I say, selecting one with a swirl of purple frosting and a sprig of candied rosemary on the top. 'Did you make them?'

She rolls her eyes. 'You've seen my baking — do they look like I could have made them? They're from that fancy patisserie in Dulwich Village.'

'Are cupcakes still a thing? I thought it was all cronuts and muffants now.'

'They looked so pretty I couldn't resist. It's all right, you can eat them — they're gluten free.'

Now it's my turn to roll my eyes. 'I'm a vegetarian, not a coeliac.'

'It's all the same thing in the end, isn't it?'

'Not really.'

'Oh well, better safe than sorry.'

I can't believe she thinks I can't eat flour. Perhaps Dad was right after all about who got the brains. I take a bite of my cake. It's as dry and as tasteless as a serviette, except for the rosemary frosting, which is just weird. I take a sip of tea to wash it down.

I watch Suzi take a bite of her cake, waiting for the full awfulness of it to hit as she chews on the first dry mouthful. Her expression gradually changes from mild surprise to disgust, and after a gulp of tea she declares: 'These are terrible!'

I nod.

'Just goes to show that you shouldn't judge a cupcake by its frosting. You wouldn't believe how pricey they were.'

I take another bite.

'You don't have to eat it,' Suzi says.

'I'm hungry,' I reply, and while I force down another mouthful, she picks at the green frosting on her cake with her fingernail, and casually asks:

'So, how's Alfie?'

'We aren't together anymore,' I splutter. 'Surely I told you?'

'You never tell me anything.'

'Oh. Well, you know now. It's over.'

'I'm sorry.' She gives my hand a commiserating squeeze. 'Did something happen?'

'No, nothing in particular.' I squirm uncomfortably in my chair and then change the subject: 'Suzi, d'you remember how you used to help me identify people when I was struggling.'

'Of course.'

'Could you have a look at these photos for me.' I show her the pictures I screen-shotted earlier.

Suzi peers at my phone. 'Ooh, a new boyfriend already. You don't hang about, do you!'

I ignore her jibe and flick between the picture of Alfie in the park, and Tom and Robbie's profile pictures. 'I need to know whether this guy on the bench is the same person as — this man — or this man?'

She takes the phone from my hands and studies it for a while before giving a defeated shake of her head. 'It's impossible to tell. The bench guy's face is way too fuzzy and shadowy to see enough detail.'

'Oh.' I let out a deflated sigh. 'What about the other two photos? Are they the same person?'

She laughs: 'No, they're definitely two different people.'

Well, that's a relief. I still don't know whether Alfie's been catfishing me, but I know that at least one of my new friends is legit.

Suzi hands back my phone. 'I know you struggle with faces, but surely the tattoos should have given you a clue?'

'What d'you mean?' I examine the photos again. I was so focussed on trying to work out whether the faces were the same that I hadn't noticed that Tom has tattoos on his left arm and Robbie on his right. Perhaps I'm not so clever after all.

Unfortunately, I can't remember which arm Alfie's tattoos are on. I picture him lying on the bed in the Tooting flat. He's bare-chested, squinting his eyes against the glare of the sun. When he raises an arm to shield his face, he exposes a dark, mossy armpit, but in this memory he has no tattoos on either arm. He's smiling at me though. An unpleasant shiver runs down my neck.

'What's the matter? Someone step on your grave?' Suzi jokes.

'No, I think it's rosemary-frosting reflux,' I reply quickly, tapping my chest and giving a little cough.

I check the time and tell Suzi I'd better be going because I'm visiting Denise.

'Thanks for coming over with Alistair's things. And thanks for finding out about Rachel Green. I might have done something very rash otherwise.'

'That's okay,' I tell her as we walk to the front door.

She places her hand on my arm and looks me in the eyes. 'You know I'd do the same for you. You only have to ask.'

She looks so earnest as she says this that I can't stop myself from puncturing the moment with a smart-ass remark: 'When you do help me out, I'll make sure I give you a better reward than a stale cup cake.'

'Oh, that wasn't your reward. I nearly forgot. Wait here.'

She hurries away to the kitchen, and I worry that she might be preparing a doggy bag of cupcakes for me. But instead she returns with some sheets of paper. I recognise them immediately: it's the pages she ripped from her diary.

'I think it's time you learnt the truth.'

'The truth about what?'

'Just read them. You'll understand. Probably I should have told you years ago, but —'

Her voice tails off and she gives my fingers a tender little squeeze. 'I was hoping to protect you,' she mutters, almost inaudibly, and I can tell by the tremulous rigidity of her body that she's close to tears.

It unnerves me. What truth have I got to learn?

Chapter 36

ACCORDING TO THE display board at the bus-stop, it's going to be ten minutes before the next 185 comes. While I'm waiting, I pick out a bunch of freesias for Denise from the flower-stall on the pavement. I remember her once saying that freesias were her favourites. But as soon as I've paid, I realise they're unlikely to have been grown in the UK in December, and I worry she won't approve because of all the air miles they'll have clocked up.

When the bus arrives it's surprisingly crowded. I go upstairs to find a seat and am still making my way down the aisle when we set off with a lurch. Because I want to sit on my own, I end up having to go all the way to the front, staggering like a night-bus drunk as I try not to crush Denise's flowers.

When we were little, Suzi and I would beg to sit in these front seats. We'd sit side-by-side with our foreheads resting against the glass, pretending to be driving; steering imaginary steering wheels and honking imaginary horns at the traffic. These days I have to avoid sitting in the front seats because it makes me feel really motion sick, and although reading's only going to make it worse, I'm too eager to find out the secrets of Suzi's diary to wait until I get home.

I take the jagged-edged sheets of loopy teenage writing from my bag and smooth them out on my lap with a sense of foreboding. As soon as I begin reading, I'm immediately plunged back into Suzi's angsty, boy-obsessed world:

Friday 9 July

This afternoon in biology Amy told me Kyle wanted to talk to me — IN PRIVATE — after school.

OMG!!!

As I approached the art block, I could feel my heart beating faster and faster, not knowing what he was going to say.

He was already waiting there for me, and he just comes out with it straight away, uber cool, no nonsense, and asks if I'm still going out with Paul because he heard from Amy that we weren't together anymore.

I told him Paul and I had broken up (Oops! Little white lie alert!!) and Kyle asked if I wanted to go to the end of term summer disco with him. I said I'd love to. He looked really made up and had such a huge grin on his face that it made me blush.

Then he leaned forward, and I thought he was going to kiss me on the cheek, but he was going in for a proper on-the-mouth kiss.

Awks!

So, our first kiss was an embarrassing half-cheek, half-mouth peck. But he laughed about it, in a nice way, and made it seem all right. He's so nice! Then he kissed me on the lips, and I melted into the floor.

Immediately afterwards I went to find Paul so I could break up with him cos I didn't want to be a liar. Technically I did two-time him, but it was only for about half an hour.

He was really upset. I was surprised because I hadn't thought about how he was going to react. He looked like he was going to cry. Maybe because I was his first proper girlfriend.

He kept asking "Why?"

I didn't know what to say. I couldn't tell him the truth i.e. that it's because Kyle is so much better looking, and because Paul's hands are always sweaty, because that would have made me seem really shallow and bitchy.

So I said "it's me not you", which is what they always say in Rom-Coms. But he didn't understand what I meant. And that's another reason to break up with him — we're just not on the same wavelength. Not like me and Kyle.

Then, and this is the really cringey bit, he said "but I love you"

Face palm!!! It was mega embarrassing for both of us and of course it's not true. I told him 'no you don't' and he argued with me and tried to convince me until I'd had enough and said I had to go.

I do actually feel really bad about it though. It's not like I don't care for him, and I definitely wouldn't want to do anything to hurt him. I worry that he'll never get over it. Things like this that happen when you're a teenager can scar you for life. He may never find love again and it'll all be my fault. I feel so bad now. I'm beginning to wish I hadn't said yes to Kyle.

Saturday 10

Soooo, this afternoon Amy texted me to ask if it's alright if she goes on a date with Paul. What the hell??!!!! And before I can take it all in I get another text saying that she's already said yes so if I'm not okay with it, it's a bit late, and Sorry.

Firstly, no it's not all right and secondly, no, I'm not okay with it. In fact I can't fuck-ing believe it. Last night I could barely sleep because of worrying about Paul. I kept imagining he was locked in his bedroom self-harming, because that's what everyone's doing at the moment. But it seems that it's taken him less than 24 hours to get over me, even though, apparently, he was really in love with me. Thanks a lot mate!!

But I can forgive him. He's just a boy and everyone knows how silly and immature boys are. But I can't forgive Amy. WTF sista!!! How could you say yes to him? Paul and I had been going out for six weeks, so it was a proper relationship, and you can't start dating your ex-best friend's ex so soon after the relationship's finished. No way. It's just not right.

Sunday 11 July

My period came on today and it's a bad one, a full-on, roll on the floor and clutch my stomach in excruciating agony one. It's like something's trying to crush me from the inside. It's so painful that I'm on the verge of crying all the time. I feel sick and dizzy too, and I think I would pass out if I wasn't lying on the bed.

Sometimes being a girl can really SUCK.

How bad is this for timing, with the end-of-term disco in three days' time?

Tuesday

I feel loads better today, THANK GOD!! Yesterday was such a shitty day, doubled up in pain and having to pretend I was fine so Kyle wouldn't find out. Luckily, because it's the last week of the school year we're not really doing much work.

We all went to the field in the afternoon to 'watch' the teachers vs pupils cricket match, which means sitting around and chatting in the sunshine, although I had to pretend to be interested from time to time because Kyle was playing.

He scored 21 runs, which doesn't seem a lot but apparently is really good, and the pupils beat the teachers by three wickets, but apparently I wasn't as impressed as I should be and Kyle said he'd have to explain the rules to me again.

Wednesday 14 July 2004

Tonight was the 2004 Meadow Park High School Summer School Disco. AND my first date with Kyle. Everyone was there, even the ones who said they weren't going to bother this year because it's really for babies. And it ended up being sooo much more fun because we were all celebrating our GCSEs being over. Plenty of alcohol was smuggled in and people were sneaking out to the park to smoke weed, and basically everyone got a little wasted, right under the teachers' noses.

The best thing though was being with Kyle. It sucks going to a disco on your own, and Kyle is one of the best-looking boys in the year.

Plus, he dances really well too.

Amy kept giving me the evils all night but our whole group is really angry with her for doing the dirty on me and we all just ignored her. She had to sit with Paul's friends all evening and every time I looked over she was looking really bored. Ha!

Kyle complemented me on my dancing and he said he liked my outfit too. When we weren't dancing, we were holding hands. I had to keep wiping my hands on my skirt to stop them getting too sweaty.

Kyle asked me to go to Marcus Channon's party on Friday. Marcus is in the year above — Kyle knows him through cricket — and his parties are legend! Last year the neighbours had to call the police because of all the noise and Kyle says it'll be even better this year because Marcus' parents are going to be away. Suckers!

The disco ended at half past ten, so we all went to the park after and hung out on the swings. I sat on Kyle's lap and we kissed for ages. We didn't speak much cos we were too busy snogging, and it was really nice but then my mouth was starting to ache and eventually I said I was too cold and had to go home.

Kyle walked me all the way home even though it's in the opposite direction from where he lives. We held hands and kissed again outside the house even though the light was on in the front room, and I was worried Mum and Dad might see me.

I assumed the light was on because they were waiting up for me, since it was past midnight and I promised I'd be home by eleven. But they were having another of their mega-rows, and so they wouldn't even have noticed if Kyle and I were having sex in the front garden LOL!

I sneaked past and came upstairs.

They're still going at it now. They're both really angry about something, and I can't sleep because of their noise, and because I'm still buzzing from the alcohol and can't stop thinking about Kyle.

Sunday 18 July, early morning

So, I decided to give up writing this diary because I've been too upset and I couldn't see the point any more. I thought why bother? It's just a stupid waste of time and who is it for anyway?

But my thoughts are so fucked up that maybe the only way to make sense of things is to write it all down? Maybe it will stop all this negativity from spinning round and round in my head all the fucking time and stopping me from ever getting any sleep.

On the other hand, I worry that putting it onto paper will make it REAL. It'll be there in black and white, and it will mean that there's no going back. And I want to go back. I want things to go back to what they were like a year ago, a month ago, even a week ago, when I was still just an innocent fifteen-year-old.

Here goes.

So, it happened on Wednesday night (though technically it was Thursday morning by then), after I got home from the disco and kissed Kyle outside the house, and after I wrote that last diary entry, saying how happy I was.

I've just re-read it, and all I can think is: you silly, silly little girl. You know nothing about the world. You think it's a nice place filled with nice people, and you hope that you'll have a nice life, but you're SO wrong.

So, what happened is this —

Fuck, I don't want to write it down, but I know I have to —

So — I couldn't sleep because Mum and Dad were still arguing and after I'd endured about an hour of it I went downstairs to ask them to keep it down.

Dad had his back to the door and Mum was standing behind him, so neither of them saw me come into the room. And they were screaming at each other really loudly so couldn't hear me either.

I saw Dad grab Mum's arm really hard. I was close enough that I could see the white marks where his fingers were digging in to her skin. Mum was struggling and screaming at him to let go.

Then: WHAM, out of nowhere, he hits her really hard across her face.

And before she can react: THWACK, he brings his arm

back and hits her with the back of his hand.

I tear my eyes from the page with an appalled, horrified gasp. My head is spinning and a queasy dread bubbles up in my throat. Is everything I thought I knew about my family wrong?

I notice that my hand has instinctively gone to my cheek, touching the spot where Alfie hit me. The same place that Dad hit Mum, THWACK. Like Mother like daughter?

Can it be true? Did it really happen the way it's described here? Or is it just some fantasy that Suzi concocted? She was only fifteen. She could have made it all up. I just can't believe Dad would hit Mum. And yet — it would explain everything.

'Could you budge up?'

A large, sweaty, mean-faced lady in a long grubby-looking puffer coat scowls at me accusingly, like I'm taking up more than my fair share of the seat. She makes me scooch over, then drops her shopping bags onto the floor, and collapses into the seat with a weary grunt.

I'm all crushed up against the side, feeling panicky and trapped. On top of that the rocking and vibrating of the bus is making me nauseous. But I have to learn the truth. I wipe my eyes and pick up where I left off.

There was a terrible, eerie silence, and then I don't know if I made a noise or something, but Mum's frightened eyes suddenly locked onto mine, and Dad turned round and saw me. His face was red and angry. I could tell he'd been drinking.

'What the hell are you doing out of bed?' he shouted angrily, as though I was the one who'd done something wrong, not him.

Mum just stood there in shock, without speaking. I didn't say anything either and ran off upstairs.

I lay in bed for ages half-expecting Dad to burst in and shout at me again, but he didn't. It was quiet downstairs now, but of course I couldn't sleep. Not after what I'd seen. I buried my head under the pillow and tried not to think about it.

But every time I closed my eyes, I couldn't help picturing the expression on mum's face. I'm pretty certain it's not the first time he's hit her, because of the way she reacted. She seemed to ACCEPT *it. It was only when she saw me, when she saw that I'd seen it, that she became properly upset.*

Thursday.

The next day I couldn't concentrate on anything at all at school. All I could think about as I sat in my lessons was the fact that my father is an abuser and my mother is the victim of domestic violence. And every time I thought about it, I felt like crying.

But do you want to know what the worst thing was? It was that I couldn't stop feeling sorry for myself. I'd think about Mum being hit and feel terrible for her, and then immediately afterwards I'd think — poor me, growing up in a broken home. Like this is all about me, when Mum is the one getting beaten up. WHY AM I SUCH A TERRIBLE PERSON?

I couldn't speak to anyone about it of course. The only person I MIGHT *have confided in is Amy, but we're still not talking. I'm sure Kyle knew something was up because I wouldn't hang out with him after school. I lied and said I had to go to the dentist, which is such a lamo excuse.*

So, I avoided everyone at school, and then Mum spent the evening avoiding me. The few times that we were in the same room together she wouldn't catch my eye, and when I tried to speak to her, she would mutter to herself and hurry off.

So I spent another night fretting about everything and stewing in waves of sadness and self-pity and guilt and not getting much sleep.

16 July.

Friday was the last day of summer term, my last day in year

11, and everyone was in such a good mood. Except me. It should have been the best day of the year, but I couldn't manage to forget about my problems (MY problems!!!) long enough to enjoy the moment.

We were let out before lunch and went to Macca D's and then everyone hung out in the high street for the rest of the afternoon. I was with Kyle, and it was okay because we didn't speak much and I just clinged (clung?) onto him. He probably wondered why I was being so clingy and not very talkative, and why I didn't mind kissing him even when his mouth tasted of burger and greasy fries.

At eight Kyle arrived to pick me up for Marcus Channon's party. He said 'hi sexy, you look nice' when he saw me, and gave me a kiss.

He'd have been in trouble if he hadn't said anything because I'd spent ages getting ready. I really plastered on the make-up, painting on a happy face because I didn't want anyone to see that I'd been crying again. I was wearing my shortest skirt: the denim belt skirt I got from Miss Selfridge, which shows a lot of midriff and a cheeky glimpse of butt cheek when I bend over. I had to sneak out of the house before Dad saw me because he would have gone ape-shit if he knew what I was wearing.

When we get to the party, I was like, WTF? Amy was there with Paul!?! I couldn't work out how they got invited, but I found out later that they'd scraped in with Andy Barnwood.

Even worse was the fact that Amy was wearing the exact same Miss Selfridge skirt as me!! When did she get that? She was with me when I bought mine so she can't pretend she didn't know I already owned it. Plus, she must have known I'd be wearing it to the party. AND she's got a new belly piercing, so it was looking better on her, especially since she's lost a bit of weight.

Note to self — next week I'm getting a piercing too.

I was in such a bad mood with the Amy situation (and of course everything else) that I was determined to get drunk. I brought a half bottle of voddie with me, and Kyle had a bottle of gin he'd stolen from his parents drinks cupboard, so I got drunk really quickly. I mean, REALLY quickly. One moment I was sober and the next it was four hours later, and I was all over the place, blazed out of my skull, shouting and dancing with everyone.

Then I was upstairs with Kyle in one of the bedrooms. There were about ten people all crammed in there, and the TV was on in the corner, but the sound was off, or maybe it was just that the music was so loud you couldn't hear it. Someone was playing The Streets new album over and over again.

Kyle and I were on the couch, and I remember that I was really impressed and kept drunkenly saying "who the fuck has a bedroom big enough to fit a couch in!"

Even though it was really hot in there, we had a blanket over us with just our heads sticking out. We were kissing, and then under the blanket he started touching my breasts through my top. Then he put his hand up my top, wormed his way under my bra and started playing with my nipples. I slipped my hand under his shirt and caressed his chest, and even though my breasts were getting a bit crushed, I was becoming really turned on and excited.

He moved his hand down to my skirt. My legs were closed together and he was trying to force them apart. I opened my eyes to look around but no-one was paying us any attention.

Then he clamped one of my legs with his leg and managed to force his hand between my thighs and started touching me through my knickers. Even though it wasn't really what I wanted, I didn't try very hard to stop him until he slipped his fingers inside the fabric.

I grabbed his hand, but he's stronger than me and I was so wasted I just thought, fuck it, and I let him slip a finger into my vagina. I could tell from his reaction that he was surprised by how wet I already was. I tried not to make a sound, but I couldn't help gasping out. He gave a sort of chuckle at this and then started thrusting into me with his fingers.

It was feeling really good, but it was also making me really overheated, like I was burning up with a fever. I thought it must be really obvious to the others what was going on, with me panting and sweating and the blanket going up and down in front of everyone.

For some crazy reason I thought that the best way to cover it up would be to talk normally, as though nothing was happening. So I started blurting out the very first thing which came into my head, which was the formula for the quadratic equation. Which was weird because I'd struggled to remember it in my maths exam a few weeks before.

"X equals minus b plus or minus the square root of b squared —" I chanted, in a strained, panting voice, struggling to sound normal.

And then Kyle took my hand and placed it on his cock, which he'd already taken out of his trousers, and I was really shocked at this. I mean, I know he's got his finger inside me and he's already touched my boobs, but his cock was so hard and big and — . I don't know, it was just so unexpected, and I didn't really know what to do with it because I've never touched one before. So I just started sliding my hand up and down, worrying if I was holding it properly, and all the time I was spouting the formula for solving a quadratic equation.

I must have been doing something right, or maybe it was the maths that was turning him on, because suddenly Kyle stops fingering me and I could feel IT tensing up in my hand, and then he goes uugh, uugh, UGHHH and comes all over my fingers. And there's a big grin on his face and when I looked around, I saw that everyone in the room was watching us now.

It was only then that I realised how drunk I really was. Kyle had his finger under his nose, giving it a victorious sniff, and people were laughing and clapping. And I realised they were all thinking what a slut I was. It was mortifying.

And then I thought, so what? I don't give a shit anymore. Next time I'm going to let him fuck me and I really couldn't give a fuck who finds out about it. I sat there burning with shame and defiance, trying to ignore everyone in the room by focussing on the music — Dry Your Eyes *by The Streets — that was blasting out from the speaker behind my head.*

And it suddenly seemed to be the saddest music I'd ever heard in my whole life, and as I wiped my fingers off on the blanket, I had to turn away from Kyle so he couldn't see that I was crying.

I walked home on my own because Kyle wanted to stay longer seeing as it was only half past eleven and 'the party's only just getting going' *but I was beginning to get that awful sobering-up headache you have when you've stopped drinking too early. And anyway, I was feeling terrible, and I just wanted to be in bed.*

It was after midnight when I got home, and I really didn't care if Dad wanted to have a go at me because I despise him and I don't give a fuck about anything he has to say to me anymore.

I slammed the front door behind me, walked unsteadily through the hallway, and headed upstairs. From the kitchen I heard him barking Susan! Come here! so I went back down and braced myself for a bollocking.

He was in the kitchen with Mum, and as soon as I walked in he started shouting at me: "What time do you call this? What are you wearing? Have you been drinking?"

Flecks of spit were flying from his lips, his face was bright red, he had a wild, scary look in his eyes, and I could tell that he was even drunker than me. He grabbed my arm and shoved his nose right into my face. "Have you been smoking?"

I told him to let go and tried to pull my arm back, but he was holding it really tight and asks again, "have you been smoking?"

I hadn't, but it was none of his fucking business. I thought of telling him: No, your daughter hasn't been smoking, but her boyfriend has. And she's had his tongue in her mouth and his dirty fingers inside her pussy and the fingers of her right hand still smell of his cum. But instead of telling him all that I just told him to fuck off.

That was when he raised his hand to hit me. His fist was clenched, and he would have punched me really hard if Mum hadn't grabbed his arm and shouted his name.

He span round and hit her really hard in the stomach. All the air went out of her, and she sank to the ground like she's been punctured. He didn't stop though, even though she was on the floor now. He kept hitting her like she was just a sack of potatoes or something and I was screaming and trying to pull him off her, but he shook me off and carried on until he'd had enough, and then stormed out of the house.

Mum was still on the floor, crying, and her face was all red and puffy and beaten-up looking, and I was crying too and didn't know what to do. She kept telling me it was all right and she was okay and was I okay and I said "yes I'm fine" and she said I'd better go to bed. I didn't want to leave her on her own, but she insisted.

Phoebe was fast asleep when I came into the bedroom. I don't know how she managed to sleep through all the shouting. Mum's gone to bed now too. Dad hasn't come home yet, but I can't sleep because I'm scared what will happen when he does. I was hoping that writing everything down in my diary would help me make sense of it all, but it doesn't and I don't know what will.

Chapter 37

IT ENDS THERE. I re-read the final paragraphs through blurry, teary eyes, and then with trembling hands, carefully put the sheets away in my bag.

Suzi was wrong. I wasn't asleep. I still remember that evening. It was my last day at juniors, and a whole gang of year sixes were going to the cinema after school. I was really excited because it was the first time I'd hung out with them. It had only taken me six years, but finally I'd been included! Just when we about to move on to our new schools and I'd have to break the mysterious code of friendship all over again.

I can't remember what film we saw or whether I enjoyed it — that didn't matter because the important thing was that I'd actually been out with *friends*. I couldn't wait to tell Suzi all about it when she came home, which is why I was still awake when she eventually rolled up.

I heard the door slam shut and then it just all kicked off. Mum's high-pitched shrieks. Dad's angry guttural rasp. And then Suzi staggered into the room, smelling of alcohol and cigarette smoke. I could see she'd been crying, but I assumed that it was because she'd received a bollocking for getting home after the curfew.

The next day a terrible, morgue-like atmosphere had descended on the house. Everyone was glaring at each other, silently navigating around our cramped little rooms like strangers.

Suzi stormed out just as lunch was being served, and I had to sit there, dolefully pushing my food around the plate while Dad scowled at the wall and Mum snapped at him over some innocuous comment he'd made. I screwed my eyes shut and wished they'd stop arguing. Or rather, I wished that Mum would stop arguing and picking Dad up on every tiny little thing he said. I thought I could see exactly what was going on. But all this time I've been mistaken.

'You all right love?' the woman beside me asks, her fleshy features bunching solicitously as she stares into my face, and I realise I've got tears dripping down my cheeks.

'I'm fine, thank you,' I say in a croaky voice, wiping them away. Her kindness towards me when I thought she was so mean is only making things worse. I misjudged her the same way I've been misjudging Suzi all these years. Suzi's had to live with the burden of this terrible knowledge while I've blundered on in blissful ignorance, feeling sorry for myself.

And worse still, all this time I've been blaming Mum — I blamed her for the divorce, for splitting me and Suzi up, for deserting me, for causing Dad's problems with alcohol — and I never realised that she was the victim, not the instigator.

I wonder how long it had been going on before she finally managed to break free. I suppose she put on a brave face for the sake of her children, covered over her bruises with makeup and grinned and beared it until finally she couldn't take any more.

The bus arrives at The Oval. It's started to rain, and I hurry along the pavement and go down to the tube in a daze. It's like nothing is real anymore. Not the digital panels on the walls playing adverts for a plastic surgery clinic in Mayfair, or the garish strip lights overhead which burnish everyone with a peculiar subterranean light, or the rubbery handrail which drags my hand backwards as I slowly descend to the station's depths.

The tube train bursts out of the darkness, then rolls

into the station and comes to a halt with a weary, rumbling sigh. The doors slide open with a little whoosh, and I get on in a bewildered haze.

The next station is Colliers Wood. This train terminates at Morden.

The train sets off and we're engulfed in darkness. I'm jolted from side to side as the carriage rattles on through the tunnel. It's like my whole life has just been shaken up and turned topsy-turvy. Everything I thought was true has turned out to be false. What I'd believed all these years — *my* truth — was just a fiction.

I get off at Tooting Broadway and make my way along the familiar route to the hospital, trying to recover some composure. I take the lift up to Denise's ward. A nurse gets in on the first floor and says *hello* in such a friendly manner that I assume she must know me. I start explaining that although it's my day off, I'm visiting a friend on Gunning ward, but I can tell from the look on her face that she doesn't know me after all, and we travel the rest of the way up to the 5th floor in an awkward silence.

When I spot Denise's pink hair and bandaged head, I give her a wave. She's sitting up in bed and looking a whole lot better.

Her face cracks into a broad smile when she sees me. 'Phoebe! Thanks for coming.'

'How are you feeling?'

'I've still got the mother of all headaches, but apart from that I'm okay. I wish they'd let me go though. What're they keeping me here for?'

I explain that because she's had concussion, they need to keep her under observation for 24 hours.

She pulls a face. 'I won't need to spend another night here, will I?'

''Fraid so. If everything's okay the doctor will

discharge you in the morning.'

'Fucking hell. Does that mean they'll be waking me up all night again to shine a light in my eyes? Honestly, I'm sure I'm well enough to go home.'

'It's for your own good,' I remind her, in the same calming tone of voice I use on patients when they're threatening to discharge themselves.

She pouts sulkily, looking unconvinced, so I hand over the freesias to cheer her up. 'I'll get you a water jug to put them in.'

Denise stops me before I can head off to the kitchen: 'It's very kind of you, but I wouldn't bother with a jug,' she says, taking the flowers from their wrapping. Half the stems have snapped, and the blooms are all crushed. It must have happened on the bus.

The ruined bouquet seems symbolic of the fact that everything in my life is falling apart around me, and I feel like crying again. I start apologising for the flowers, but I'm not making much sense and Denise says *it's okay* and *it's the thought that counts* and *come here* so that she can give me a hug.

She's got a fearsomely tight grip — clearly the blow to her head hasn't damaged her motor function — and by the time she releases me, I've calmed down a bit.

She launches into a minute-by-minute account of the terrible night she's just had, and I sneak a surreptitious glance behind me to the bed in the bay where I encountered Nisha last night.

She's still here. The bruises on her face are visible even at this distance. She must really have had a battering.

'Oh my God!' Denise shrieks, gripping the sheets and sitting up.

'What?' I look round in alarm.

'Bernard! My baby! I'd completely forgotten about him. He's not been fed since yesterday morning. He'll be starving!'

I haven't broken the bad news to her yet. I should tell her, but one look at the anxious creases on her face, and I chicken out. Which is pathetic really. Part of my job is having to talk to people whose loved one is dying, and yet I can't face telling Denise about her cat. I convince myself that in her present condition it's best not to put her under unnecessary additional stress. So instead I say: 'You don't need to worry about him.'

'He'll be hungry —'

'He won't be hungry, believe me,' I say evasively.

'You've fed him?'

I purse my lips before replying, unable to look Denise in the eye. I'm hopeless at lying, and one lie always leads to another.

'He's been fed,' I say, but refrain from adding: *to a fox*.

'Is he okay?'

'The last time I saw him he was lying down in the front garden.' Well, it's the truth.

'That's a relief!' Denise pats my arm and I force a guilty smile, pretending to be distracted by some lint on the bedsheets.

I steal another glance round at Nisha. She's got a visitor with her now: a guy in a blue polo shirt, holding her hand and leaning close to whisper something in her ear.

My heart skips a beat. Alfie? It has to be. But before I can get a proper look at him, Nisha spots me and scowls. I quickly turn away in a panic. Surely it's only a matter of time before Alfie spots me too.

I take a deep breath and tell myself to start thinking rationally. What can he do to me here? And anyway, maybe it isn't him? I shouldn't keep jumping to rash conclusions.

'Denise, d'you see the guy in the blue shirt behind me?'

She starts craning her neck to get a better look, and I have to tug at her sleeve and hiss: 'Don't let him see you looking!'

'Okay, okay.' She lets her gaze slide slowly from my face. 'You mean the guy sitting with the girl in bandages?'

'Yes.'

'Who is he? Someone you know?'

'I think it might be Alfie.'

Denise pulls a sour face. '*That* Alfie?'

'Maybe. I don't want him to see me. Can you describe him for me?'

'Okay. He's white. He's got brown hair. A short beard. Good looking, well-dressed. He obviously works out. Probably spends too much time in front of the mirror.'

I check off each point against my mental database of known Alfie facts. Tick. Tick. Tick. And tick.

'Does he have any tattoos?'

'Yes. One arm's covered with them.'

It's Alfie! I'm sure of it. But before I can ask *which arm*, Denise tenses up, and with excitement in her eyes exclaims: 'He's getting up! He's coming over.'

I look round. Alfie's striding across the ward towards us, a black jacket slung over his shoulder.

'I've gotta go! I'll ring you,' I say, scurrying off towards the emergency exit at the end of Denise's bay, which is used by staff to access the lift that takes you down into A&E.

I'm in luck: the lift's here and the door is open. I jump inside and press the button for the ground floor, jabbing at it frantically even though I know it won't make the doors close any quicker, and muttering *c'mon, c'mon, c'mon.*

Alfie bursts through the double-doors and marches purposefully across the lobby towards me, his expressionless face as fearsome as The Terminator's.

But he's too late! The lift doors are already closing. They snap shut, the lift starts to move, and I slump back and let out a huge sigh of relief.

Chapter 38

MY RELIEF QUICKLY turns to confusion when I realise that the lift's carrying me up, not down, and I start to freak out all over again. It doesn't make sense: the only thing beyond the 5th floor is the helipad up on the roof, but you need a special key to take the lift up there. And if an air ambulance was on its way, the alarms would all be going off and the emergency team would be rushing up to meet it.

The lift stops at the 7th floor, the doors open, and I step out into the glass lobby. I was half-expecting to see porters and emergency medical teams, but there's nobody around, and it's eerily quiet. Too quiet. I feel uneasy. I'm not supposed to be up here.

I cup my face against the glass and peer out into the night sky. I've only been up here once before, on my induction day. It was gloriously sunny and the views across London were amazing. You could see the Gherkin, the Shard, and the Walkie-Talkie building in the distance, but it's pitch black out there now, and lashing it down so much that I can barely make out the metal rampway that leads up to the heliport. Perhaps all the heavy rain has caused the lift to malfunction?

There's a metallic creaking and a clunk behind me: the lift doors are closing. My first instinct is to hop back in, but what if Alfie summoned it? It will take me down to the 5th floor, the doors will open, and he'll be waiting for me. It's too risky. I'll have to take the stairs. I open the door to the stairwell, but freeze in my tracks when I hear the echo of heavy footsteps. He's on his way up!

I rush back to the lift, but it's already left. There's nowhere in the lobby for me to hide. Alfie will be here any moment, and I'll be trapped. I've no choice — I force open the big double glass doors and run outside into the rain.

I'm immediately buffeted by a huge gust of wind which would have blown me right off the building and into the netting below if I hadn't been holding onto the railing. But I fear that Alfie will spot me if I wait by the doors, so I'm forced to set off into the blackness.

As I make my way up the steep, wet, switch-back rampways, the wind behind me howls like a wounded animal, blowing into me with such power that I'm driven to my knees. Something behind me catches my attention and I squint my eyes to peer back through the heavy sheets of rain. A dark shape is coming up the ramp. It's Alfie! He's waving his arms and shouting, but I can't hear what he's saying because of the wind. I press on.

When I finally reach the helipad at the top, I have to stop because there's nowhere left to run. I stand on the white H in the middle of the exposed platform, bracing my legs against the fierce wind. The lights of the city twinkle bleakly through the darkness on all sides and I've never been so terrified in all my life.

Alfie's stopped running now. He doesn't have to because I'm trapped here. He casually ambles across the helipad towards me, water dripping off his face, his hair plastered to his head.

'Aren't you scared out here?' he shouts when I'm within earshot, raising his voice to be heard above the wailing wind. 'I thought you hated heights?'

The revulsion I feel for him is far stronger than any fear of heights, and I stare back at him with defiance, determined not to let him hurt me again.

'Don't worry, you're safe now. *I'm* here.'

He tries to take my hand, but I duck away, pivoting round on my left foot, and swinging my right leg up to deliver a powerful jabbing kick right in the centre of his chest.

He wasn't expecting that. He staggers backwards with his eyebrows raised in surprise. 'Nice move! Did you learn that in your kick-boxing class? I don't know why you have to be so aggressive towards me. I only want to speak to you.'

He thinks he can talk his way back into my life, make me think everything's okay, that it's all been in my head. But I'm wise to him now. His mask has slipped, and I see him for what he is: a silver-tongued feral animal.

A sweeping light suddenly pierces the darkness of the sky, and I can hear the distant thwup-thwup thrum of the HEMS helicopter, growing louder as it approaches: the air ambulance is on its way.

Alfie turns and stares, as if mesmerised by the light as it rakes the roofs of the buildings all around. I see my opportunity to escape. I scurry across the helipad and am running back down the ramp before he's even noticed.

Although I've -got a head start, I know he's much quicker than me, but I push on, fear and adrenaline powering the muscles of my legs. The driving rain stings my cheeks, but I tell myself not to give up. Almost there. Not much further to go now.

I grab the railing and make the 180 degrees turn onto the final section of rampway. I can see Alfie above me now, racing down in the opposite direction, his mouth twisted with exertion and his eyes shining with pleasure.

He makes the turn, and now he's behind me once again. His thudding footsteps on the metal are getting closer and closer, but I can't run any faster than this. Out of the corner of my eye I see him reach out to take hold of my arm. I think it's all over.

But suddenly he loses his footing and falls. I don't stop to look round. I sprint on down the ramp, charge inside the building, slam the double doors shut behind me and slide the bolt.

Chapter 39

FUCKING BITCH HAS locked the door! I give it a really hard punch out of frustration, but the glass just flexes a little and my fist bounces right back off. Fuck it! I can't believe I slipped and let her get away. So now I'm stuck out here in the rain, on the roof of a fucking hospital, and I suppose I've got to wait until that fucking helicopter arrives before the door's unlocked and I can get back inside. How mental is that? And on top of all that, the hand I punched the door with is beginning to hurt like fuck.

But I'm not gonna let it get to me. Seeing as I'm trapped out here, I may as well go and watch the helicopter land. It'll be interesting.

I stop near the top of the ramp and peer out over the edge. The swirling wind tugs at my jacket and sharp prickles of icy cold rain stab at my cheeks. As the throbbing growl of the approaching helicopter grows louder, a delicious tingle of excitement travels from the tips of my fingers up the nape of my neck.

I close my eyes and stretch out my arms as though I'm Jesus Christ on the cross. Or Leonardo DiCaprio in *Titanic.* Or I'm a fucking super-hero in a cape about to swoop down to rescue a heroine from certain death.

Except in this story, I'm the super-villain, not the hero. I wonder what my super-power should be. It's a difficult decision because I've got so many qualities to choose from. Charm? Good looks? An unshakeable sense of my own self-worth? The ability to lie with a straight face? Modesty?

The helicopter suddenly sweeps down from nowhere, its rotor blades buffeting me with icy blasts of air. My nostrils become overwhelmed by the smell of diesel and the noise is so painfully loud that it feels like my ears are being scoured out with balls of wire wool.

All my senses are firing at once. I'm a flickering flame of raw being. It's as if nothing exists in this world except me. The only thing that matters is what *I* think. What *I* want. What I *do*. I feel an exquisite sense of freedom.

They tell you it's wrong to be selfish, but the truth that everyone is too scared to admit, is that selflessness and altruism *always* makes people unhappy. Parents who stay together for the sake of their children? It makes them miserable and it's a sure fire way of screwing up their kids. Or what about nurses? Slaving away in a broken-down health service for rubbish pay, rubbish hours, and a rubbish quality of life, out of some misguided sense of duty? What a fucking waste of time.

Bracing myself against the downward force of the helicopter, with my arms outstretched, I savour my freedom. I'm a slave to nothing and to no-one. I jut my chin out into the wind and, at the top of my voice, shout: '*I'm the king of the fucking world*!'

The thwopping sound of the helicopter's blades suddenly drops an octave. When I turn round I find that it's landed, and an orange jump-suited crew has already got out and is wheeling a patient on a stretcher down the ramp. They're so absorbed in their business of saving lives that they haven't noticed me yet. When they reach me, I adopt a tone of authority and direct them down the slope, telling them: *this way*.

They don't bat an eyelid. They've no time to stop and wonder what a guy in civilian clothes, drenched to the skin, is doing out here on the roof. It just proves that you can blag your way out of anything if you've got enough confidence and don't give a fuck about the consequences if you're caught.

I follow them through the doors into the lobby, where a crowd of porters and nurses are waiting to take the patient down in the lift. I casually slip past and take the stairs to the ground floor, then nonchalantly stroll through the A&E department and leave via the main entrance.

I don't have to wait long for the Uber, but by the time it comes, and I'm sat in the back in my wet clothes making a damp patch on the seat, the thrill of excitement I felt on the roof has completely evaporated.

For a few moments up there, I felt invincible! It was like an electric current was flowing through my veins. My whole body burned brightly, like the filament of a light bulb. But unfortunately that delicious feeling of being alive never lasts long with me. As soon as the current is switched off, the filament stops glowing and the light inside me goes out. All I feel now is a muddy sort of irritation at the fact that Phoebe managed to escape me so easily. These trainers sell for three hundred quid, so you'd think for that kind of money they ought to be able to cope with a bit of fucking rain.

I scoot across the seat and position myself behind the driver so he can't see me take a baggie out of my pocket and chop a little line of coke to try and get back my high.

I snort the powder and lick my fingers clean, savouring the buzz as it numbs my tongue and hits the back of my throat. But it's a scuzzy sort of artificial high, lacking the purity and clarity of a real, lived experience.

I take out my phone to check the surveillance cameras I installed in Phoebe's flat. I wasn't really expecting her to be home yet, but there she is already, at the top of the stairs. How the fuck did she get back so quick? She heads for the bedroom, and I switch cameras to watch her changing out of her soggy clothes.

Her wet jeans are clinging to her legs, and she has to

sit on the bed to tug them off. Next, she crosses her arms, grabs the hem of her top, pulls it over her head, and I'm instantly hard. I slip my hand inside my jeans. Even though this is like the mildest porn you'd ever see, every part of me is throbbing with anticipation because this is real, not faked, and she has no idea she's being spied on.

She reaches behind her back to undo her bra, and I unzip my flies. But just as I'm about to whip out my cock, the picture stutters, freezes for a moment as it buffers, and then cuts out completely.

Fuck it! Just as it was getting good! I try reconnecting but it's no use. It's that shitty knock-off gear I got from the guy I met in the pub. I can connect to the camera in the kitchen, and even to the new little one I installed in the hallway, but that's fuck all use when all the good action's happening in the bedroom.

Although it's not a long journey, the traffic's pretty heavy because of the wet weather, and by the time we're pulling up outside Phoebe's house on Laithwaite Road, I worry that the show will be over.

I keep my head down as I scurry up the path to the front door of the house opposite Phoebe's. It was a stroke of good luck finding this place. It couldn't have been closer, and the front garden's so overgrown that no-one can see me coming and going.

I go round the back, climb in through the broken window, pass along the narrow hallway and head upstairs. It's bloody freezing in the house and the smell of damp's getting worse because the gas and electricity's been off for months and there's no heating apart from the three-bar electric fire I've got running in the front bedroom. I managed to hook it up to next-door's electricity, and I leave it on constantly so at least one room's always nice and toasty. I've actually made it quite cosy and homely in there now. I've got a decent mattress on the floor, a table and chair set I found in the garden shed, a TV I nicked from a house up the road, and the microwave and kettle I took from Nisha's.

I strip out of my wet clothes and drape them over the back of the chair to dry off in front of the fire. Then I grab my binoculars and go over to the window.

It always takes me a while to locate Phoebe's room because everything's so magnified. First I'm looking at the roof, then I'm looking at the garden — a full-on close-up of those bastard gnomes that I daubed in sacrificial blood and then had to scrub clean again — and then my gaze travels up the side of the building until I finally lock in on the ill-fitting curtains in Phoebe's window. From this angle I can see right into the whole bedroom.

And just on cue, there she is, slinking across the room with a hairdryer in her hand, her naked shoulders glowing damply in the soft light. She's got a towel wrapped turban-style around her head, and another wrapped tightly around her middle, and I can see the tops of her breasts. She looks beautiful.

She sits on the edge of her bed with an absorbed, abstracted expression on her face as she rubs her hair with the towel, oblivious to the fact that she's being watched from across the street.

I start to recover that buzz of excitement that I couldn't get from the coke. It's not just sexual, it's the feeling of control and power over another person that thrills me. I can't help smiling. I wonder how long I can keep this going — the accent, the fake Facebook profile, all the hair gel I'm slapping on. She hasn't got a fucking clue about her helpful neighbour Robbie. Sometimes I almost feel sorry for her.

I don't feel sorry for Denise though, nosy bitch. I didn't plan for her to get hurt, but it's her own fault, snooping around like that. Luckily it was dark, and I don't think she got a proper look at me. If she had, there's a chance she might have recognised me because she already caught me loitering outside the flat once before. I'd just finished repositioning Phoebe's stupid tennis ball in the hallway and was carefully shutting the front door when Denise popped her fat head out to see what was going on. I pretended I was a Polish delivery driver, looking for a non-existent address.

It's almost insulting to me that Phoebe thought she'd be able to catch me using a tennis ball. It's so retro, so low-tech, compared with the spyware I've installed on her phone and the spy cams that are fixed all round her house.

The only fly in the ointment is that bastard Tom, but hopefully that relationship's been knocked into touch now. Planting that *Guess Who?* card on him was a fuckin' stroke of genius. I had to think quickly when the opportunity presented itself outside the coffee shop, and I couldn't have wished for it to work out better. The look of horror on Phoebe's face when the card flipped out of his pocket and onto the floor was priceless.

I don't think she'll be wanting to see any more of the lovely Tom, which means that the path's clear for Robbie to make his move. Last night was the last time I'm going to let her mug me off. Next time I'm not gonna accept no for an answer.

Chapter 40

I SIT ON the bed and let the warm air from the hairdryer blow into my face. I'm still in a state of shock, unable to get over seeing the look in Alfie's eyes up there on the roof. I think he was quite capable of killing me.

And this is the man I was in love with? How come I didn't see anything before, when apparently it was really obvious to everyone else that he was rotten to the core? Though I did see it. I saw lots of signs. I just ignored them. Like the fact that he was constantly sponging off me. Like the fact that he was never able to arrive anywhere on time. Like the fact that he'd disappear off into radio silence and I wouldn't hear from him for days on end. Like the fact he constantly criticised my appearance, telling me that my outfits didn't suit me, that I had a rubbish dress-sense and needed to go on a diet. Why didn't I listen to my gut instincts?

I switch off the hairdryer, take off my towel and stand naked in front of the mirror. I might not be able to recognise my face, but my body is all too familiar to me. I try to study myself dispassionately, as a stranger might, examining the pale, silvery-white flesh with all its bumps, hollows and little dimples. I place my hand on my tummy and suck it in. It's not that bad a body, is it? I'm sure there are thousands of women out there with less shapely legs, less toned arms, saggier buttocks and flabbier bellies. So why was he always telling me I could do with losing a few pounds?

The only thing he really seemed to like about my body was my breasts. They fascinated him. He'd prod and poke and grab at them as if they weren't actually a part of me, and when I got annoyed with all the unwanted attention, he'd tell me I should feel flattered.

I rummage around in the drawer for underwear. I've got skimpy little thongs in every colour you could imagine, but since splitting up with Alfie I've stopped wearing them, finally admitting to myself that not only are they really uncomfortable, but unless you've got a pert, toned, size 6 bottom, they're just going to make your bum cheeks look flabby. From right at the back of the drawer I fish out the biggest, comfiest, most Bridget Jonesiest pair of knickers I own. They're so old I don't even remember buying them. Alfie definitely wouldn't approve, and even though we broke up months ago, it still feels kind of subversive to be putting them on. Like I still need his approval for everything I do.

I keep catching myself doing this. It's like he's watching and judging me over every little decision I make. How long will it take to shake free of this feeling?

I shudder to think of all those months I spent as one of *those* women. The sort you meet from time to time who seem perfectly intelligent, with a good job, a nice flat, a person who in every other respect seems to have everything going for them — and then you meet the boyfriend or girlfriend who treats them like crap. I never could understand why anyone would stay in that kind of relationship. Well, now I know.

When we first started going out I believed Alfie was the kindest, most considerate man I'd ever dated. It was really hard shaking this notion, no matter how shitty his behaviour became. When he wasn't being nice to me, I'd tell myself well, no-one's perfect, no-one scores a ten out of ten, and if he's scoring a six or a seven, then I should count myself lucky. I kept telling myself *maybe he'll change.*

Deep down though, I think my problem has been that I didn't feel worthy of being loved by someone who treated me decently. It's most likely all tied up with the rejection I felt after Mum and Suzi moved out. But now that I understand the reasons why Mum had to leave, perhaps the burden of worthlessness, which I've been unconsciously carrying around, will be lifted? For the first time in eighteen years can I finally let myself believe I'm worth something? That I was loved? That I'm worthy of love?

I get dressed and finish drying my hair, letting the high-pitched whining of the motor drown out my thoughts. But then my twisty little brain makes a connection between the sound of the hairdryer and the roar of the helicopter. In an instant my head's flooded with memories of my encounter with Alfie on the roof.

One little memory in particular stays in my mind like a lump of grit caught in a sieve. At first I don't know why I keep coming back to it and then all at once I realise what's bothering me. After the roundhouse kick I did on Alfie, he said *nice move, did you learn that in kick-boxing?* But I only started kick-boxing classes *after* I moved to Clapham. And apart from Suzi and Denise, the only people I've told are Robbie and Tom. Which proves that Alfie has definitely managed to inveigle himself back into my life.

My stomach makes a sickening leap into my chest at the realisation I've been duped. But which one of them is it?

Robbie? Witty, confident, helpful and kind. Who somehow keeps turning up to offer help to a damsel in distress just when I need it. Who had blood all up his arm last night which he claimed was just from clearing up all the mess.

Or Tom? Charming, gauche, funny and sincere. Who keeps randomly bumping into me at the coffee shop. Who had a *Guess Who?* card in his pocket which he denied knowing anything about.

My head says it must be Tom because I can't see why else that *Guess Who?* card would be in his possession, but my gut instinct tells me I can trust him. So it must be Robbie, right? But he was already living across the road when I moved in, wasn't he?

Then in a facepalm-worthy moment of clarity, I realise that Denise didn't have the chance to tell me which arm Alfie's tattoos were on before he spotted me and chased me up to the roof. My hands tremble with anticipation as I ring her number.

'Hello?' she drawls wearily.

'Hi, it's me, Phoebe.'

'What? Is that Phoebe?'

'Yes!' I take a breath to try and calm my voice. 'Sorry, were you asleep?'

'I wish! I've been lying here, wide awake.'

'How are you feeling?'

'Bored. I can't wait to get home and crack open a bottle of wine. Are you just ringing for a chat, or did you want something?'

'Actually I've got a really quick question I need to ask you.'

'Okey dokey, fire away.'

'You remember when I spotted Alfie in the ward earlier?'

'Oh my God, I'd completely forgotten. I think the pain killers have made me a bit spacey. What happened? Did he catch up with you?'

'No, I managed to give him the slip. Listen, you know you told me that Alfie had a sleeve of tattoos on one of his arms?'

'Yes.'

'I need to know which arm it was.'

'Erm, let me think. The right arm?'

'The right arm? Are you sure?'

'I think so.'

'Please Denise, it's important. It was the right arm?'

'Yes. Definitely the right.'

So, it's Robbie. My eyes flash to the window and I examine the building opposite with a newly-formed sense of fear. But it doesn't make sense. Would Alfie really have gone to the trouble of renting a house just to be near me?

'Denise, do you know the guy who lives in the house directly opposite us?'

'That big derelict house?' She sounds surprised. 'No-one lives there. It's empty.'

I feel like I've been doused with icy water. 'Empty?'

'It's been empty for months.'

So, that confirms it. A grinding sense of dread descends, and I experience that vertiginous feeling which comes with cognition, as all my memories of Robbie flash through my brain and are reclassified. Not Robbie. Alfie.

I tell Denise I have to go.

The foreboding building across the street seems empty at first, until I notice a dim orangey glow coming from one of the first-floor rooms. I press my nose up against the glass and as my eyes adjust to the darkness, I'm able to make out a figure standing at the window — a figure that is staring back at me through a pair of binoculars.

Sudden panic tears through my system and an involuntary gasp is forced from my lips. I duck down and crouch under the window, my legs trembling, my skin slick with anxiety.

Alfie's watching me. He's been spying on me all along, preying on my fears, conveniently on hand to help clear up the mess he created. Oh God, he was in here last night. Anything could have happened.

Fear paralyses me. I can't get to the door without being spotted. My only hope is to make a break for it when he gets bored of spying on me.

One minute. Five minutes. Ten minutes. I don't know how long I've been crouching here, but finally my curiosity becomes too much. With my heart thumping in my chest, I grip hold of the windowsill with my fingertips and slowly pull myself up.

He's still there! A dark shape by the window, dimly illuminated by a gentle orange light. At first I think he hasn't noticed me peeping out, but then he raises his arm and waves.

I drop back to the floor in panic and cower beside the skirting board. A clammy shudder passes down my spine. What now?

Bzzzzz Bzzzzzz

I'm shaken out of my trance by a loud noise coming from the other side of the room.

Bzzzzz Bzzzzzz

It's my mobile, vibrating away like mad on the bedside table. My eyes widen in fear. Is Alfie ringing to taunt me?

Bzzzzz Bzzzzzz

The phone is insistent, like an angry wasp trying to escape from an upturned glass, and I wish it would stop. I can't stand it! Why won't it go to voicemail?

Bzzzzz Bzzzzzz

I've had enough. I crawl over on my hands and knees to reject the call, but the phone slips out of my sweaty fingers and falls onto the carpet. A muffled voice is speaking: 'Hello?'

It's a woman. I pick up the phone gingerly, as if clearing up fragments of broken glass, and say a tentative 'Hello?'

'Phoebs, it's me.'

I almost cry with relief at the familiar sound of Suzi's voice. 'Suzi! Thank God it's you. I'm in trouble. I need your help.'

'Hold on a sec —'

'Hello?'

'That's better. I'm in the car and the line was bad. Can you hear me okay now? What were you saying?'

My words come out in a jumble as I explain about Robbie and Alfie and how he's living across the street from me and spying on my house and now I'm frightened to death. She listens patiently, and then tells me that everything's going to be all right. She tells me I'm not to do anything rash, and that she's turning the car around and will be with me in twenty minutes.

Emboldened by our conversation, I'm able to crawl across to the opposite side of the room. I reach up, switch off the light, and scuttle out of the bedroom to wait in the lounge for Suzi to arrive.

Chapter 41

I KEEP GLANCING towards the door, fretfully wondering where Suzi's got to. Surely she should be here by now? She said twenty minutes and that was half an hour ago.

After another five minutes my phone gives a short buzz. It's a message:

Phoebe, I'm stuck in traffic. There's an accident and the road's closed. Don't know when we'll be moving again, but hopefully not too long. Sorry :(Love Sz xxx

My anxiety levels start to rise. I pick up a teaspoon from the draining board and tap it nervously on the countertop. After another five minutes I receive another text:

Traffic still not moving. Will look for an alternative route. Sorry. I'll be as quick as I can. Sz xxx.

My anxiety levels crank up another notch. I can't bear the uncertainty of not knowing when she'll arrive. She could be trapped in the traffic jam for hours. I throw the teaspoon into the washing-up bowl and begin pacing the flat like a caged animal. First I check the front door, then I march back through the hall to the kitchen and rattle on the back door handle, averting my eyes from the bedroom each time as I pass. I'm not sure how much more of this I can take. In desperation I call Tom.

'Phoebe?'

At the sound of his placid, sober voice I blurt it all out.

'Calm down and take a breath,' he tells me when I've finished. 'Are you safe at the moment?'

'Yes. But I don't know what to do — I'm scared!'

'Don't panic, it'll be all right. I'll be right over.'

'How long?'

'Give me ten minutes. Just don't open the door to anyone else.'

'How will I know it's you?'

'Won't you recognise me?'

'I need some kind of signal.'

There's a pause and then he suggests: 'I could hum you a few bars from *The Barber of Seville* if you like?'

I go downstairs and wait for Tom by the front door, chewing nervously on my thumbnail, my ears pricking at every little sound. Finally I hear footsteps, and the bell rings.

I place my head to the door and in a tentative voice call, 'Hello?'

'Phoebe, it's Tom.'

'Yes?' I'm not going to open the door until I'm absolutely certain.

'Hang on a moment while I catch my breath. Okay — hmmm.'

At the first sound of humming I slide the door-chain and fling the door open. Tom's standing in the rain, his hair plastered to his scalp, a look of consternation on his face. 'I got here as fast as I could,' he says, panting heavily.

I usher him in wordlessly, casting a nervous glance to the house across the street.

'You okay?' he asks.

I nod, still unable to speak.

'It's gonna be all right,' he tells me, 'but I really think you should go to the police.'

I start to protest but the determined expression on his face stops me short. Perhaps the only way to end this nightmare is to involve the police, even if it means having to tell them about *that* night.

I agree to go with him to the police station straight

away and we head up to the flat to get my coat. I ask him to fetch it from the bedroom for me, because I'm too scared to go in there. He opens the door and reaches for the light switch, and although I shout *no!* I'm too late. The naked bulb flashes on and the room's lit up like a Christmas tree.

'He'll see you!' I shout, quickly switching off the light.

Tom apologises sheepishly and goes over to spy through the gap in the curtains. 'Which house is it?'

'Directly opposite. The window on the first floor with the faint orangey light.'

'I can't see anyone.'

I join him at the window but can't see anything either. Is Alfie still lurking there in the shadows? Maybe he's gone out? Or did I just imagine it all?

'He was there earlier,' I protest. 'Honestly.'

'Quick! Someone's coming!' Tom barks, jerking his head back.

A man's striding up the path. I pull away from the window when he glances up, but I'm pretty certain he saw me.

The doorbell goes. It's Alfie.

The bell sounds again, and when no-one comes, he starts thumping on the door with such violence that the windows rattle in their frames.

I grab Tom's arm.

'Don't worry, I won't let anything happen to you.' He tries to sound convincing, but the hammering on the door's becoming increasingly frenetic.

'I'm frightened!'

'Is there another way out of the building?'

'There's the fire escape.'

We hurry to the kitchen, through the back door and out onto the fire-escape. It's still raining and our feet clank on the wet metal steps as we descend into the darkness. Then we're splashing through muddy puddles along the little alley at the back of the houses, emerging on the corner of Laithwaite Road.

I glance back and spot Alfie coming out of the front garden onto the street. He sees us and starts running in our direction. A sinking inevitability bears down on me, rooting me to the spot, and Tom has to grab my hand and give me a tug to snap me out of my despondent trance.

We set off for the police station at Lavender Hill. Although we had a good head start on him, Alfie's slowly gaining ground. I can tell that Tom's keeping himself in check, but I'm running as fast as I can and I'm already breathless.

The pavements are deserted because no-one else is foolhardy enough to venture out in this rain, but the roads are really busy. Cars blare along the street beside us, pluming through the surface water, making us drenched.

'Don't keep turning around,' Tom tells me, so I keep my head down and focus on my feet as we splash through the puddles. I try to ignore the complaints from my aching legs and keep running, with my eyes half-closed against the rain, like a sleepwalker moving through treacle. I'm soaked to the skin, I've got a stitch in my side, my breasts are hurting, and my sodden shoes are rubbing my feet raw.

'Are we nearly there?' I pant, in a hoarse, wheezy voice. 'I don't know how much longer — I can — keep — going.'

'This way!' Tom shouts, making a sudden right-turn between two tall buildings. We pass along a narrow, shadowy passageway, and when we come shooting out at the other end I give a gasp of surprise: rearing up out of the darkness ahead of us, as though a giant pool table had fallen out of the sky and landed right in our path, is a red-brick, Art Deco monolith, with an elegantly-turned white chimney at each corner: Battersea Power Station.

It's a dead end. There's construction work on the land all around the power station, and everything's boarded up. The road ahead is blocked by gates locked with thick chains and heavy padlocks, and there's prison-grade barbed wire along the top of the fence.

'What now?' I ask in dismay. If Alfie has spotted us slip through the alleyway, we'll be trapped here like rats in a drainpipe.

'I know a short cut,' Tom says crouching by the fence and prising one of the boards loose to create a gap that's just wide enough for us to squeeze through.

Chapter 42

THE BUILDING SITE is much larger than I imagined. Towering, half-completed glass-fronted blocks of flats gleam with menace. Giant cranes strung with red and white lights shoot up out of the blackness. Desolate mounds of earth have been gouged out of the ground, leaving murky, rain-filled pits dotted all around. Tom weaves a zig-zag path around the heaps of rubble, skirting the harsh shadows cast by the floodlights on the perimeter fence. I can't shake the impression that we're crossing a stage set used for faking the lunar landings or something.

We seem to be heading towards the derelict-looking building at the centre of the site, which is constructed in the same monolithic Art Deco style as the power station. When we reach it, we head up a broad metal rampway which leads to a cavernous, open-fronted entrance hall. A safety light in the ceiling gives off a weak, sickly-red glow that's just bright enough to make out the heaps of sandbags covered with blue tarpaulins that are scattered around the room. In the far corner there's a large rusting metal door, which looks as if it hasn't been opened in years.

'Let's rest here,' Tom says, slumping exhaustedly onto a pile of sandbags.

'Aren't we going to the police?'

He gives a weary smile. 'There's no hurry. No-one's going to find us here.'

I feel my ears prick at his words. It's the same feeling you get when a musician hits a wrong note, even if they're playing a piece of music you've never heard before.

Something he just said seems a little off, and I study his face in the dim red light for a couple of moments before realising what it was:

'No-one?' I ask with trepidation.

He smiles indulgently at my misreading. '*Alfie* won't find us here. We're safe and it's dry. I don't know about you, but I'm soaked!'

He takes off his jacket and begins rolling up the sleeves of his jumper, exposing the head of a serpent on the underside of his wrist — the underside of the wrist of his right hand!

It's Alfie!

The tattoo snakes up his forearm, encircles his elbow, and disappears into the bunched up wet sleeve of his jumper. The blood rushes from my head and I'm gripped by such an intense sense of fear that my legs buckle, and I stagger back onto a sandbag.

'You alreet?' Alfie asks in a Geordie accent which no longer sounds convincing.

I tear my eyes from his tattoos so he won't notice I'm staring, and force myself to look up into his face, faking a smile. Everything seems to come into sharp focus. A moment ago, when I thought I was with Tom, I felt safe, protected and secure. Now I've never felt more afraid.

The phone in my pocket starts buzzing. Probably Suzi or Tom — the real Tom — ringing to find out where I am. But I can't risk Alfie hearing, so I double over and pretend to have a coughing fit to drown out the noise.

He's watching me with his best Tom-appearing-to-be-concerned smile, but it's just an act. It's always been an act with him. Well, two can play at that game. By the time my phone's stopped buzzing, I've come up with a plan.

I thump my chest and cough a couple of times, pretending to clear my throat, and then in a clear voice say:

'Tom?'

There's a slight hesitation before he looks up and says, 'Yes?'

'I've lost my phone!' I whine, screwing up my face in dismay. 'I think it must have fallen out of my pocket by the fence where we came in.'

As I make my way towards the ramp, in a calm voice I tell him: 'I'm just going to look for it. I won't be long.'

'Hang on!' Alfie shouts in a sharp, not-very-Tom-like tone, grabbing his jacket and jumping to his feet. 'I'll come with you.' And then, after composing his features into a more sympathetic expression of concern, he adds: 'It's not safe for you to be out there on your own. We might have been followed.'

He's obviously never going to let me wander off alone, so I try a different tack: 'Oh God, you're right!' I exclaim with a shudder, hoping I'm not laying it on too thickly. 'Could you go and look for me?'

Annoyance flickers across his features. 'It could be anywhere!'

'Please!'

'I think it would be a waste of time.'

'Please Tom! Don't you remember telling me yesterday that you'd do anything for me?'

'Yes,' Alfie replies uncertainly, uncomfortable at being backed into a corner.

'Then surely you'd have a look for my phone?'

'Okay, I'll go,' he agrees with a reluctant sigh. 'But you have to promise that you'll wait here where it's safe. Promise?'

I tell him *I promise* and watch him pull on his damp jacket and set out into the rain.

He won't bother looking for my phone, of course. He'll make a pretence of hunting around in the darkness for a little while before returning empty handed. But a little while will hopefully be long enough for me to phone for help.

Tom's phone goes through to voicemail, but Suzi answers straight away:

'Phoebe? I'm at the flat. Where are you?' Her voice sounds anxious, breathless.

'In the building site next to Battersea Power Station.'

'Battersea Power Station?'

'Suzi, you have to listen because I don't have long. I'm with Alfie.'

'Alfie?'

'I can't explain now. The thing is, I think he may turn violent. Can you call the police?'

'Okay, but how will they find you?'

I give her directions and a rough description of the building, but have to break off before I can tell her anything more because I can hear footsteps clanging up the ramp.

Alfie's feigned expression of empty-handed regret quickly sours when he spots me trying to stuff my phone away into the pocket of my wet jeans.

'I found it!' I say, holding it up triumphantly.

'Who were you talking to?' he demands, coming towards me.

'It was only my sister' I say, wondering how much of the conversation he heard.

'You phoned for a cosy little chat?'

I shrug as casually as I'm able.

'Did you tell her where you are?'

'No — Tom.'

The word *Tom* sounds forced and unnatural, like the dull chime of a cracked bell, and I wince as soon as the word's out of my mouth.

He examines me suspiciously. Does he suspect that I know his real identity? I flash him a little smile. I only need to tough this out long enough for the police to arrive. But before I can put my phone away it gives a buzz and flashes on, lighting up the whole room. The words *Tom CoffeeShop* appear on the screen.

An oily chill runs down my spine: Alfie knows for certain now that his subterfuge is exposed. A malevolent scowl spreads across his features. Wordlessly he prises the phone from my fingers, runs over to the entrance, and hurls it out into the darkness. The phone flashes briefly in the beam of a security light, before being swallowed up in the inky maw of the night.

'Well, well. So you've got it all figured out, have you?' he sneers, dropping the Geordie accent. 'Perhaps you aren't as stupid as I thought. So, what do we do now?'

'I've called the police.'

'Really? That's a shame. Why did you want to go and do that?'

His tone is so casual you'd think we might be discussing the weather, but his lips are tightly pursed, his face is ashen with fury, and I know what's coming next.

He raises his hand to strike me, but I'm ready for him. My kick-boxing training kicks in again. I roll with his punch, tipping my head to the side so he barely makes contact and is thrown off balance. He takes a couple of staggering steps, and by the time he's regained his footing, I'm already darting away towards the door at the back of the hall.

I give it a desperate shove, expecting it to be rusted shut, but by some miracle it flies open. I hurry through and slam it shut behind me, fumbling with the stiff bolt while Alfie starts pounding on the other side. I only manage to budge the bolt an inch or two, but hopefully it'll buy me enough time to get away.

When my eyes have adjusted to the darkness, I find myself in a long, low, windowless corridor with a faint light coming from the far end. I start running towards it. I'm about half-way there when the door behind me crashes open. Alfie's footsteps echo behind me, the strange acoustics of the corridor making it impossible to know how close he is.

At the end of the corridor, I reach a broad stairwell. I frantically scurry up the concrete steps, some innate instinct keeping me going upwards, like a forest animal moving to higher ground to escape a flood. There's a door at the top of the stairs, leading to a high-ceilinged room with glossy, milky-green tiles on the wall. The windows are all smashed in, broken glass is strewn across the puddled floor, and thick tree roots have forced their way through cracks in the ceiling.

I hear Alfie's footsteps coming up the stairwell, and I scan the empty room in a panic, but there's nowhere to hide. I'm trapped.

I run over to a window and poke my head out into the rain. The building's crumbling brickwork is covered in scaffolding and supported at its base by thick, rusting, metal props. There's a scaffolding board running just below the window. Perhaps I can hid out there? I gingerly steer my leg over the jagged teeth-like shards of glass that are embedded in the window-frame, and cautiously step outside.

Squally gusts of wind buffet me as I edge my way along the scaffolding board; icy fingers of rain rake my face; and I have to keep ducking to avoid the ropes and pulleys that are whipping around wildly in the gale.

I make it to the far end and start climbing a ladder that's lashed by thick rope to the scaffolding poles. My feet keep slipping on the wet rungs, but I tell myself *keep going, only a little further now, the police are on their way, just don't look down.*

Half-way up I feel something grabbing at my ankle. I peer down in alarm and find Alfie yanking my foot. I kick out desperately, trying to shake free, but he's got too firm a hold. Suddenly I lose my grip and come crashing down, landing in a painful heap at the bottom of the ladder, and he's looming over me with a manic look in his eyes.

Chapter 43

I REACH OUT a hand to help Phoebe to her feet, but she recoils from me and shuffles away on her bottom like a dog with worms. This is becoming tiresome! Why is she so determined to make things difficult? The rage that's been brewing up within me for weeks finally reaches boiling point. Something inside me snaps. An acrid taste fills my mouth and adrenaline pumps like molten metal through my veins. Everything in the periphery of my vision darkens, allowing me a laser-sharp focus on this one fragile thing that cowers on the ground in front of me.

A vivid image of my fingers around her neck comes unbidden to my mind. It's so palpable that I can almost feel the soft skin on her throat stretching and straining as my thumbs dig in and her life ebbs away. A gentle calmness sweeps through my body. I inhale deeply and savour the cold damp air as it enters my lungs. I feel alive again!

Then Phoebe goes and ruins the moment: 'Whatever you're thinking, it's too late. The police will be here any minute.'

The defiance of her words enrages me. I grab her wrists and jerk her to her feet. I twist her arms, pin them behind her back, and march her over to the edge of the scaffolding. I put my mouth close to her ear. 'Are you sure the police are coming? Can you see them?'

When she doesn't reply I yank on her arms, making her squeal in pain, and ask again: 'Can you see them? I don't think they're coming. Perhaps you need a closer look?'

I grab the back of her head and bend her over the

guard rail. I stand behind her, grinding my groin into her buttocks as if we're fucking. 'No-one's going to find us up here,' I hiss.

I lean all my weight against her, sliding my hands to her neck and reaching my fingers around her throat. Her neck is warm and surprisingly small. A feeling of power surges through me. How easy it would be to snuff out her life. She's a baby bird that's fallen from its nest and won't survive on its own. Or a sick puppy that has to be drowned in a sack.

I start squeezing my fingers together until I feel the resistance of the tendons of her neck. The knowledge that it will only take a tiny bit more pressure to extinguish her life is dizzying. Excitement courses through my blood, making my skin tingle as though it's caressed by hot feathers.

She was always trying to buy my affection through expensive gifts, but I can't think of a more precious gift than giving me her life. The last voice she'll ever hear will be mine. I press my lips to her ear, and in a breathy tone ask:

'Do you love me, Phoebe?'

When she doesn't answer, I tighten my grip, as if I might squeeze a response out of her, like I'm squeezing the last of the toothpaste from the tube.

'What's the matter?' I grunt with effort as I dig the tips of my fingers into the tender flesh at her throat. 'Cat got your tongue?'

Chapter 44

I CAN'T SPEAK, I can't breathe, I'm gasping for air and thrashing my legs in a wild panic. But it's no use. I'm too weak and jerking around just makes the searing band of pain around my throat worse.

The floodlit building site below me becomes blurry and seems to be spinning. Then everything turns red. I feel the blood draining away from my head and have the sense that my brain is powering down.

Like a swimmer who's become exhausted after a long struggle against the current, I allow myself to sink down into the turbid depths of this blood red ocean, and the overwhelming feeling of terror is finally displaced by a calm sense of acceptance.

Chapter 45

I FEEL HER body go limp in my hands and release my grip on her throat. She slumps onto the floor. *Is she dead?* I wonder dispassionately, bending over to put my ear to her mouth. I don't think she's breathing, but it's hard to tell with the wind roaring so loudly through the scaffolding.

I'm neither disappointed nor pleased. Alive or dead, it doesn't really matter. The fun is in flipping the coin and marvelling at the laws of physics as it spins through the air, rather than caring whether the coin comes down heads or tails.

But if the police *are* coming, I suppose I'd better finish the job. Can't have her telling them about our fun and games, can we. If I push her over the edge, perhaps it'll look more like an accident. Just picturing her rag-doll body falling through the air and landing with a splat on the concrete below, causes a satisfying glow of pleasure to spread through my system.

I put my hands under her armpits and try lifting her onto the guardrail, but manoeuvring a dead weight is harder than I'd supposed. So I squat down, wrap my arms around her legs, and employing all the power of my thigh muscles I'm eventually able to heave her up.

I stare at her lifeless, jack-knifed body slumped over the metal rail, balancing half-way between life and death, and for some reason I find the sight almost touching.

'Goodbye Phoebe,' I mutter tenderly, crouching down to give her upside-down face a Spider-Man style kiss.

As I ready myself to topple her into the abyss,

something crashes violently into the side of my skull and I'm sent reeling across the planking, staggering unsteadily backwards. The dark sky swings round above me, the wooden scaffolding boards rush up to meet me from below, and just before my head strikes the ground, I see that bastard Tom scowling at me, holding a metal pulley in his hand.

Chapter 46

A VOICE IS speaking, but I can't make out the words because they're all muffled, as though they're floating to my ears through a dense body of water. I kick free from the seaweed that seems to be entangling my legs, and swim upwards towards the voice. The words become clearer as I rise through the water, there's a sudden rushing in my ears, and then I'm bursting through the surface, opening my eyes and gasping for air.

At first I can't make anything out because my vision's blurred and everything's strangely discoloured. But gradually my eyes adjust enough for me to see that someone's leaning over me, calling my name.

The burning pain in my throat makes it hard to catch a steady breath. My neck is sore, my head throbs, my arms and legs are hurting, and I'm so confused that it makes me queasy. Who is this man in the sopping wet jacket with water dripping off his hair, and why is he right in my face?

'Thank God you're alive!' he exclaims, touching my cheek with his cold fingers.

I turn to find that I'm on some kind of scaffolding. It's pouring with rain and so windy that the plastic sheeting above me is billowing like the sails of a yacht. When I try lifting my head I find that I'm too weak and too dizzy. I've no memory of what has happened.

'Where am I?' It hurts when I speak and my voice sounds scratchy and raw, and not like my voice at all.

'Battersea Power Station,' the man tells me.

And suddenly it all starts coming back to me. My

hand flies protectively to my neck and I jerk back with a gasp: 'Alfie!'

The man silently moves aside to reveal a spreadeagled body on the floor behind him.

'Alfie? Is he — is he dead?' I rasp.

'Just unconscious, I think.'

I switch my gaze back to the man standing in front of me, still struggling to get my brain into gear. My mouth is dry and my heart is hammering madly. Is this Tom, my coffee shop guardian angel, materialised out of nowhere to save me? Or is it Alfie playing yet another trick on me.

'How did you find me?' I croak.

'I followed you all the way from your flat, and then lost you when you entered the building site. I'd never have found you again if it wasn't for this —'

He fumbles in his pocket and hands me something. Despite the fact that the screen's cracked and it's all streaked with mud, I recognise my phone.

'It landed on the ground right in front of my feet,' he says.

There's no way Alfie could have got hold of my phone again after hurling it out into the night, which means that this man kneeling before me must be —

'Tom!' I exclaim. A wave of giddiness passes over me as I try to get to my feet.

'Whoa, steady!'

He catches me and steers me over to a stack of planks so I can sit down. 'We need to get you to safety. Are you able to walk?'

'Yes—' I begin, but my reply turns into a horrified shriek of alarm as a figure comes lunging out of the darkness towards us.

Alfie crashes violently into Tom. The momentum makes them stagger together across the scaffold boards, clutching onto each other as if in a grim, drunken embrace, and then they slam into the guard rail with such force that they both topple over the edge.

I rush to the spot where they fell, and peer down through dense sheets of rain into the darkness below. We're so high up here that surely no-one could have survived that fall.

My cheeks are wet with rain and with tears, and I let out an exhausted, despairing sob. The wind howls in response. It's an unearthly, chilling noise which could almost be human. It almost sounds as if someone is calling my name.

'Phoebe!'

I give a start, jerking my head to look around me.

'Phoebe!!'

It's coming from beneath my feet. I get onto my knees to peer down through the gaps between the boards. Two figures are clinging precariously on to opposite ends of a long scaffolding plank which is suspended on a thick rope that's tied around its middle.

They're calling up to me, frantically trying to get my attention. But what can I do? They're trapped beneath the platform I'm standing on, and I can't think of any way of helping them.

Suddenly the rope gives a convulsive spasm, and I watch powerlessly as the plank and the two men holding on to it, drop down — and then, just as suddenly, jerk to a juddering halt.

Although they've only descended a few inches, the plank has begun a slow, unwinding rotation, and it's clear that the fraying rope isn't going to hold much longer. The situation is hopeless.

One of the men is gesticulating at something, and it takes me a moment to realise what he's getting at. Then I realise that the slow circular rotation of the plank is carrying him out beyond the edge of the scaffolding. I might be able to grab hold of him.

I hook my feet around a scaffolding pole, and inch myself out under the guard rail. Silvery trails of rain streak past my face as I reach down as far as I can and wait for the figure clutching onto the end of the plank to slowly circle into view.

When he sees me, he gives a desperate shout and stretches out his arm. But just before our fingers touch, I panic: what if it's Alfie? If I save him first, then Tom and I will both surely be doomed. I snatch my hand away.

'Phoebe!' the man implores, but I'm frozen by indecision, and a few seconds later it's too late to change my mind because he's circled away and carried beyond my reach.

I'm hanging upside-down, the blood rushing to my head, trying to study the two men desperately hanging on to the plank. It's so dark that it'd be a struggle to tell them apart even if I *was* able to recognise their faces.

A sense of helplessness threatens to overwhelm me, but I fight it, and tell myself: *trust your gut.* I close my eyes and picture Alfie's body as he lunged towards me in his flat. I recall how he shifted his weight onto his right foot when he drew back his hand to hit me; how he arched his body while he lay on top of me; how he tilted his head to one side as he told me *thanks babes*.

When I open my eyes, I know. The man spinning into reach, holding his hand up for me to grab, is Alfie. When I don't make a move, he bellows my name in confusion: 'Phoebe! It's me! Tom!'

I resist the urge to respond, and let his impotent pleas be carried away on the wind as he disappears back under the scaffolding.

Then I stretch down my arm in readiness for Tom —

the real Tom? — to come into reach. I feel the touch of his fingertips, a hand clamping around my wrist, and then my arm feels like it's being wrenched out of its socket as I take his whole weight.

At that same moment an anguished scream slices the air as the plank slips the rope and Alfie — please God it *is* Alfie — plummets down into the darkness.

Tom is dangling from my arm, and I don't think I can hold on much longer. 'You'll have to climb up me!' I shout, bracing myself by tightening my legs round the scaffolding pole.

Hand over hand, using my arm like a rope, he slowly makes his way up. The pain's almost too much to bear, but just before I think I'm going to pass out, he manages to grab onto something and haul himself up.

And now he's pulling me up, helping me to my feet, wiping the rain from my face, staring concernedly into my eyes. It's all over. I'm safe! Unless —

I think it's Tom, but now I'm starting to doubt myself. 'Show me your arm,' I tell him.

He seems confused.

'Please!' I say. 'Just roll up your sleeve.'

He reaches for his left cuff.

'No, the other arm.'

He shrugs puzzledly, then rolls up his right sleeve, revealing a shadowy mark on the underside of his wrist.

I give a horrified start as my eyes fly to his face. Alfie!

Oh God, what have I done? An image of Tom sliding down into the blackness of the night flashes through my mind. When I saved Alfie, I condemned myself and Tom to death. But for his sake I'm going to face my fate with stoicism. *Be strong* I tell myself, raising my head defiantly.

Alfie's finished rolling up his sleeve, exposing the pale, wet *blank* skin of his arm. I was mistaken: I see now that what I took to be a tattoo on his wrist is just a splatter of mud. But just to be certain I get him to roll up his other sleeve. He's got some sort of Celtic design with knots, crosses and geometric patterns, and not a serpent in sight. It's Tom!

I can't help laughing at his soggy, bunched-up sleeves, and the bewildered expression on his face. The laughter seems to open the flood gates and, as a huge tidal wave of relief washes over me, I start to cry.

Tom takes me in his arms and holds me tight. Although I'm sore all over from being half-strangled to death and used as a climbing rope, I cling on to him and don't want him to let go.

Police sirens wail in the distance and we watch in silence as the blue flashing lights make their way through the building site towards us.

We meet the police and paramedics at the building's entrance, by the spot where Tom fished my mobile out of the mud. When I try to explain what happened, I find that my throat's become so swollen and sore from being strangled that I can't speak, so Tom has to do all the talking.

He goes off with two policemen to help locate Alfie's body, while I'm examined by paramedics. And then I have to wait on the steps of the ambulance, wrapped in a blanket, for someone to come and take my statement.

Tom returns with news, his face flushed with excitement. But I'm too exhausted to follow what he's saying and it's only when the ambulance crew are wheeling a stretcher across the bumpy ground that I realise what's happened. By some devilish miracle Alfie managed to survive that fall.

As they're loading his trolley into the ambulance, he turns his blood-streaked face and his eyes lock with mine. A dismayed chill riffles right through me. I thought it was all over and now I'm scared I'll never be free of him.

But when I study the livid, bloody gash running from his eyebrow to his chin, I realise everything's going to be okay. I know enough about cutaneous scarring to be certain that the wound on his face isn't going to heal without severe disfigurement. I'm never going to have a problem recognising him again.

Chapter 47

CHRISTMAS DAY, AND I'm waiting on Suzi's doorstep, rubbing my hands together and huffing clouds of frosty breath into the crisp air with a kind of surprised sense of disbelief that I agreed to spend Christmas Day with her for the first time in I don't know how long. And not just with Suzi, but with the entire Hertfordshire contingent of the Fairleigh-Granger tribe too.

Suzi insisted: 'You must come, or it will be me on my own again, hopelessly outnumbered by Alistair's relatives. I'm sick of the pitying glances I get around the Christmas table when the crackers are pulled, and they start singing this Christmas song which is some sort of family tradition. There are so many of them, and it's just little orphan Annie me.'

Mmm, she makes it sound so appealing. Eventually I relented, but only on the condition that she wouldn't make me sit next to Charles again. And then Tom decided he wanted to be with me on Christmas day. He's driving up this morning from his sister's in Kent and when he gets here, there'll be three of us batting for Team Suzi.

Tom and I have spent a lot of time together over the past two weeks. It turns out that saving each other's life is quite the bonding experience. We've been interviewed by the police half a dozen times and having to relive everything we've been through over and over again has been quite intense.

Alfie's out of hospital now. Aside from the cut to his face, the only damage he suffered after that fall was three broken ribs and a tibial fracture. He's in custody and awaiting trial. They're probably going to charge him with attempted murder, which carries a hefty prison sentence if he's found guilty. But these things take a long time, so I'm trying to put it out of my mind by getting into the Christmas spirit. I'm usually a bit bah-humbuggy but this year I've been embracing it fully.

I can hear the click-clacking of heels on the parquet flooring, and then the door's opened by a flustered-looking blonde woman wearing a fussy-looking fuchsia pink dress, with an incongruous plastic apron bearing the wildly inaccurate slogan *World's Greatest Cook*.

She gives me the double nod. 'Phoebe! Thank God you've arrived! Hold this for me?' She hands me the wooden spoon she's carrying and reties her apron before giving me a big hug. 'Happy Christmas!'

'Happy Christmas!' I croak. They told me my voice would be okay after a couple of days, but I'm still rasping like a sixty-a-day smoker. Tom thinks I sound very sexy though, so I'm not really complaining.

Suzi eyes all the bags piled up round my feet. 'Are you planning on moving in?'

'It's Christmas presents. I wasn't sure whether I was supposed to be buying for Alistair's family. And there's three bottles of parsnip prosecco for you from Denise.'

She gives a short dry laugh. 'Thanks! I can't wait to see Charles's expression when he tries that. He's a terrible wine snob you know.'

She leads me through to the kitchen. There are messy half-filled pots, pans, dishes and bowls piled up on every surface. It looks even more bomb sitey than I'd expected, as though the meal's already over, and it's time to scrape the leftovers into the bin and start on the washing up.

'Are the Fairleigh-Grangers here yet?'

'They're in the lounge knocking back the Bucks Fizz.

I told them lunch would be ready at two, but I've not finished chopping the vegetables yet, and I haven't even started on the bread sauce. I don't know what Alistair's doing. I asked him to lay the table, but that was half an hour ago.'

'Relax, I'm here now,' I say, putting my hands on her shoulders and giving her an encouraging smile. And despite the fact that my culinary skills are even more rudimentary than her's — unfortunately neither of us inherited the cooking gene from Mum — Suzi seems reassured.

She passes me an apron with an apologetic shrug. 'Sorry, it's all I've got.'

I pop the strap over my head and then look down at the slogan emblazoned across my chest: *Sexy Beast*. It's even less accurate than *World's Greatest Cook*.

'It's Alistair's,' Suzi explains.

Sexy Beast? I can't help imagining Alistair's naked, hairy, pale, out-of-shape Dad bod under the shiny fabric, and a surprised *oh!* is forced from my lips.

'It's supposed to be ironic,' Suzi says.

'Obviously! I mean, not that he isn't, you know —'

And then, as if on cue, Alistair enters the kitchen.

'It's the Sexy Beast himself!' Suzi exclaims.

'What? Oh yes, of course. Hello Phoebe. Happy Christmas!'

'Happy Christmas!' I say in return, watching as his expression becomes more serious, and in a concerned voice he asks:

'How are you doing? Are you okay?'

'I'm fine, thanks,' I reply self-consciously, hoping that the make-up I applied to hide the purple bruising around my neck hasn't already rubbed off.

'It's really good that you decided to spend Christmas with us this year. It means a lot to Suzi having you here. And to me of course. When you're ready, come through and I'll introduce you to the family.'

He laughs at my reaction. 'Don't look so worried. They don't bite. They're quite harmless really, aren't they Suzi.'

'Yes,' Suzi says, shaking her head *no* for comic effect.

Alistair laughs indulgently. 'Actually, I thought it might be a bit overwhelming for you, with so many unfamiliar faces, so I printed off some name cards which I'm going to put round the meal table —'

Suzi interrupts him: 'D'you mean you haven't even finished laying the table yet? Alistair!'

'I'm just about to do it,' he mumbles, and hurries off.

Suzi rolls her eyes after him and in an exasperated tone tells me: 'He's hopeless.'

'But you love him really. Aren't you glad you didn't leave him because of Rachel Green?'

'Actually, I've got something to tell you.' Her eyes are shining, and she beams at me with barely suppressed joy. 'We've decided to try for a baby.'

'Suzi!' I exclaim with a broad smile. 'But I thought you never wanted children?'

'No. I said I wasn't ready for children. I've always wanted them some day, and now that day has come. And before you say anything, I know there's a chance it won't happen. But we're going to give it a try.'

'That's wonderful,' I say, giving her hand a gentle squeeze.

'Don't let Alistair know I told you though. He didn't want me telling anyone, but we're sisters, and sisters tell each other everything.'

I squeeze her hand again, almost as pleased by the fact she wanted to confide in me as I am by her news.

The doorbell rings and I go to answer it. A handsome young man wearing a Santa hat is standing on the doorstep with his hands behind his back.

'Tom?'

'Happy Christmas Miss Sexy-Voice,' he replies, whipping out a sprig of mistletoe and holding it over our heads while he leans in for a kiss.

I have to suppress a knee-jerk reaction to pull my head away. I still flinch when anyone comes near me, and I guess it's going to take a long, long time to come to terms with what happened. I've decided to seek professional help in the new year, so that will be a start I suppose.

'I wasn't expecting you for another half hour,' I say.

'Yeah, the roads were practically empty.'

'Are you coming in then?'

He doesn't move. 'I've something to show you first?'

'What is it?'

I wait expectantly as he brings his left hand out from behind his back, but it's empty. Then I notice there's a new tattoo on the back of his hand — a little espresso cup with three coffee beans on the side and a curl of steam rising up out of it.

'Oh!' I exclaim, getting it immediately. 'Tom Coffeeshop!'

'So you'll always be sure it's me.'

'Wow! That's quite a permanent statement.'

He blushes, and mumbles something about liking coffee, and before he says anything too cringe, I give him a kiss.

'I love it. Thank you,' I tell him, then take his hand and lead him into the house. 'Come on, let's go and meet the Hertfordshire Horde.'

Printed in Great Britain
by Amazon

21929969R00162